Praise for

little black lies

"I've read and loved every single one of Tish Cohen's books. _Little Black Lies_ is her best book to date."
—Lauren Baratz-Logsted, author of _Crazy Beautiful_

"Tish Cohen is a master storyteller who gives me everything I long for in a book and then some. . . . Made me sadder than sad, and bursting with hope. This book makes the world a better place."
—Sheree Fitch, multi-award-winning author of _The Gravesavers_

"Social misfit Sara Black's account of her year at America's premier institute for hyper-over-achievers is full of gut-punch emotion and compelling insights from a smart girl forced to navigate the treacherous hallways of Anton High—a school of piranhas in kilts and knee-socks. This is a place where good things only seem to happen to bad kids and a good kid has no choice but to do bad things."
—Lesley Livingston, author of _Wondrous Strange_ and _Darklight_

"_Little Black Lies_ is a funny, poignant tale of high school intrigue taken to the nth degree (and occasionally times Pi). . . . A brutally honest book with a fabulous sense of humour that keeps you turning the pages right until the very end. In other words: (wicked sense of humour) + (awesome characters)(searingly astute observations)-(sentiment) = (one great read)"
—Adrienne Kress, author of _Alex and the Ironic Gentleman_

"Cohen's creative intelligence and sure-footed prose style ensure the novel is both lively and humourous. Her pacing is sharp, and her language has the capacity to surprise. . . . A mature and more substantial alternative to some of the other high school novels out there."
—_Quill & Quire_

little black lies

tish cohen

harper*trophy*canada™
an imprint of harpercollins*publishers*ltd

HarperCollins Publishers Ltd
2 Bloor Street East, 20th Floor
Toronto, Ontario, Canada
M4W 1A8

www.harpercollins.ca

Library and Archives Canada Cataloguing in Publication

Cohen, Tish, 1963–
    Little black lies / Tish Cohen.

ISBN 978-1-55468-461-8

    I. Title.

PS8605.O3787L58 2009   jC813'.6   C2009-903452-2

Printed in the United States of America
HC 9 8 7 6 5 4 3 2 1

Interior design copyright © Egmont US Inc

For Lisa Posluns,
who loved nothing more
than life itself.

ACKNOWLEDGMENTS

Special thanks go out to so many: Jacqui Goodman, for giving me an up-close glimpse of life at an elite school. Marysa MacKinnon, Max Cohen, and Lucas Cohen, for their ever sage adolescent counsel. John Lindsay, for reading with such enthusiasm, and to my husband, Stephen Cohen, for reading each new draft as if it were the first. Patry Francis, for janitorial wisdom and early reads, and Jessica Brilliant Keener, for her sharp eye, thoughtful reads, and familiarity with the neighborhoods of Boston. Regina Griffin, my editor at Egmont, for caring so much about the book. Elizabeth Law, Doug Pocock, Mary Albi, and all the terrific folks over on Park Avenue South. Lynne Missen, my editor at HarperCanada, for getting behind the book from the start. Also at Harper, Melissa Zilberberg, Charidy Johnson, and Liza Smith Morrison, for your support. As ever, Kassie Evashevski at United Talent Agency. I'm beyond grateful to my agent, Dan Lazar, at Writers House, for believing in me no matter what, and to the tireless Stephen Barr and the lovely Maja Nikolic, for all they continue to do for my books.

CONTENTS

little black lies

chapter 1
first day of school

Ants have a complicated social structure made up of infertile female workers, as well as winged males and females who reproduce.

"What the . . . ?" Gripping the vinyl passenger seat of the VW bus, I try not to hit the window as my father takes a corner too fast in his rush not to be late for our first day at Boston's illustrious Anton High School.

"Language, Sara," he says, shooting me a stern look.

"I didn't say it."

"You didn't need to." He rolls his window halfway down. "It was implied."

The rush of September air is so cool and crisp it almost shatters. You can practically hear the cracking spines of new textbooks in the wind, and my finger is already bleeding from the jagged bite my three-ring binder will give me in class later today.

Another corner so tight the van nearly flips. This time, my cheek hits cold glass. "Are we on the run?"

He pats my knee and I notice he smells like cologne. Upon further inspection, I notice he's shaved his normally short gray hair even closer to his head and carved his tidy beard's edge to perfection. "Didn't count on this much traffic. Rule number one for starting a new job: Be on time."

1

Rule number one at Anton High—crowned "North America's Most Elite and Most Bizarre Public School" by *Time* magazine—no one is admitted after the ninth grade, no matter how thick their Coke-bottle glasses are.

Think about it. A tuition-free school that practically guarantees a kid's admittance to the Ivy League college of her choice. In a leafy, historical neighborhood with a low crime rate. Its doors flung open to kids from all walks of life. The American Dream with lockers, right? Wrong. Whoever created the place didn't count on the scholastic hysteria it would breed among the privileged. Regular families, no matter how brilliant their kids, can't compete with moneyed parents willing to do anything to guarantee little Thompson or Oleander's future. Even if it means paying $15,000 per year for a cram school created to prep their wheezing, sneezing urchins for one sparkly moment—the Anton High School entrance exam.

After writing the entrance paper—a brutal test some 11,000 gifted students take in March of their eighth-grade year—only 175 get in. They're the Cream of the Gifted Crop. The other 10,825, the Lesser Gifteds, have to live with that failure the remainder of their suddenly pointless lives. That Anton is tougher to get into than Harvard will do little to soothe their scrabbed-up egos. Ant grads go on to become U.S. senators, Nobel Prize and Academy Award winners, astronauts, Olympic athletes, and international chess champions. There was also that brainy Miss America who contorted her body into the Nike symbol for the talent segment, but rumor is she never finished senior year.

All of which explains why the school is considered elite. Why it's called bizarre is too obvious to mention.

It's 100 percent stocked with nerds and brainiacs. Forget quarterbacks, starting pitchers, and pom-pom-wielding cheerleaders. If they exist at all, they're probably ashamed of themselves. The real royalty of the school are national robotics warlords, science wizards, and mathletes. I've even heard there are two kids who are published authors. With all this brain muscle crammed into one Boston high school, you've got to expect a whole lot of deviant behavior, right?

So how was I, Sara Black, long-standing math geek from Lundon, Massachusetts, allowed to take the Anton High School entrance exam the summer before eleventh grade and get admitted to the most sought-after school in North America?

Simple. My father is the new janitor.

"Rule number two," Dad continues, "is dress professionally. I've even ironed my socks and underwear."

I let out a long sigh. "You're going to fit right in."

"Your wardrobe influences how you are adjudged by new people." He glances over at my Dubble Bubble T-shirt, graffitied jeans, cherry red Doc Martens. Turning back to the traffic, he mumbles, "Your father wants to be seen as a sanitation professional right down to his underclothes."

As nervous as I am, I allow myself a smile. "Adjudged?"

"Adjudged."

You wouldn't know it based on his career choice, but my dad reads all the time. He practically lived at the Lundon library, hauling home every book ever written about vintage cars. When I was really young, he read me bedtime stories from *Car and Driver* magazine. Some kids' nightmares are populated by the bogeyman creeping out of the closet. Mine were haunted by the snaggle-toothed muscle car that growled at me from the garage.

Dad pulls the van onto Beacon Street, where we inch along in Tuesday-morning traffic. On our left is a sunken park, sheltered by towering trees all dressed up in velvety moss. Between their meaty trunks, a wading pond flashes and sparks with sunlight. This is Boston Common, one of the oldest parks in the country. An oasis of September-tinged nature wearing hot dog stands and T-shirt kiosks as ironic trash jewelry.

The sidewalk gets bushy with teenagers hauling backpacks and lunch bags, and we pull into a driveway between two buildings, passing beneath a polished steel sign announcing ANTON HIGH SCHOOL. Students—they call themselves Ants—stream along wide pedestrian path-ways, and it isn't until now that I notice they're all wearing white shirts, navy vests, and plaid skirts or gray pants. I look at my father, shocked. "Uniforms?"

He shoots me an upside-down smile. "Sorry, sweet pea. There was a parental vote a few years back. They felt it would remove the disparity between the students' finan-cial situations."

Sliding down in the passenger seat, I close my eyes and try to ignore the battery acid in my stomach. The fear of walking around a new school without the comfort of my red Docs is rising up my throat like vomit.

The driveway opens into a courtyard at the back of the school, which looks just as jail-like as any other learn-ing institution—about five stories of prison windows, flat roof, wide steps leading to a set of scratched metal doors.

4

Concrete stretches right up to the base of the building, so right off the bat you know there'll be no digging out of this place with a click pencil and a protractor.

The lane circles around to the doorway, and parents slow their cars to spit out bright and shiny offspring. In the center of the roundabout is a parkland being trampled flat by backpacks, bicycles, and teenagers; wasps patrol the grass at their feet, inspecting discarded coffee cups and other bits of trash.

Homesickness pricks my eyes. I was nervous all weekend and thought my anxiety had peaked on Labor Day, but today, after seeing the kids, the uniforms, the school itself, I'm terrified. What if I'm not smart enough?

Dad looks at me as if he's read my mind. "It'll be a better life here in Boston, honey. I promise."

I wish I could believe him. "I still don't get why you took another high-school janitor job. The other job would have paid way more money."

"They didn't call after the interview."

"Should you have called them, just to check? Maintenance manager of an office building would have been so much better. And it was in Lundon."

"I don't have energy for people who don't have energy for me. Besides, Anton High School is a legendary establishment. I'm honored to come on board."

"But you're supposed to avoid cleaning."

Charlie has obsessive-compulsive disorder—a condition that launches him into pointless and repetitive rituals. But as with a tide choking on a flotsam of fish bones and jagged glass, OCD ebbs and flows. Sometimes you might think it's gone because he's stopped washing his hands until they bleed or stopped scouring toilet bowls until the brush snaps, but it's only because the problem has fooled you by morphing into another form. One behavior gets replaced by another. If you're lucky, that new behavior will be something inconspicuous. If you're not, that behavior could make an appearance in the most public of places. School. Last year he fixated on the liquid soaps in the Finmory restrooms. Draining them of liquid, scrubbing the containers, and refilling them every single morning just in case bacteria had bred in the soap overnight. He was warned several times to cut it out, but nothing could get him to stop. The principal kept Dad's behavior hidden from the students, which I appreciated beyond belief, but it was clear from my parents' repeated arguments that if the board hadn't switched to antibacterial soap a few weeks later, Dad would have been out of a job and my family would have been out of a house.

"Is this about leaving your old school?" Dad says. "Because Anton is a huge opportunity for you too."

"I had a huge opportunity at Finmory. Everyone said I would have been valedictorian next year. Please know you're ripping that experience right out of my hands and annihilating my one and only chance to scar my enemies and frenemies for life."

He pats my knee and grins, his clipped beard spreading thin across his jaw. "Sara, you're sixteen. You won't know what scars you need to inflict for another ten or fifteen years. Until then, it's your parents'—" He looks out the window, then back at me. His voice softens. "It's your *father's* job to tell you."

An uncomfortable silence fills the van. The same uncomfortable silence that has filled our lives ever since the last day of school, when Mom's exit destroyed any hope of Dad staying in his comfy position of Finmory janitor. If only to break up the deafening quiet, he announced it was time to "start fresh." So here we are and I have a formula to prove it. (Me + Dad − Mom) × (brainiacs + prison windows − beloved red boots) = starting fresh.

"She left another message for you last night."

"Don't go there. Not today."

"You have to talk about your mother sometime. You have to talk *to* her sometime."

I say nothing.

"She walked away from me, Sarie-bear. Not you."

I pull a sweater out of my book bag and tug it on—stupid when you think about it. I'll have to take it off again in about five minutes. But this isn't just any sweater. It's a vintage beaded cardigan with sleeves that end at the elbow. Itchy. Dark green. Smells like cigarettes. My mother picked it up at a flea market in Vermont and wore it all the time because it matched her green eyes and dark blonde hair. The day she announced this whole "trial separation," she said I had the same coloring; maybe I should try the sweater on. She offered to try to find me one in Paris once she got there, then explained that overseas shipping rates weren't nearly as high as people think.

So I did what any other girl would do. I stole the freaking thing.

Dad pulls into an empty spot at the far end of the teachers' parking lot and kills the *putt-putt* sounds of the engine. After stepping out of the van in navy pants and a light blue short-sleeved shirt, he reaches into the backseat for the Anton High custodian jacket they gave him after his interview and pulls it on. The oversized patch on the left side, over his heart, says *Charlie*. He zips up. "So how antediluvian do I look?"

"If that means wicked ghastly, I'll give you a ten. Out of five."

He pulls a huge key ring out of his pants pocket—strung from it are keys of every shape, size, and color—and jams it into his jacket pocket. "Let's go. First impressions."

I slide out of the van and trot across the parking lot after him. An empty footpath leads us along the side of the school to the front, nose to headlights with a sleek black car that has just pulled to the curb. Dad nudges me. "Ever seen a Bentley up close?"

I shake my head. Amazing—this gleaming heap of metal, rubber, and polished glass probably costs more than our house back home.

"It's a bit new for my taste," Dad says with a sniff. "Now if it were a '35 Bentley Cabriolet three and a half liter with six cylinders and a flying lady mascot hood ornament, that would get my attention."

The driver's door swings open and a chauffeur climbs out. I can't get a good look at his face, but from behind he's a study in opposites. From the neck down he looks every bit the dedicated chauffeur, crisply outfitted in a charcoal uniform and shiny black shoes. But from the neck up he looks like a druggie—long reddish brown dreads tied back with string and dirty black baseball cap with a broken fastener at the back. He pauses to polish a spot on the hood of the car, then, keeping his eyes to the ground, he marches around the back of the Bentley to open the rear door by the curb. A long, muscular thigh emerges, followed by a student—a tall girl with magnificently wavy, summer-faded brown hair all flipped over to one side as if she's been hit by a major gust of wind.

I slow my step and try not to stare. Against toasted skin, her pale turquoise eyes shine like the community pool back home. Her face is strong and boyish—thick eyebrows, square jaw, long, sharp nose—refined against the wild hair. She swings a backpack over her shoulder and stares at the building. "Welcome to my nightmare," she mutters in a voice that is deep, gravelly.

Her driver climbs back into the car, leans one arm out the window, and waves good-bye with a couple of fingers. She bends down and flips him off.

Halfway up the school steps, Dad looks back at me. "Hurry up, Sara."

Dropping down on one knee, I pretend to fuss with my laces. "You go ahead. I'll find the office for myself."

"Ask for Mrs. Pelletier, the vice principal," he calls. The bell rings and he waves to me before trotting toward the main doors. "And remember the rule about cell phones. Turned off during the school day, just like at Finmory."

I nod and he disappears inside.

The girl stomps toward the stairs, her jaw muscles bulging with fury, and slows to give me a long, aggravated glance that starts at my boots and travels up my shins, past my Dubble Bubble–covered chest, then up to my braided hair. I seem to bore her instantly and she looks away. Once the Bentley is out of sight, she lifts her jean jacket and rolls the waistband of her skirt way up. But when she hoists her

9

backpack up again, the back hem of the skirt gets caught. It lifts high enough to expose her pink cotton underwear. She starts up the stairs and I panic. People will see. It would be mortifying and I'm not altogether certain this girl can handle it. I want to call out to her but it's dangerous. I'm the new kid. I'm nobody.

Truth is, I wasn't such a somebody back in Lundon either. I was the quiet girl who wore the same red boots every day, stood up in math class to solve thorny-looking formulas in her head, and cozied up to inverse trigonometric functions and secondhand novels on Friday nights. Not exactly a girl people wanted to sit next to in the cafeteria. Still, my own particular flavor of strange wasn't what drove my social life straight over the cliff. My mother accomplished that for me.

Bentley Girl is almost at the door now. New girl or not, I have to say something. "Hey!" I race up the stairs until I'm so close I can nearly touch her. "Your backpack's swallowing your skirt."

She spins around and looks down at me. No. Not at me. Through me. "Did you just diss my skirt?"

"What? No, I . . ."

She spins around and I stand there like an idiot. As she runs up the remaining steps, I find myself staring up at her impertinent ass. Apparently not even days-of-the-week panties can keep this girl in line. Just before she pulls open the massive wooden door, I see she has SUNDAY IS THE DAY OF REST written in green across her perfect bottom.

It's Tuesday.

chapter 2
the little zygote that could

Between the abdomen and thorax lies the petiole—a narrow segment that forms the ant's waist.

Bentley Girl vanishes inside the school, leaving behind the zingy scent of tangerines, fresh wool, and something else I cannot quite decipher. Acid reflux? Bad dreams? I pause for a moment on the steps and try to calm myself before going in.

My parents will never admit it, but I was born about a decade too early. All because of a cat who decided to nap behind the left rear wheel of my grandmother's Toyota. The horror of having killed an innocent creature made her forty-five minutes late in arriving home from work, giving Charlie and Tina just enough time to push their usual after-school routine (necking until they heard her car engine in the driveway) three bases too far. By the time Grandma pulled up in front of the old brick bungalow at 67 Norma Jean Drive, I was a freshly pollinated zygote clinging to a uterine wall, waiting to force two randy teenagers into a marriage that never should have happened.

My untimely birth blurred any focus my parents might have had on the pursuit of education and profitable careers. After I was born, my mother worked nights to free up her days to care for me, eventually working her way up to head chef of a French restaurant in a neighboring town. Dedicated father that he was, still is; passionate car nut that he was, still is; Dad snatched up the first job that promised decent health benefits and summers off to tinker with the crotchety engine of his VW love of the time—an orange two-door Karmann Ghia with the world's smallest backseat. He became the custodian of a middle school in the southwest corner of Massachusetts.

That he never aspired to more, that he rendered all his self-schooling useless by doing nothing constructive with it, was something my mom held up as proof that he was lazy. Unmotivated. Unfair to his family. It drove Mom crazy. More than crazy. It drove her far, far away to a cooking school in France.

My entire existence is an accident. Had one cat felt *marginally* more energetic, my fingers wouldn't be wrapped around the cold metal handle of Anton High School's front door right now.

The foyer, more like that of a shopping mall than a school, with escalators and koi pond surrounded by tropical plants, is about four stories high and is capped with skylights that offer peeks at the clear September sky. All the doors and window frames are reddish brown wood, as are the trophy-filled cabinet cases along the far wall. The floor is a mosaic of teensy colored tiles intricately arranged in the pattern of a warm sunburst.

The office is just to my left and appears to be bursting with activity. With my bag pressed tight against my chest, I shuffle over to the counter and say to the closest secretary, "Hi. I'm new here."

★   ★   ★

Mrs. Pelletier, the vice principal, wraps a measuring tape around my waist and cinches it tight, making me catch my breath. The plastic is icy against my shivering flesh. As she bends over to get a good look at the numbers, several strands of pearls too white to be real clatter forward from her neck and I get a noseful of hairspray from her floppy bun. "Twenty-four inches." She scribbles it down on a chart. "My waist was twenty-four inches once. Four children and two husbands ago."

She motions for me to follow her into the storage room, a big closet lined with metal shelving that boasts every kind of school supply you could ask for. Zillions of spanking-new pens, highlighters, and staples. Towering stacks of textbooks and cellophane-wrapped packages of blank notebooks. Fully aware of how very geeky I am for even having this thought, I fantasize about winning a shopping spree inside this cupboard. I have a big weird thing for fresh, unmarked notebooks.

As she walks toward a closet with double doors, I lean against a tall wooden filing cabinet. It comes up to my shoulders and is so ancient the top edges of the four drawers are worn down like the edge of a pillow. I realize too late my sweater is caught on a splinter in the ancient wood, and as I work to free the green wool, I notice tarnished brass squares hold labels that announce each drawer's contents, from AHS EXAMS—FRESHMEN at the bottom to AHS EXAMS—SENIORS at the top. Strange, this small cabinet contains the key to so many students' futures. Do well, you're golden. Flunk and, well, bye-bye, Harvard.

Mrs. Pelletier yanks open a set of narrow locker doors.

Inside are dozens of plaid skirts, gray trousers, navy vests of all sizes—some fraying at the seams, some brand-new. White shirts sway in the draft from the air vent overhead. Two cartons sit on a shelf, one labeled KNEESOCKS, the other labeled TIGHTS. She points at the boxes and asks which I prefer. Desperate for a bit of warmth, I shrug. "Tights, I guess."

"Lucky for you, the students of Anton High are fairly careless with their belongings," Mrs. Pelletier says, handing me a folded pile of black Lycra. "And their parents rarely take the time to label, so our Lost and Found is something of a free-for-all. Of course, *everything* is laundered before it's hung in the closet."

I nod to show her I would expect nothing less.

"It gives you a great stockpile to choose from." She admires the orderly clothing. "One of my children came in last week and helped organize the closet."

"Do your kids go to the school?" I ask.

"My youngest, Daria. She graduated last year and is just starting at Columbia."

"Did she take her uniform from the Lost and Found?"

"Oh, heavens, no. This closet is only for proven financial cases. Recent immigrants, struggling fam—" She stops and looks at me, her expression now one of mild horror. "Anyone who needs the help."

A prickly silence follows, during which I pray that the floor will buckle and swell, crack open along the seams of the tiny porcelain tiles, and, with a mighty belch, suck me inside. Mrs. Pelletier didn't mean to degrade me. But that only makes it worse.

"Sara, there's something I'd like to speak to you about.

Not many staff members' children have even attempted the entrance exam, so it's fairly unusual for us to have a family member on campus. This is a competitive school and we have a policy in place to discourage favoritism. If one of our staff knows a coworker's child is a student, he or she is not to divulge it to the other teachers. Whether or not you choose to tell the students is your own choice. Okay?"

"Okay."

Another silent funk settles over us. I point toward the uniforms. "I'm pretty sure I'm a size six."

"Great. Let's see what we can find." She runs her finger along the clothing rack, eventually pulling out the following:

One plaid skirt (looks brand-new)

Two white blouses (both with puckered collars)

A navy vest (looks itchy)

One pair of hideous black leather shoes (Doc Marten is stomping in his grave)

Holding the skirt up to me, she clucks her approval. "Looks about right. Go ahead and try everything on. If it fits, we'll be able to get you to class before attendance is called." She heads out the door. "Call me if you need anything."

She closes the door and, ignoring the rule about cell phones, I pull out my phone and turn it on long enough to send my best friend, Mandy—who is probably standing at her new locker at Finmory High right about now—a text message:

MANDY-THEY HAVE UNIFORMS HERE. SAVE ME.

I jiggle the doorknob, praying it locks from the inside.

15

It doesn't. Throwing the skirt, vest, and blouses onto a chair, I drag it to the entrance, where I undress with my back firmly pressed against the door. I squirm into a blouse as quickly as I can and button up. The skirt looks a bit small, but judging from the sounds in the office, I'm in very real danger of being invaded, so I step into it and fasten. It's tight. The door handle turns and I throw my weight onto the door, calling out, "Changing in here!"

A female voice mutters, "Sorry," and I hear footsteps patter off.

I pull on a pair of tights, thankful for the insulation they provide against the air conditioning blasting down from the ceiling. They hide my freckled legs. But best of all, I won't have to risk anyone reading my underwear—not that it has anything interesting to say.

I slip my feet into the ugly shoes and stuff my boots and clothing into my bag. Just before I head out the door to ask Mrs. Pelletier for my class schedule, I notice a rectangular piece of fabric dangling from the side waistband of my skirt. It's the tag of some student with a weird name. As hard as I try, I cannot rip it off, so I tuck it in and vow to cut it off at home later.

Parking me in front of a large mirror in a hallway lined with long benches outside the principal's office, Mrs. Pelletier smooths my shirt upon my shoulders. "Seems to be a good fit. We don't have a locker available for you just yet. Check back again in a couple of days."

I thank her and turn away.

"And Sara?"

"Yes?"

"Welcome to Anton High School, dear."

chapter 3
saint sarah

Ants have terrible vision and communicate with one another by releasing chemical scents called pheromones.

Room 217. Peering through the window of the closed door, I pray I don't pass out with fear. I turn the doorknob with great plans to slink in quietly, pass my new-student slip to the teacher, and find myself an empty desk at the back. But the squeaky hinges give me away. About thirty kids spin around to stare.

My cheeks burn so hot it's like I've been slapped.

"Welcome to Honors Math," the teacher says to me, pushing up the sleeves of his jacket and loosening his tie. "I'm Mark Curtis. I was just explaining that I'm here to make your lives miserable for the next few months. By the time you encounter me again as a senior, you'll be thankful you've been broken in. Grab a seat, we've got a lot to cover today."

The ripple of groans that follows is a nice distraction from the strange kid at the door. Unfortunately it's short lived. All eyes return to me as I walk across the room to hand him my office slip. "I'm new."

He glances at the paper. "Welcome to the class, Sara. Ever heard of Saint Sarah?" he asks, rubbing his chin and

looking up. "More than one author has suggested Saint
Sarah was the daughter of Mary Magdalene and Jesus.
History's most perfect union."

A few kids smirk from the front row.

I start to hunt for a seat, when he continues. "This theory
was used in Dan Brown's *The Da Vinci Code*. The daughter
of Jesus. Fairly illustrious parentage, don't you think?"

I offer him a watery smile.

He grins, his grayish hair swooping down over one eyebrow. "Now that I've destroyed any shot you might have
had at a social life, you can go ahead and find yourself a
seat."

There's an empty desk next to a girl with layered hair
dyed so black it's nearly blue. As I pull my binder from
my book bag, I realize Bentley Girl is right in front of me.
Thankfully, her underwear is covered.

I notice her bare knees right away and scan the other
girls. Sure enough, every female in the class is wearing
kneesocks. No one is in tights but me, and I feel like a
kindergartner. I'm tugging my skirt down over my knees
when Mr. Curtis asks Bentley Girl about her summer
vacation.

She flips her hair and turns sideways in her seat,
crushing her mouth into an irritated smile. "I spent six
weeks sunning myself in the courtyard behind the Queen
Elizabeth Theater, where I was meant to be sorting sweat-
soaked costumes for the cast of my dad's new musical
while he howled at the orchestra for butchering the music
he spent two years writing. But this old fungus-face of
a lead actor kept hitting on me, so I bailed." She snaps
her gum and looks around at the class before her blue-

green eyes rest on me. As hard as I try, I can't stop staring. Before she turns away, she adds, "Don't ever let anyone tell you showbiz isn't freaking glam."

The redheaded boy next to her scoots his chair closer. He's so small his overstuffed pencil case could practically crush him, and with his plump cheeks and soccer-themed backpack, he looks to be about nine or ten. He reaches for her hand and starts to scrawl something on her palm. "Take *my* number," he says through a nose stopped up with rhinovirus. "I'm younger and way more flexible."

Bentley smacks the pen to the floor. "We need to get Little Man Griff a blow-up doll before he hits puberty and implodes. He clearly can't handle the estrogen around here."

"That'll be enough from the two of you." Mr. Curtis crosses his arms. His head tilts to one side as he stares at the girl next to Bentley. "How about you, Sloane? Do anything interesting?"

Sloane slumps lower in her seat, causing her too-tight vest and shirt to ride up and expose her slender waist. She nudges Bentley Girl. "I spent the summer texting my poor friend from my dad's office." She pushes a tangle of chestnut hair from her face to reveal eyes the color of smoke and a pouty lower lip that gives her a drowsy sulk. She looks as if she'd like to go back to bed. Not necessarily alone. "It was boring. All I really learned was that you can't get a good cell signal in the basement of Mallory, Mallory, and Montauk unless you sneak out into the rat-infested back alley and risk the plague."

"Don't think I didn't appreciate it, Sloaney," says Bentley Girl.

"Rats didn't cause the plague," says another girl, haughty and offended. Unlike Bentley's, this girl's voice is shrieky and metallic, like a spoon scraping against the bottom of a mixing bowl. Her yellow bob is tamed by a velvet headband. Everything about this girl looks fragile, from her thin legs to her papery fingernails to her dangling butterfly earrings. "It was fleas that carried *Yersinia pestis* and they transmitted it to the rats. In fact, rats carry very few zoonotic conditions. *Leptospirosis*, maybe, but you'd basically have to lick rat urine while it's still wet to catch that, and it isn't even in season during the summer." She settles herself back in her seat and folds her arms across her chest, satisfied. "Not outside of the tropics, anyway."

Sloane blinks at her as if too tired to push her features into any sort of expression. "Is that information meant to kill me, Isabella? Because it might."

Isabella doesn't answer. Just adjusts her headband and turns to Bentley Girl. "Anyway, what about me, Carling? I braved old fungus-face every Tuesday to meet you for lunch. Don't I get any credit?"

Carling. Wait a minute . . . I suck in my stomach and fumble around inside my too-tight waistband to pull out the dangling tag on my left. It says *Carling Burnack*. My stomach flips over as I realize I'm sitting in Bentley Girl's cast-off skirt. After class, I should go back to Mrs. Pelletier. Tell her this skirt isn't lost. It escaped. From the girl with the composer father and randy old actor and the chauffeur with the dreads.

Carling reaches over to slap the blonde girl's forearm. "Isabella gets a love smack."

This pleases Isabella so much I have to look away.

Though, on some level, I understand her fascination.

Mr. Curtis turns to a girl with smooth black hair pulled back into a high ponytail so glossy it could be made of strands of satin. Her eyes are enormous, her dark-skinned face heart-shaped. Her shirt is buttoned to the chin. She launches into an explanation about helping her right-brain father choose scuff-proof hotel wallpaper and helping her left-brain mother develop an industrial robot system to vacuum each floor, and I realize who she is. Willa Patel from Patel Hotels. I hear they're so completely computerized, the front desk is notified electronically when a room's toilet paper is low.

"What about you, Saint Sarah?" says Mr. Curtis when Willa is done. "Do anything special over the summer?"

Everyone turns around to look at me. They're waiting for me to hold up my superior genes for all to see. My mother's law firm, my father's robot army. But all I have is a hole where my mom used to be and my jilted dad in his really bad janitor uniform.

"I just moved here from Lundon."

"*London*," says Carling, kicking one leg out in front of her in despair. "I'd kill to live in London. They're about two years ahead of us in style. Whatever they're wearing right now, you can be sure we'll be wearing our freshman year in college."

"No," I say. "Not Lond—"

Mr. Curtis interrupts. "If that's true, Carling, you should probably take your new classmate with you on your next shopping excursion. Sara, do you have advice about next year's skirt lengths or must-have accessories?"

For a moment, I'm full of promise. Kids, mostly the

girls, especially Carling and her friends, look at me as if I hold the key to their long-awaited transformation from wool-wrapped super geeks into world-weary It Girls poised on the knife-edge of global miniskirt fashion. Then I open my mouth. "I never, um, never really paid attention to that sort of thing."

Carling, Sloane, and Isabella look disappointed. One by one, they spin around in their seats and face forward. There's nothing to see back here.

"Figures, the daughter of Jesus is an Ant," mutters the dark-haired girl beside me. As Mr. Curtis scrawls a complicated formula on the blackboard, I look up to see she's filming me with a large camera.

I hold a hand up to shield my face. "What?"

"Most insane school in the country. Figures you'd go here." Pulling back from the camera, she squints at it, presses a few buttons, and resumes shooting me, this time leaning closer. The blue circles beneath her eyes, set against her ultra-white skin, combined with the wild black layered hair, make her look like she's been exhumed from a grave.

I'm the daughter of somebody all right, but after spending ten minutes in this class, I'm not sure I should say whom. "What's with the little boy?"

She whispers, "That's Griff Hogan—an eleven-year-old perv-sicle genius who scored higher on the Ant admission test than anyone in history and will probably rule the world one day and force all women to walk around in rubber chaps and pasties. He's in the news all the time and they make him out to be this model student. What never makes it into the papers is that he's more interested in bra sizes than algorithms. Total deviant and not once in the two years has his sniffer been mucous-free."

She's funny, this girl. I wonder if she has any openings in the friend department. "But how does he not get trampled in the halls? He's, like, three feet tall."

She shrugs. "Brains are revered around here. And no one is brainier than Griff Hogan. His family lives in a shack in the South End that should be condemned, but his dad's some famous researcher who won the Nobel Prize in physics about a million years ago. There's some serious cerebral wattage in that family. Any one of us could be begging him for a job one day and we know it. Like I said, Hogan's going to rule the world."

The parents who voted for uniforms were wrong. White shirts and ties might be able to camouflage Griff Hogan's crumbling house, but the real inequality between these students and me can't be erased. The cerebral wattage of my genetic background is comparatively low in volts and all the entrance exams and wool skirts in the world won't change that. Even the poor kids, the ones too gifted to need cram schools and tutors, come from brilliance. I don't belong.

I nod toward Carling. "And her?"

"Carling Burnack is kind of like the school mascot, our crazy-faced lunatic. The daughter of this major award-winning Broadway composer whose career is now seriously wounded. The chicks making googly eyes at her are her minions. The blonde, Isabella, is a prickly little know-it-all, totally devoted to Carling. The brunette who can't keep her eyes open is Sloane Montauk, about the laziest human you'll ever meet. If the boys offered to carry her from class to class on their shoulders, she'd be up for it. These girls all hang out at the Petting Pool at lunch."

"Petting Pool?"

She writes something on a scrap of paper, folds it a few times, and slaps it down on my desk. "Here's my number. Stick with me and you'll be okay. I'm Poppy, by the way. We should totally hang out."

"That would be cool," I say, trying not to sound too eager. When she moves in close with her camera, I laugh. "What's with the short-lens-stalker thing?"

A boy with acne-scarred cheeks and greasy hair grunts from behind her. "Poppy's mom is Kiki Chan."

"The director? Seriously?"

"Don't get all excited about the DNA," the boy says, giving the back of her chair a few playful flicks. "There won't be any Oscars for Poppy. She'll be more into shooting cheating husbands through restaurant windows . . . maybe a few porn flicks to keep her creative edge."

Poppy frowns, lowering her camera for a moment. "I can't even believe you said that, Landau."

Landau squints. "I was joking. Chill."

"Yeah, right!"

"I actually think he was," I say, baffled by her overreaction.

"Oh. So you're taking his side?" Her voice rises into a pathetic squeak.

"No. I . . ."

"You know what, Sara? I've changed my mind. Don't call me."

Mr. Curtis's voice booms from the front of the class-room. "Can we have a little less chatter back there?"

I flip open my binder, mortified. And once I'm certain Poppy isn't looking, I slip her phone number into my pencil case. An overly sensitive friend is better than no friend at all.

chapter 4
molly maid

An ant's social position is clear the moment it breaks out of its pupal casing, fully grown. A wingless female is destined to be a worker.

After class, I follow Poppy into the hall hoping she'll laugh, tell me she was totally joking. But she just vanishes into the crowd of uniforms without so much as a backward glance. Sad part is, I scanned the class while Mr. Curtis was talking and realized there weren't many options in terms of potential friends. A trio of girls in one corner was busy arguing about when the first programmable humanoid robots were built. There was a huge girl hidden behind masses of frizzy hair who refused to acknowledge me when I asked to borrow her eraser, just zipped up her pencil case and looked the other way. Another girl was scribbling what looked like poetry in her journal when the bell rang. When I passed by, she covered it with her hand as if I might steal her haiku and submit it to the *New Yorker* as my own.

I miss Mandy more than ever.

At the escalator I pause to allow Carling, Sloane, and Isabella to step on before me. Sloane immediately drops her books onto the escalator steps and sits down as if hoping to be served fresh-squeezed orange juice before we reach the ground floor.

Carling hoists herself up onto the moving rubber hand-rail, completely oblivious to the forty-foot drop onto cold, hard tile behind her. The open foyer echoes with teenage voices, slamming doors, and the splashing of the water fountain, but I'm inches from these girls and can hear them speaking about some kid rumored to have walked into the office this morning and scrawled on the counter, *I QUIT*.

It was his first day of twelfth grade. He'd just turned seventeen. Word is, his act this morning was a final salute to the extreme pressure he faced from his parents. Nothing less than 100 percent was acceptable to them. Apparently, after this kid received a 96 in biology, his father called the teacher to ask why his son was doing so badly.

"I heard his parents pushed him like mad," says Sloane. "They made him go to Saturday school, which meant even more work. He never got any sleep."

"Who sleeps? I haven't slept a full night since middle school," Isabella says with a sneer. "You don't see me quitting. Anton High has never been known as a warm, fuzzy, make-up-test kind of place. It's Ant eat Ant."

"You're just hip-deep in your Ayn Rand phase right now," Sloane says. "Only the selfish survive and all that tiger-eating shit. You exhaust me, Izz."

"I'm only saying what's true," says Isabella. "Tommie's parents did nothing wrong. They didn't want their son to face a future like theirs—so what? Would you want your child to run a twenty-four-hour grocery store in a seedy part of town?"

Carling bounces her heels against the glass of the escalator. "As long as my brats don't grow up to be moody

composers or horny eleven-year-old juniors in high school,
I'm good with it."

"Yeah, well, it's enough pressure around here without
having your parents on your back at home," Sloane says.
"He'd have been better off if they'd left him alone."
Isabella blinks down at her. "That's a bit naïve."

"Why?" asks Carling.

She lowers her voice. "Tommie probably didn't have
what it takes. He was born to a couple of uneducated
grocers. Just because Tommie *got* in, doesn't mean he
was going to *stay* in. That's all I'm saying. It's a matter of
genetics."

"You, Latini, are a snob," says Sloane.

Carling tilts her head back and lets the breeze from the
massive foyer finger her wild hair as if she's posing for the
cover of *Maxim* magazine. She's gorgeous and it's pretty
clear she knows it. Then, watching her friends' reactions,
she slowly allows herself to fall back farther and farther
until the black handrail lifts up on one side, straining
against her body weight. "I feel so free," she says.

"Stop it, Car," says Isabella. "You're scaring me."

Carling lets her bottom sink lower until only her hands
and the undersides of her knees have contact with the side
of the escalator. Her skirt has risen up to her waist. Grinning, she pokes Isabella with her feet. "Promise to help me
get through math this year?"

"You know I will," says Isabella shrilly, trying to stop
Carling's shoes from touching her uniform. "Just climb
back up before you kill yourself."

Sloane says, "She's just messing with you. She won't let
herself fall."

"You didn't help me with the final last year," Carling sings. "Maybe I should punish you." She lets one hand drop behind her. "Look, Isabella! I'm falling."

The escalator jerks to a stop and an alarm sounds in short, staccato, buzzing beats. Kids start pushing past as if they're well used to Carling's antics.

Isabella grabs uselessly at Carling's calves. "Hurry! Before Mrs. Pelletier comes and suspends you."

I don't mean to edge closer. I don't mean to reach past Isabella and wrap my fingers around Carling's wrist. I don't mean to snap at Sloane, "Don't just sit there, help me pull her up!"

"Get your hands off me, London," says Carling.

"No," I say, pulling harder. Furious at Sloane and Isabella's lack of help, I look back at them. "What's wrong with you people? Help me!"

They don't move. Carling struggles against my grip and loses the hold she had with her other hand. Just before the rubber rail threatens to pop right off its track and send Carling plummeting to the floor below, I'm pushed aside by an old man in a suit covered in chalky handprints. His splatter of white hair disappears over the edge as he takes her by the upper arm and muscles her up and over the railing. Red-faced, he sputters, "Hardly the behavior of a junior at Anton High School, Miss Burnack."

"Thank you, Mr. Snyder." Carling coyly adjusts her skirt and pouts. "I slipped."

"You are just like your mother," he says over the echoing alarm. "If we'd had the escalator in place during her days here, she'd have done the same bloody thing. Goes right back to the Genius Theory, which you'd have learned if you'd signed up for my class last year. See me in my office right away."

The escalator starts moving again and, thankfully, the alarm stops droning. Carling and Sloane gather their books and handbags. As Mr. Snyder steps onto the tile floor and begins to burrow through the clusters of kids milling around in the foyer, Carling calls out to him. "Mr. Snyder?" She tilts her head to one side and starts blinking. "Can you explain the Genius Theory? I've always regretted not taking Intelligence Studies."

She's the most seductive girl I've ever seen, twirling her hair and twisting her body side to side as she flirts with this dusty octogenarian. No surprise, he's falling for it. His pinched face loosens and he reaches up to straighten his tie as students jostle and bump him from behind. "Francis Galton came up with a hypothesis called the 'Genius Theory.' He suspected human intelligence was hereditary and studied the similarities between twins who were raised apart from one another."

"Wild," she says. "What did he find?"

"That their intelligence wound up being very much the same in the end, and his conclusion was this, and I quote, 'Education and the environment produce only a small effect on the mind of anyone, and most of our qualities are innate.' The Genius Theory states that you're born into your future."

"Wow," says Carling, grinning at her friends. "You have a wicked memory, Mr. Snyder. Not every teacher around here is so sharp."

One rheumy eye pinches into an aged and sardonic wink. "I am sharp enough to know when I'm being snookered."

Carling feigns shock. "I would never—"

He starts to walk off. "Not to worry, Miss Burnack. I'll let your behavior go this once if you agree to keep yourself intact for another academic year."

As he toddles away, Carling mutters under her breath, "Asshole."

Isabella says, "See? It's exactly what I said about Tommie."

"What?" says Sloane with a snort. "That he was destined to flunk because his parents aren't rich? Neither are yours and you still won the Hawthorne-Tate Math Prize last year."

This was clearly a prickly spot for Isabella. "My mother's books have received international recognition, in case you've forgotten. Great literary novelists don't always get rich. It's not what they're after. They want to achieve excellence."

"Okay, so your mother serves you literary excellence for dinner. Remind me to eat first next time I come over."

"This conversation's boring me," Carling says, joining arms with the girls. She looks up to see me passing them by and calls out, "Hey, London?"

I can't believe she's talking to me. "Yeah?"

"Question. How is it you got into Ant as a junior and the rest of us had to start when we were fourteen? And don't say you hooked up Mrs. Pelletier with one of the Royals because Izzy tried that and failed."

"Did not!"

I try to come up with a good reply. A reply that is witty enough to impress the most charismatic girl in math class,

if not the entire school. Sadly, I've got very little. I shrug.
"Witness Protection Program."

They glance at each other, disappointed, and walk away.

As I follow them around a corner, I smell the chemical
tang of cleaning product and my pulse races. With all the
strangeness of the morning I completely forgot my dad
is in the school. Sure enough, there he is, pushing a big
sloppy mop. If we were back at Finmory I'd have waved
to him. But here that feels wrong. This place seems to be
splitting me in two. Part of me wants to call out, make a
joke about not missing a spot or something equally lame,
if only to see him look up and grin. But a bigger part of
me freezes.

A tall girl with curly auburn hair trots across the foyer
with a round-shouldered guy and drops her breakfast-bar
wrapper on the floor right in front of him. Charlie stops,
glares at her, incredulous, then picks up the wrapper and
tosses it into the trash.

Isabella whispers, "You know what Francis Galton
would say about the DNA of this guy's offspring. . . ."

Carling mouths the words *Molly Maid.*

chapter 5
lucky girls

Ants are omnivorous; they can eat anything deemed to be edible.

The next night, Dad falls asleep on the couch in front of the news. Since dinner, I've been trying to come up with the nerve to talk to him about Anton. To point out this school is very different from Finmory and that maybe it might be best for everyone involved—namely, me—if we keep our relationship private at school.

Perching myself on the arm of his chair, I shake his shoulder and he opens his eyes, yawns. "Did I drift off?"

"It's okay."

He starts to get up. "The dishes, I forgot—"

"I did them, it's okay."

"What about the spaghetti pot? Sometimes the linguine sticks. You have to let the pot soak in a little olive oil—"

"Got it covered, Dad. It's clean and dry and put away in the cupboard. We need to talk about school."

"Nice staff over there. You getting along okay with your teachers?"

"Yes."

"Good. What about the kids? Are they as smart as you imagined?"

I think back to pre-law this morning and how Carling,

when the teacher asked us what we knew about the Sixth Amendment, cited from memory the 1973 case of *Strunk v. United States*, where if a defendant's right to a swift trial was deemed to have been breached, his or her case is thrown out of court or his punishment removed. All I really know about 1973 is that my dad wants a VW camper bus from that year. "Yeah. The kids are pretty smart. And different too. Not like the kids back home."

"Well. You can't top the Finmory kids."

"Yes. They were especially great to you," I say, nudging his arm. "They loved their Charlie."

He smiles, nods, remembers.

"At this place, students might not be as cool. They probably don't bring in their mother's oatmeal raisin cookies for the custodians, you know? I'm just thinking we should be prepared."

"Prepared for what?"

"For things to be weird here. For them to be dorky about you and me, you know, being at the same school and all that. Mrs. Pelletier said if I don't want to tell anyone, I don't have to."

Dad pulls my head closer with his paw and kisses my nose before standing up and turning off the TV. "If there's one thing I've learned about kids over the years, it's that they live up to our expectations of them. And I expect these kids to be just as terrific as the kids in Lundon. And I expect you to give them the very same opportunity. Deal?"

I try not to look nauseated as I nod. "Deal."

Half an hour later, I lie on my bed, staring up at the ceiling, listening to the sound of relaxed snoring coming from

Dad's room. Things are so simple for adults. They go to work, do their jobs, and come home. No social minefields to tiptoe across, no independent study assignments or exams, no hiding at lunchtime so people won't see how alone they are.

I notice there's something nightmarish about my new room. The walls are lined in fake wood paneling that some child has crayoned all over and, in spite of Dad's scrubbing, the room still smells like a hamster cage. The dirty ceiling slants down like a barn roof, and the wooden floor isn't quite level, so it's hard to find a right angle to stabilize my soul. It's like a giant grabbed hold of my room, rolled it around in his hand, and pushed it back into place, all twisted and wonky. Not a healthy habitat for a linear math brain like mine.

My cell phone vibrates from where it sits on my night table. I snatch it up quickly and almost cry when I see it's Mandy. "It's you," I say with a sigh.

"All I've done since you left is listen to the saddest elevator music and weep." She has music thumping in the background and I'm quite certain it's never been played in an elevator.

"Liar."

"You go first. How geeky are the kids there?"

"They try to get out of phys ed so they can work on trig assignments, they hold Sudoku tournaments on the floor in front of their lockers, and I can pretty much guarantee there's no wood shop."

"In other words, you fit in right away," she says with a giggle.

"No. I managed to stand out just as much as I did at

Finmory. Ate my egg-salad sandwich on a bus-shelter bench down the street from the school."

"Aw, dude. That makes me weep all over again."

"Why? I ate lunch at the bus shelter near Finmory tons of times until I met you. Teenagers don't like me. I'm used to it."

"They're just like the idiots at Finmory. Jealous as all hell because they know you're going to cream them in life. You'll be the serious brains of the school."

I grunt. "I wish. These kids are way beyond me, Mand. I'm completely lost in pre-law and it's only the end of the second day. You should see the stack of homework on my desk. I couldn't even finish it all. And none of the other kids seems to be freaking out. They're all totally used to it."

"Yeah, well. Wait'll they see you in math. Will it help if I tell you I have the sweetest news ever?"

"Let me guess. Eddie proposed to you and wants you to blow off high school so you can follow him around the country and keep the groupies from getting fingerprints on his guitar." Eddie Wilcox is Mandy's long-term boyfriend. A full two years older than her, he manages Video Invasion back in Lundon by day and wastes away his weekends trying to reinvent 1990s boy-band songs with his fellow idiots in his mother's garage. Mandy is completely smitten with him, which baffles me because he has cheated on her twice—that we know of. Besides, I think he looks like a cartoon baby, only stretched out, rubberized, and without the zingy one-liners.

Mandy bites into something crisp—sounds like an apple or a carrot. "Hey, that's the father of my future dropouts you're knocking."

"Sorry. I'll make it up to them in candy and violent video games. What's up?"

"Remember Jessie Clarke's cousin used to have a horse she kept outside of town?"

"Sure. She never let you ride it, no matter how much you hinted. So what?"

"The cousin has scoliosis."

"Wow. That's brutal."

"She needs someone to ride him every day and muck out his stall. And it's going to be me."

"What's the pay?"

"I don't want pay. I want to ride Bojangles."

I consider this. "Not to burst your thought bubble, Mand, but what about homework? You can't just goof around in a barn all year."

"I've come up with a new life ambition. Stable manager. There's a course I can take in Cohasset and, believe me, my grades are not going to matter. Hanging in a barn will be like doing homework."

Mandy has always loved horses but her parents could never afford regular lessons. I know this is a dream come true for her. So why do I feel like throwing up? "That's cool," I say.

"It gets better. Remember my great-grandma died?" she asks. "I guess she's been stashing money under her lumpy mattress or something, because we just found out she left us money. My brother and I are each going to inherit thirty thousand dollars when we graduate high school. I'm going to use it to start my stable."

Mandy is getting to ride a horse for free, inheriting a wad of cash, *and* she gets to stay at Finmory High? I force a smile. "That's amazing! You're so lucky."

"What about you?" she asks with her mouth full. "Is your new house totally gorgeous?"

I glance at my window frame, which still has bits of tinfoil stuck to it. "It's not exactly a house. It's an apartment. Above a hardware store."

"Huh." Mandy is quiet for a moment. "Anyway, I can't wait to come visit next month. Will your dad pick me up?"

"Of course. God, I can't *wait*."

"I wish he'd let you go on Facebook. A few guys friended this *Cosmo* model and she answered them. Bobby asked her out, the moron."

"I'd have loved to have seen her reject him." I laugh. "But you know my father—no Web presence for little Sara."

"Once more, I weep for you."

"Please do."

I hear shuffling from the hall and my dad's sleepy head pokes into my room. "Sara? Are you on the phone?"

I whisper, "Gotta go," snap my phone shut, and pretend to roll over in my sleep.

chapter 6
lockers, unlike mothers, are for life

The little black ant, or Monomorium minimum, *is commonly found in homes and remains active day and night.*

Late Thursday night I sit at my desk, the surface of which is littered with notebooks, open textbooks, an empty package of Oreos, dirty dishes, and a yellow highlighter whose lid has been swallowed up by confusion, exhaustion, and what should be an illegal amount of homework.

I was finally assigned a locker this morning. Apparently lockers are for life since Anton students are assigned a locker number their first day of freshman year and keep it until they graduate or, considering the pressure, go AWOL. Whichever comes first.

All of which means Tommie, the senior who dropped out so famously on the first day of school, left behind something much more exciting than a juicy exit story. He left behind an empty locker. So guess whose new locker is on the third floor with all the twelfth graders? Mine. Doesn't sound like a big deal, but if you think about it, high-school students don't have recess, so where do they make social plans and get to know each other? Hanging around their lockers, of course. It's a pathetic formula.

1 lonely kid + 0 people her age = a whole lot of Saturday nights alone playing Scrabble with Charlie.

It's 12:37 a.m. My eyes itch and ache, and the strain of keeping them open is making me think of using toothpicks as props, like in the old *Flintstones* cartoons. But I still haven't finished my calculus, and after that, I have to read over two case studies for pre-law. Now I'm reading the first three chapters of *Crime and Punishment* for Nineteenth-Century Lit.

I thought I'd hate it. Truthfully, I'm more of a Jane Austen fan. Give me Miss Elizabeth Bennett and her pert opinions over a bedraggled Russian loner in a garret any day. But the main character in Dostoyevsky's book, this Raskolnikov, he had me at *rascal*. I can actually relate to him. His crappy room, his isolation, the way he's afraid to bump into his landlady in the stairwell. I bumped into our landlord, Mr. Ness, in the lobby this morning, and I have to say, was mighty creeped out by the way he looked at me in my skirt. It's not that Rascal thinks his landlady is hot for his bones, he's just a little lean on rubles and it's been awhile since he's paid any rent. But here's what really got me: Rascal hates his ragged clothing almost as much as I hate my new uniform. He's embarrassed to meet with anyone from his past and to this I can totally relate.

Dad knocks on my door. I spin around to find him yawning and scratching his stomach in the hallway. "Fell asleep watching a sitcom."

"Don't torture me with tales of life as I used to know it. Because that would be cruel."

He wanders in and perches himself on the edge of my

bed. "It's a bit late for *Crime and Punishment*, Sara. Why don't you pack it in for tonight?"

"No can pack. I'm nowhere near finished."

"You've been at it for hours and you need your rest."

"Tell it to the Antmasters."

"The workload here does seem to be pretty intense, doesn't it?"

"A heavy workload I can handle. This workload is pulverizing. By the time I'm done I should be milled into a finely ground powder."

Dad doesn't say anything right away. He's been unusually quiet since he started his new job. I can see he's worried he's done the wrong thing, moving me to such a school. He stares at my desktop. "This kind of pressure isn't acceptable. We're going to have a rule around here. Books packed up, lights out by midnight."

"Midnight? I worked longer than that the first day of school!"

He leans close to kiss my cheek, then stands up. "Whatever work you haven't finished by midnight will just have to wait."

"But that's not fair! Or realistic . . ."

"Maybe not, but it's the way it's going to be. Anton students may maintain nothing is more important than getting into an Ivy League school, but I don't. It doesn't matter to me where you attend college as long as you—unlike your feckless father—actually attend." He walks toward the hallway, keys jangling in his pocket.

"Where are you going?" I ask, doing nothing to hide the sarcastic edge in my voice. "It's *after midnight*."

"Just out back to check the doors on the van."

"They're locked. You asked me to check earlier, remember?"

His footsteps echo from the front hall. "I'll sleep better if I've checked myself." And the door slams shut.

There's only one reason my father is a janitor. She's five foot six, with dirty blonde hair and a highlighter that is dying a slow aerospheric death atop her unfinished schoolwork. I wouldn't know it for another sixteen years, but that speck, that poppy seed that was me, that inseminated crumb would force her parents to marry too young and abandon any larger ambition that may have involved postsecondary education.

And if just one event hadn't happened, they might be married still.

It happened back at Finmory, back in tenth-grade science class. All because of an empty water bottle and a kid with lousy aim.

"Students brave enough to hurl their trash at the receptacle from as far away as you sit, Miss Black, generally have better aim. You'll stay after class." Mr. Nathan glared at me from the science-room blackboard where he'd just drawn a lima bean with four teensy sea-turtle flippers and written *five-week-old human fetus* underneath.

Great, I thought. My mom was supposed to pick me up in front of the school after class to take me to the dentist. Isaac Walters threw the empty bottle, we all saw him. But you didn't rat on a kid whose parents had lost their assembly-line jobs at the car-parts factory that just shut down, and who now had to share his grandparents' house with his entire family tree.

The bell rang and as everyone filed out, Mandy gave my shoulder a sympathetic nudge and whispered, "Nathan's such a dick."

Mr. Nathan dropped a battered science book on my desk, flipped it open, and pointed at the left page, toward a faded and fully labeled illustration of a little girl fetus. A long pink umbilical cord wriggled its way out of the baby girl's belly, dipped down into the gutter of the book, and snaked up onto the right-hand page, ultimately latching on to the uterus of a naked lady who, judging from the way she let her unborn child float all the way over to page 232, was probably not going to be much of a mother.

"Copy this illustration on a blank piece of paper, color and label it. I'm going to head out for the day, so you can leave it on my desk when you're finished," he said.

I lowered my head and began to draw.

Once I had filled in the baby's face with closed eyes, pudgy nose and heart-shaped mouth, I paused, staring at the illustration. When a baby is born, she comes out in a whoosh of amniotic fluid and blood, with umbilical cord and placenta still attached. Doctors take hold of the slippery baby and placenta, then sever the thick, flopping cord, immediately compressing the end of the stump with a plastic clamp that remains until the cord dries up and falls off, usually one to three weeks later.

My mother hated the sight of an ugly yellowing stump and blue plastic vise on my body after I was born and dabbed it with rubbing alcohol at every diaper change to dry it up. But as badly as she wanted it gone, I refused to let go of my connection to her womb. The grisly remains of my umbilical cord didn't fall off for a full twelve weeks, prompting the pediatrician to joke that I'd probably be the kind of kid who lives in her parents' basement at thirty.

I've always hated that story. It makes me look needy.

Mom breezed into the classroom and pointed at her watch. Her hair was caught up in a high ponytail and she was wearing black yoga pants, white T-shirt, and white hoodie, making her look younger and more energetic than me. I didn't like her coming right into the classroom. She's flirty—and way too pretty for me to feel comfortable with it. It always made men in our neighborhood stop too long and smile too wide as they walked their dogs or taught their kids to ride two-wheelers in front of our house. "We don't want to keep the dentist waiting, Sara. Let's get moving."

"You must be Mrs. Black," said Mr. Nathan. "Nice to finally meet you." He set down his jacket and briefcase as she told him to call her Tina. Suddenly the man was magnetically incapable of leaving the room.

"I'll just be a few more minutes," I mumbled.

Mom glanced down at my drawing. As she stared, I noticed the way the umbilical cord bulged in spots, like it might burst with pressure, then grew as narrow and limp as overcooked spaghetti. She ran her finger over the amniotic sac. "That looks great. Especially the baby's face. She has a nice smile."

"That's not the baby, Mom. That's the placenta."

"Are you sure?"

"Pretty sure."

"Huh." She studied it. "Oh, right. I see it now."

I grinned, shaking my head. "Liar."

She giggled and leaned over me, pressing a kiss to my

cheek. "Never mind, sweetie. You're a whiz at math and science. As long as you don't become an obstetrician and throw out the baby and hand the mother the smiling placenta instead, you'll be fine."

"I'll watch out for that," I said.

"Sara is definitely one of my better students," Mr. Nathan said. "Tell me, Tina, does she get her talent from her mother's side or her father's?"

Tell me, Tina. That crawled under my skin a bit. And anyway, Mr. Nathan knew my dad was the school janitor—what kind of question was this?

Mom raised her brows. "Well, one can accuse Charlie Black of many things. But being a science whiz wouldn't be one of them. You'd be more likely to find him under the hood of an old car than behind a microscope. He's always been that way. Mechanically inclined."

It wasn't her words but her tone that knocked Dad. I slapped my finished assignment on Mr. Nathan's desk, but neither of them noticed, just kept chatting about science.

Mom sneezed a girly sort of sneeze. Delicate, with a baby chick sort of peep at the end. Her ponytail swished from side to side. If I'd known I would have only 125 more days of her, that after June 27, all I'd have left of her was a green cardigan with beaded roses sprinkled on the shoulders and a fistful of phone messages, I'd have scanned her face for details, committed them to memory.

Did her nose crinkle when she sneezed?

Had springtime freckles begun dusting her cheeks yet?

Were her eyes more hazel or emerald?

"Mom?" I tapped my watch. "I'm ready to go."

She looked at me. "Right! You have some teeth to get

45

cleaned." She glanced at Mr. Nathan and rolled her eyes. "Well . . . off to the dentist."

For a terrible moment I thought he might scoop up his briefcase and follow us to Dr. Pape's. Instead, he waved good-bye, picked up my drawing, and frowned.

Mom was right. I wasn't good with umbilical cords.

Now, sitting at my cluttered desk, waiting for Dad to come back up from the parking lot, I think about his new rule. It will squash me. Which means I need to come up with a quick way around it. Fighting my father is not going to work—his stubbornness is immovable. What I'll have to do is crawl into bed and turn off the lights at twelve o'clock, wait until I hear Dad snoring, then get out of bed and get back to my new friend, Rascal, and toil until I finish my homework. Starting tonight.

Flipping my books shut, straightening my papers, stacking my dirty dishes, I arrange my desk to make it look as if I've actually finished for the night. In the bathroom, I scoop my hair into a ponytail, reach for a bar of Ivory soap, and scrub my face. It isn't until I'm uncapping the toothpaste that I hear the front door thump shut. He's back.

Dad pokes his head into the bathroom and nods his approval. "That's my girl. Night."

"Night," I say with a mouthful of Crest. I spit into the sink, rinse, and reach for a towel to wipe my lips. As I'm rehanging the hand towel, I hear Dad's keys jingle. I wander into the hall to find him heading for the front door once again. "What are you doing?"

He looks sheepish as he steps through the door. "Just realized I forgot something. Off to bed."

I do what I'm told. I climb under my covers, turn out my light, and stare at the shadows until I can get up and start breaking his impossible-to-follow new rule.

I open my eyes to see it's 3:07 a.m. Throwing back my blankets, I jump out of bed, relieved I woke before morning. No sounds come from Dad's room, no snoring, no loud breathing. I'm certain he's submerged in the most cavernous stage of sleep, but I pad to his room to check, with the plan to grab a Coke from the fridge and get back to my homework. His bed is empty. I wander the apartment to find no sign of my father.

Not in the bathroom.

Not in the living room.

Not in the kitchen.

I run out of rooms to search at the exact same moment I run out of calmness. It makes no sense. My breathing grows spiky and thin as I try to think of where he could be.

In nothing but a baggy T-shirt and underwear, I stuff bare feet into my school shoes and race out the front door onto the landing. I peer over the railing—see nothing but dirty steps—then rush down the stairs, praying I don't find his lifeless body. I don't know, exactly, what I'd like to find. But not that. Please not that.

No sign of him in the stairwell. After what seems like days, I reach the door to the back alley and, finally, I see him. Relief thunders headfirst into me, nearly knocking me backward onto the floor. My father is safe.

Only he isn't.

It's happening again.

I press my face to the icy cold glass and watch. He's out there in his pajamas, walking around and around the van, checking each door handle, then staring at it as if it might jump and run off the moment he turns his back. The freakishness of it hits me in the parasympathetic nervous system, completely obliterating my breathing reflex.

It's after three in the morning and I could die from wondering how many times he's checked those doors.

OCD has no logic. Although I've heard it can make people count things. Which, to me, hardly classifies as a problem. I wish that were the kind Dad had. Numbers give me comfort. I could totally handle Dad zigzagging around the apartment grouping things in fives or sevens. On a subconscious, super-geek level, I might even feel a certain pride. But never quite believing the doors are locked baffles me something ferocious. It's like that terrible never-ending hole Dad dug in middle school.

The summer before I started seventh grade was prickling hot. Not a drop of rain fell in two months. With weeds and bushes so dry they sizzled and cracked as you passed, with air so heavy with smog you had to part it like jungle brush, the people of Lundon got a little edgy. But no one worse than Charlie. His mother, my grandmother, died that July, and Charlie spent the rest of the summer inside the house trying to decide where to bury her urn full of ashes. The best way to come to a decision, he found, was by nonstop checking that the windows were spotless and the stove was turned off. The VW—his best friend—sat in the garage and sulked, devastated by his absence.

One evening in late August it started to rain. Not

buckets of rain, as we would have liked. But a noiseless, maddening mist that frizzed up your ponytail and tickled the back of your neck like a mosquito. Just after it began, Dad announced it was time to bury Grandma, went outside with his spade, and headed straight for the front garden at the base of our veranda, determined to dig the perfect hole for the woman who raised him.

But the hole didn't cooperate. The sides had to be straight and smooth or he was a terrible son, he said. Over and over he carved into the earth, only to have the muddy walls cave in on themselves. With water drizzling down his beard and his hair sticking up like Einstein's, he widened the hole, digging up the roses and geraniums and leaving them in a massacred heap on the walkway. Mud gurgled from their roots and streamed down toward the driveway like rivers of blackened blood. Next he excavated the thorny bushes and the newly planted birch sapling and tossed them onto the pile of corpses. Then, once he'd exhumed all vegetative life forms from the bed, he dug wider and wider until Grandma herself could have lain down inside it. It was a full-sized grave.

Then he was on his hands and knees, crawling through the trench to perfect the corners, his face striped with mud. When the corners refused to behave, he shouted at them, his cries loud enough to bring Mom running out of the house in her pink windbreaker, holding a *Good House-keeping* magazine over her head.

I stood on the walkway and watched, helpless. Sometimes I look back on that day and think if Mom hadn't been terrified enough to smother his dripping, earth-smeared face in kisses and promises of a better marriage, if she hadn't led him dripping and sputtering into the house, he might be there still.

It wasn't until Dad was safely inside that I noticed the funereal crowd huddled under a web of spindly umbrellas. Once the umbrellas lost interest and scuttled off down the sidewalk, all that remained was twelve-year-old Ryan Hawthorne from school, his yellow eyes flattened into gloating slits, his patchy buzz cut repelling the rain. I actually watched his smudge of a soul leave his body and rise behind him all green and black like a terrible cartoon smell. It was clear what he was thinking, but he told me anyhow.

"Your dad's a freak."

"Shut up, Hawthorne."

"This is going to make the first day of school *so* much more fun."

I stepped over the pile of muddy roots and headed toward him. "Don't say anything or I'll tell that your sister's pregnant. I saw her tanning her giant belly in your backyard last week."

"At least she doesn't flirt with married guys, like your mother."

I shoved him to the ground so fast he didn't have time to break his fall and his head brushed against the edge of a prickle bush. I stepped on the edges of his sopping wet AC-DC T-shirt. "Shut your filthy little face about her and swear you won't tell. Or I'll push your bald head right back into this bush."

"Okay, get off me. I won't tell!"

"Swear to God?"

"Swear to God."

Five days later he told.

It took the dilution of a high school that fed from four different middle schools for kids to stop calling me "Gravedigger." Until then, my only friend was Mandy.

But shortly after the mud-bath incident, maybe because Mom took him to get help, maybe because he was put on super meds, his OCD began to fade. Other than Dad's getting up early to meditate, other than the bare earth where the prickle bushes and the birch tree used to be, other than the soap-dispenser debacle in tenth grade, it was as if the whole thing never happened.

I was stupid to relax. OCD is like a puffy white dandelion wishie. With the slightest breath, its feathery seedlings tumble up into the air and disappear. But they aren't gone. They will find a place to burrow and, sooner or later, will sprout again. It's the only thing in life I'm certain of right now.

Watching Dad circle the car in the dark, I press my face into the glass. I know I should be worried for his health. His sanity. But I have only one thought.

Please don't do this at school.

chapter 7
blinking back stupid

Periodically, the fertile and winged males and females rise up into a short-lived mating flight, after which the males die.

Friday morning I wake up exhausted. After finally convincing Dad to come upstairs to bed, after finally getting back to bed myself, I couldn't sleep. I knew Dad's locking of the van doors would be waiting for me in the morning. In full daylight. Right behind Anton High School. Will it be a repeat of last night? There is no way of knowing until it happens.

Hunched over his second cup of coffee at the breakfast table, my father seems remarkably well rested for a guy who spent who-knows-how-many hours in a parking lot in his pj's.

I wrap my arms around him and give him a peck on the cheek. His skin is smooth, soft. It smells like Christmas morning and makes me sad as I sit down in front of a bowl of Cheerios. "Do you ever do that meditation routine anymore, Dad? The one you did when I was in middle school?"

"Too much work."

"But it calmed you down, remember? It was good for you."

"Took nearly an hour. I'm a single parent; I don't have that kind of time."

But he has the time to circle the van all night long. This is the thing. At some point he stopped taking care of himself. *Refused* to take care of himself. Stopped meditating, stopped seeing his psychiatrist, stopped taking his meds. It almost cost him his last job. It played no small role in my mother's decision to leave. And all the while he's the most lovable man on earth. It's crazy-making. "Pretty wild night, huh?"

He loads two spoonfuls of sugar into his cup and looks up. "Excuse me?"

"You know . . . with the door handles."

After sipping from his cup, wiping a dribble of coffee from his chin, he nods. "They're not in great condition, those handles. It's impossible to tell whether they're locked."

I stare at the fake wood pattern in the Formica table. There's one pear-shaped black knot—fake knot—that is tightly wrapped in long, swerving lines. The lines nearest to the knot follow its shape closely, but as they get farther and farther away, the lines begin to lose their fruity direction, until they eventually run so straight they cannot possibly know the knot exists. "That's not what I meant," I mumble.

"Hmm?"

"Nothing."

"I spent three hours working on the transmission a few weeks ago and just *listen*." Charlie pulls the sputtering van into the school laneway and I forget any fears of

53

door-handle checking because horrendously loud explosions have begun shooting out the back end like muffled mechanical farts, creating a ripple of excitement among the students in the parking lot. I bend down and pretend to dig something out of my backpack to avoid detection as he continues his rant. "It's as if she's in agony. I have half a mind to turn around and spend the rest of the day under the hood."

The sun hangs so low I wonder if I might reach up and twist it from the sky, blackening the whole city and rendering me invisible. If only. "It's just a car, Dad."

"No such thing, my girl."

I sink lower in my seat, sickened to be attracting such gaseous attention. Dad coasts into a parking spot mercifully close to the edge of the lot, kills the already dying engine, and climbs out. He reaches into the backseat for his jacket, pulls it on, and locks his door. Without checking to see if it really is locked, he walks around to my side and stares at me. "Coming?"

There's no way I'm climbing out of this vehicle. Not until anyone and everyone who witnessed our entrance has lost interest and toddled away. Still ducked down, I hold up one shoe and tug at the laces. "Leave me for dead. I'm having footwear issues."

"They look just as loathsome as anyone else's. What's the problem?"

"They're pinching. Go ahead."

"Just don't forget to lock up. It might not sound so hot, but this bus is a classic."

"If someone steals it, they won't get far without attracting attention. Let that be your comfort."

"I'm being serious, Sara."

"I'll lock up. Go forth and do that uniform proud."

He doesn't move right away. Just chews on his cheek and considers the pragmatics of walking away and leaving his girl here unprotected. The van, not me.

I decide to appeal to his sense of responsibility. "Dad, the bell's about to ring. You don't want to be late. First impressions, remember?"

It works. Dad lifts his hand in a half wave, half salute and says, "Right. You have a good day, hon. Try to get your homework done right after school so you can get to bed at a reasonable hour."

He vanishes into the maze of vehicles, leaving me squatting on the dirty floor mat, blinking back stupid, and trying to figure out what's happened to our lives.

My Nineteenth-Century Lit teacher doesn't seem to belong at Ant any more than I do. She's not from Boston— you can tell from the way she pronounces words like *get* as *git*—and it's clear she's intimidated by the students, probably because she's practically still a kid herself. She gets flustered and blushes when she loses her place in the lesson. Then, once she figures out where she left off, she giggles and runs a hand through her cropped curls as if in apology. The gesture slices into me, somewhere deep, right in my very center. If anyone gets what it's like to be the outsider, it's me.

Luckily the students at Ant are too grade-centric to give her a hard time. If Ms. Solange stood before a Finmory class and showed herself to be this unsure and timid, the kids would eat her alive, the way they once made

it a schoolwide goal to ensure any substitute teacher quit
before the end of her first day.

It's not a very popular class; only half the seats are filled.
There are a few kids I recognize—Willa's up at the front,
and there's a guy from pre-law near the door. And Poppy
is sitting to my right. As I watch the teacher unpack today's
lesson, I wonder if she takes the poor turnout personally. I
hope not, but I'm sure, on some level, I would.

Poppy slides a peppermint onto my desk. "Hey."

I pick up the candy, pleased she's being friendly again.
"Is this for me?"

She unwraps another one and pops it into her mouth.
"Yep. I have plenty more. One for each period. Eat it."

"I will."

"Eat it now." Her fingers are wrapped around the
camera on her lap.

I just finished a honey-almond granola bar and am
quite happy with the current taste in my mouth. "I can't
do mint this early. Late-rising tastebuds."

She's quiet, fidgeting with her camera and staring into
her lap. Finally she says, "It's because it's from me, right?"

"That has nothing to do with it." I can see her mouth
tighten and I'm terrified we're on the edge of another
snap-at-Sara episode. "You know what? I will eat it now." I
unwrap the candy and pop it into my mouth. "I love it. It's
so . . . pepperminty."

She seems reassured and starts filming me as I suck on
her striped lozenge. I don't dare do anything but make the
candy dissolve as fast as possible.

Ms. Solange steps in front of her desk and leans back
against it. "If you did your reading, you'll know our friend

Rodion Raskolnikov has hazy, unformed theories forming in his pretty head as he sits in his horrid coffin-shaped room."

Willa waves her hand. "I liked the inconsistency between Rodion's good looks and the squalor of his apartment. A lesser writer would have made him look despicable, don't you think?"

"Nice observation, Willa. I couldn't agree more."

"I actually read *Crime and Punishment* over the summer and wrote an essay about it," says Willa. "His clothing was ragged, so was everything around him, yet his face was beautiful. Said a lot about his soul."

"Excellent, Willa," says Ms. Solange. She turns back to the class. "Now, young Raskolnikov's ideologies are so imprecise you'll later see they actually contradict each other. This was not accidental on the author's part. Raskolnikov gets busy with his borrowed theory that the end justifies the means. And if a desired outcome brings about a situation that benefits humanity, the extraordinary man is justified in using any means to make it happen. Which is how Raskolnikov comes to plan the murder of the old pawnbroker who beats her—"

There's a knock at the door and a guy with dark eyes and sandy hair pokes his head in. "Excuse me, Ms. Solange." He points across the room. "I forgot my stats textbook. You mind if I just go grab it?"

Ms. Solange waves him in and starts pacing. She's lost her place. Sure enough, her hand goes up to hide in the curls. I can't stand it. I park my mint in the pouch of my cheek and say, "Ms. Solange? The old pawnbroker was known for beating her sister, wasn't she?"

"That was smooth." Poppy is still filming me.

Ms. Solange looks at me, relieved. As she details the way the craggy Aliona owed the cleanliness of her furniture and floors to her severely underappreciated sister, the guy weaves his way through the classroom and stops right in front of me. He's wearing the silver tie pin that shows he's a senior. He grins, his lips parting to reveal smooth teeth. "Mind if I dive under your desk?"

I look down to see a textbook near my foot. Quickly, I scoot back to give him space. "No. I mean, sure. Go ahead."

He climbs down onto the floor and his shoulder brushes against my knee. I pull it away and rub it until the tingling stops. As he withdraws, he bumps his head on the underside of my desk and stands up laughing, embarrassed. He salutes me with his *Statistics Today* textbook, winks, and leaves the room, not quite closing the door.

"Turn this way," whispers Poppy. "I need a close-up."

I don't turn. I don't even acknowledge her. I can't. I'm too busy staring at the doorway.

chapter 8
skirtie come home

The thief ant is known for setting up its nest adjacent to or inside larger ant colonies, making it relatively simple to steal food and pupae from its host colony.

Anton High has its very own store, located right behind the office. I saw it on my way to pre-law after a very lonely lunch hour during which I hid in an empty classroom, ate a dried-out tuna wrap, and sent desperate text messages to Mandy about my father.

The store, matter-of-factly called Store, has huge display windows on either side of the door. One is decorated with textbooks, packages of highlighters, and leather-bound weekly planners. Handmade thought clouds offer tired motivational messages such as FAILING TO PLAN IS PLANNING TO FAIL.

The other window is dressed more like the Lost and Found closet, only this clothing definitely hasn't been left in a forgotten heap under the bleachers. Mostly the display shows spirit wear, like navy Anton varsity jackets and striped scarves, though school spirit really only extends to the robotics and math teams. Apparently it's difficult to get students to support a basketball team that hasn't won a game in fifty-three years.

Seeing as I'd already failed to plan in my choice of socially acceptable hosiery and moved straight to plain old failing, I've been promising myself all afternoon on Friday that I'd treat myself to kneesocks. I considered going back to Mrs. Pelletier, there was that box of unloved cable knit socks—but I can't. Or won't. The twenty dollars in my backpack should be enough to buy me a few pairs of kneesocks.

After school, the shop is infested with Ants—some still in uniform, some in phys-ed clothes, some who've changed into jeans. A bell chimes as I walk in and a security guard makes me stash my backpack into a cubby in the interest of preventing theft. I take out my wallet and hand over my bag.

Inside the store, girls slip in and out of curtained dressing rooms to admire themselves in full-length mirrors, squealing hellos to people they haven't seen all summer while their hips gyrate to the punk music thumping from speakers that hang from the ceiling. I grab a wire basket and head down an aisle, hoping no one will notice I'm the only one, besides the student cashier and the backpack bouncer, who's friendless.

The back corner is dripping with ties, undershirts, and kneesocks. I throw three pairs of socks into my basket. Beside me, a girl holds a pair of blue yoga pants against her body, then reaches for two more pairs in gray and stuffs them all in her basket. When she leaves to join her friend at the cash desk, I run my hand along the cool stacks of Lycra. Knowing full well I have no way of paying for them, now or in the near future, knowing I'll only have to put them back on the shelf and walk away depressed,

I hunt for a pair of size 6 longs, lay them over my arm, and, keeping my head down, bore through the crowd at the back and disappear into a dressing room.

I can't strip fast enough. Skirt and tights drop to the floor. I pull on the yoga pants and realize, too late, that there are no mirrors inside the tiny stall. My love affair can continue only if I slip out from behind the safety of my curtain.

Tripping over my cast-off uniform as I leave the dressing room, I bundle my shirt and vest at the waist and emerge.

The pants are gorgeous and make me look as if I actually do yoga. Which I don't. They're probably well over seventy bucks, and I know Dad would never agree to such a purchase, plus he'd hate the Anton logo on the right butt cheek, but I let myself dream for just a few more minutes.

A girl with a snub nose and short mahogany hair looks at me. "Those look so good on you. You should totally get them."

"Thanks." I yawn, wondering if I dare catch a nap on the bus ride home. "Maybe I will."

What a lie.

Anxious to escape her roving eyes, I yank back a curtain and walk straight into the muscled chest of a guy. But not just any guy. A nearly naked guy. Well, naked other than the underwear or bathing suit or whatever. It's hard to get past the beefy pecs fairy-dusted with blond hair, which trickles down his tire-tread abs and into his . . . into his low-slung boxers.

I peel my hands off his chest, my face burning with flustered giggles, and look up at his brown eyes. It's the guy who burst into lit class this morning. The twelfth grader who forgot his textbook. "Sorry," I mumble.

Instead of breaking into a smile and making some lame sexual innuendo, like any of the guys at Finmory would have, this guy's face darkens and he snatches up a T-shirt. As he tugs it over his head, I notice his chest and shoulders are stippled with dozens of tiny scars, as if something exploded and he'd been caught in the fiery spray. I can practically smell the sizzling flesh.

"Seriously," I say, backing up. "This no-sleep-by-night is getting to me."

The scars are safe under the T-shirt now. He looks at me, his mouth a grim line that slopes down on one side. No sign of the sweet guy who bumped his head on my desk. "Try opening your eyes by day," is all he says.

I fumble with the twisted curtains and bolt. Back in my dressing room, I fall to the floor, fighting not to drop dead of mortification. I can just see him in the halls later, pointing me out to his friends, mocking the idiot who copped a feel and kept right on gawking.

Those scars . . . I can't imagine what caused them. In such a concentrated area too. His face was unmarked; so were his abs. Whatever it was, it had to have hurt like hell.

On the other side of the curtain, life goes on as if nothing happened. The beat of some song I'm too uncool to recognize. A cashier telling kids they have ten more minutes until closing. A girl with a deep voice wondering why she suddenly has two skirts with her name sewn in them. Her friends laughing.

I compose myself and reach for my tights. But where's my skirt?

I peer through the curtain. It's not out there. My heart starts to pound again. This makes no sense. How can a piece of clothing just disappear? It isn't possible. A wool skirt doesn't just walk away.

"You're such a brat," says a bored voice. "That's what you get for owning, like, *six* school skirts. They're dropping from the sky."

Another voice, this one jingling like thin gold bangles. "It doesn't make sense. Seriously, did you wear two skirts to school?"

"As if! I didn't even know this skirt was missing."

That third voice. Deep. Raspy. I've heard it before.

I remember. In Honors Math. One row up. Wearing Sunday underpants on Tuesday. Carling Burnack owns that voice. Not only that, now she owns my skirt. Which was, of course, her skirt all along.

I peer through the curtain to see Carling examining my pleats. I want to call out to her. Explain what happened. Promise to return it to her in the morning. Point out that while she has too many skirts for one girl to manage, this one is all I have to wear home. But I can't do any of that. It would mean admitting that I went shopping in the Lost and Found.

Sloane sits cross-legged on the carpet. "Maybe Izzy stole it, so she could feel closer to Carling at night."

"Shut up," Isabella hisses. She flashes Carling a smile. "I know what happened. The poor skirt got lost and traveled hundreds of miles to find its way back to her crotch. Kind of like Lassie. I think it's sweet."

Carling pets the skirt like a bedraggled collie. "Poor baby. We should re-create its journey across the country and shoot it for film class." She presses a kiss to the rumpled fabric. "Skirtie Come Home."

A guy's voice utters something I can't hear and my blond dressing-room victim strolls up to Carling. He's all smiles now as he slings one arm around her shoulder and plants a kiss on her mouth.

Anton's boy genius—redheaded Griff Hogan from math class—interrupts the kiss. He grabs the skirt and pushes his snout into it.

"Griff, you're *such* a pig." Carling snatches up the skirt and pushes it into her bag. They all turn and head down one of the aisles.

I close my curtain. So that's it. I'm officially screwed. I can't approach the cashier and explain. Too risky. She's definitely a student here—she was still in her uniform. There's no way I can trust her. I have no choice but to go home wearing nothing but a pair of black tights and a white shirt that doesn't even come close to covering my behind.

Unless.

I think of Rascal, stashed away on his fraying sheets. I know what he would say. If you prevent some calamity or unpleasantness from befalling society, if you are truly a great dude, any crime is justifiable.

Surely it cannot be fair to the good people of Boston to have some girl from Lundon climbing onto a city bus in her tights. It would be some kind of unpleasantness, there's no mistaking it. And this is a definite calamity. Besides, it wouldn't be murder.

I stare down at the pants, then bend over and run my hands along every inch of fabric, feeling for an antitheft device. All I find is a bar-coded tag hanging from the waistband. The thing is, I've never done anything like this before. I wasn't one of those toddlers who reached for lollipops in the grocery store and by-accident-on-purpose dropped them into her stroller. I've never stolen anything in my life. I generally walk around this planet feeling I don't belong, so why add to the misery with guilt?

Sucking in a deep breath, I picture Rascal one more time, then rip off the tag and head for the cashier to pay for my socks. As I make my way toward the exit, I pass Carling and her posse by the varsity jackets. I feel her eyes on me as I leave.

At the door, the guard smiles, tells me to have a nice day. It's all I can do not to peel off the pants and hand them over. My face burns as I hurry past him, unable to choke out a reply. My hands start to tingle as I realize there is no turning back. I'm a thief now. A thief! Even if I grow up to end wars, cure diseases, or find lost puppies, I can never erase today.

Saint Sarah, I guess.

This was a huge mistake. I would have handled bolting in my ratty underwear better than I'm handling this.

I head out into the hall in search of a water fountain. Cold water on my face, that's what I need right now. As I march down the corridor, I hear footsteps keeping pace with me. I spin around to find myself staring at Carling Burnack. It's the same thing every time I see her. I get a thrill. A jolt. Like I've spotted a celebrity.

She walks toward me, her hips swinging with the kind of confidence I've never had. "You're some kind of new girl, aren't you, London?" When I don't answer, she laughs. "That's okay. If I were you, I wouldn't bother defending myself either." She reaches out and pulls the stretchy fabric from my thigh, then lets it go with a snap. "Not if I was wearing the evidence."

"It's not what it looks like. I was in the changing room and "

"Lose the sob story, London. I don't want to hear it. Besides, I'd rather be friends with a thief than a liar."

chapter 9
burn baby burn

Unlike most species, the fire ant both stings and bites, creating an intense burning sensation at the site.

At one point on the bus ride home, I actually press my fist into my lips so I don't throw up. Could it have gone worse? Carling Burnack knows what I did. She could do anything with this knowledge. Anything. Turn me in, blackmail me, tell the other kids.

Then again, she did say something about being friends.

I stopped by the Lost and Found before leaving the school. My plan was to find Mrs. Pelletier and tell her what happened. Explain that I had no choice but to leave the changing room in my tights. But Mrs. Pelletier is so kind and so trusting it hurts. As soon as I told her I lost my skirt, she made some joke that misplacing my skirt is proof I've assimilated. She looked almost proud of me as she led me into the closet. How could I tell her I stole from the school when she was being so good to me? While she thinks I'm a decent person?

I took the coward's way out. Made sure to stand a few steps back so she couldn't smell the newness of the yoga pants. Believe me when I say, no pants on earth have ever smelled this pristine. It was making me dizzy. I choked back my guilt, popped another skirt in my bag, thanked her, and hopped on a bus.

Our apartment building has a climate all its own—not unlike the inside of a casket that's been underground for a few years. The air, what little of it exists, is so dark and dense you have to gnaw on it, soften it, before every breath. It's foggy with dust and dander, so much so that I've taken to waving my hands in front of my face as I walk, to clear myself a path.

The foyer is lined in bare brick with nothing more to dress the walls than a handwritten poster reading *NO PeT. Absolute NO EXePtion.* And whatever effort the owners didn't put into ventilation and signage, they made up for with a peculiar choice on the floor. Below my feet, the buckling wooden floorboards are coated in chipped pink paint so thick it could be dried-up frosting.

Still reeking of guilt and factory-fresh Lycra, I trudge to the bottom of the narrow wooden staircase and start the long, airless climb to the fourth floor.

Halfway up the second set of stairs, I detect the peppery sweetness of weed wafting out from under someone's third-floor door. All three entryways on this floor are unpainted wood, and there's a sickly tree in a plastic pot beside 3B that may or may not be dying of secondhand smoke. I slow down in front of each door on Cannabis Row, trying to determine who's doing the dirty deed, but cannot detect any difference. Maybe the smell's coming from all three.

I slow as I pass 3C because the door is cracked open just enough that I can peek inside. From what I can see the place is nearly empty but for a wooden futon with rumpled pillows and bedding, two overturned milk crates functioning as a coffee table, and a sheet nailed to the window frame.

Suddenly a guy in surfer shorts and a *South Park* T-shirt appears. His skin is pasty, and he's thin enough that his bones threaten to pierce his skin. In his hand is a smoldering joint, which makes me feel marginally better. There's another person breaking the law today, and he's not even worried about keeping it secret. As he tosses his head, a snarl of dusty dreads swings forward like decaying snake skins, and I realize I'm staring at the driver of Carling Burnack's Bentley. "Hey," he says, shutting the door before I manage to squeak out a "Hey" of my own.

As soon as I'm through the threshold of our apartment, I pull the pants down to my ankles and stumble to my room, where I kick them off and cram them behind the unpacked boxes in my closet. I dump a handful of old books and clothing on top. Then I slam the closet door shut and lean back against it as if the pants might try to dig their way out of their makeshift grave.

I miss my old life so much it hurts. Mandy's been calling me every night to rave about her new horse. She's planning to spend tomorrow hacking him in the woods, oiling his hooves, and trimming his tail. After, she and Eddie will go to a big party at Vince Martin's house, where Leeza Owens is supposed to show up with a tattoo that goes from her shoulder to her elbow.

Normal teenage existence seems so far away. A life where I'm not monitoring my father's condition and pulling all-nighters and contemplating being expelled for theft seems so out of reach I wonder if I ever knew it at all.

I roll over onto my side to see a small envelope waiting on my nightstand. It's dirty and tattered to the point of being fuzzy at the edges and is addressed to me. There's no sender information, but the thin, weblike handwriting gives it away even before the French postmark. It's a new tactic from my mother—a letter in disguise. Slipping a fingernail under the sealed flap, I pause. Do I really want to hear what she has to say, especially since her departure is the reason Dad's obsessiveness has shown up again?

Then again, maybe something has changed. Maybe she hates the taste of French tobacco more than she hates life with me and Dad. Maybe she's coming home. Maybe she can save me from my new life.

I tear open the envelope and pull out a thick letter. A photo falls to the floor, landing faceup. As soon as I see it, I realize I'm a stupid girl who gets what she deserves. I knew not to open the letter and I opened it. There, lying on the rug, is the black-net rocket of the Eiffel Tower piercing a bleached white sky. Worse, standing at its base is my smiling mother. Whomever she is arm in arm with has been cut out in a lame attempt to crush me slightly less, but I recognize the fur on those burly forearms. It's the man I despise more than anyone on earth. The reason she went to a French cooking school in the first place. Her bilingual boyfriend got a job so good she just couldn't help herself.

I snatch up the photo, the letter, the filthy envelope, and push it into my metal wastepaper basket. Then I heave my window open, set the can on the sill. I light one of the

Benson & Hedges from the package I swiped out of my mother's purse, drop it into the garbage can, and watch the Eiffel Tower curl up and burn.

Once the smoke in my bedroom has cleared and my mother has vanished—yet again—I wander into the kitchen and pick up the ancient wall phone to check for messages. The beeping dial tone raises my hopes that Mandy has called with more delicious news from Lundon. But after punching in our password, I hear a man's voice.

"I'm looking for Charlie Black. . . ." He pauses, shuffling a few papers. "I hope I have the right number. This is Ryan Talbot from Eastern Property Management. We'd like to offer you the position you interviewed for. Give me a call at the office when you get a chance."

I knew it. Dad should have called them after his interview instead of jumping at the first janitor job that came his way. Wait a minute. This means we can move back home!

So many happy thoughts swarm my head they get all tangled up. The vision of a full night's sleep bumps into the thought of hanging out with Mandy again. The joy of being absent from Poppy's future movies collides with the hope that Dad's locked doors will settle down if we go home. Best of all, I can escape Carling and whatever it is—or isn't—that she might do to me. Before I know it, I'm wrapping myself in the phone cord and wondering, with all the extra money Dad will be making, if we'll be able to afford to live in the two-story house next to Mandy's.

Just then, Dad's key turns in the lock and I race to throw my arms around him. He kisses the top of my head and tosses his keys into a bowl on the hall table. "Do I smell smoke?"

"You got the job, Big Charlie!" I'm on my toes with excitement. "The guy from the property-management company left a message. He wants you to call him right away!"

He pulls off his Anton High jacket, looking confused. "The job in Lundon?"

"Yes. Which means we can go home! I can burn my uniform and my books, you can ditch your janitor suit, and we can go back to Lundon! Isn't that sweet?"

Dad wanders into the kitchen and pulls a beer out of the fridge like he hasn't a care in the world. He leans against the counter and sniffs the air. "Did you start burning your clothes already?"

"Did you hear me?" I hop up onto a barstool and spin around and around. There will be no greater feeling on earth than walking into school Monday morning and dumping my uniform on the counter in the office. And I'll pack up my room, leaving nothing but the yoga pants behind. "Maybe we can buy a house on Mandy's street. You know that place next door to hers, the one with the porch that wraps around the whole place? It's been for sale forever."

"Sara . . . ," Dad says quietly.

"Listen to the message. The guy actually says the job is yours."

"Honey, I don't want that position. Today was a great day. I formulated a new tracking procedure for the supply room next to the gym. Repaired the cooling system in the south building—it hasn't functioned in three years. The principal himself came down to the custodian's room and welcomed me. Said from what he hears, in another month I'll have this place running so smoothly—"

"But the other job pays, like, twice what Ant pays you. You said it yourself. And it's a huge step up. You'd get to hire *other* people to fix cooling systems. You'd get to be the Big Cheese!"

Dad reaches into the fridge and pulls out two pork chops, unwraps them, and puts them on a plate. He pulls out the frying pan and peers closely at it. "Doesn't look quite clean." Holding it under steaming hot water, he scrubs at it until I think the sponge might scratch right through the metal. Then he dries the pan, inspects it, shakes his head, and begins scrubbing all over again.

"Dad," I say, putting my hand on his arm. "It would be so good for you to get away from cleaning. . . ."

He shuts off the water and drops the pan to the counter with a clatter. After a deep breath, he says quietly, "Not everyone is cut out to be the boss," and walks off toward his room, leaving me alone with the uncooked pork.

I stand perfectly still for a moment, blinking back hot tears. My father makes no sense. It's like he's avoiding any positive action in his life, and I have no choice but to pick my way through the rubble of his decisions. I know life isn't fair. I've heard the propaganda. But come on, is hoping for a little normal paternal behavior really asking so much? He doesn't even shout and swear when he gets mad! Instead, he gets quiet. He disappears. It doesn't happen often, but his near silence can crack your eardrums.

I can see now my mother was wrong about Charlie's being unmotivated when it comes to his career. There was something in his face as he scrubbed the pan. It was fear. My father hasn't been a janitor all these years because he's lazy. My father is terrified to try for more. He's convinced he is exactly where he should be, convinced if he pretends nothing is broken, it isn't. Just like he did with my mother.

It was early June, the sixth, to be exact, and I was sitting at my desk in my old bedroom pretending to be studying for my English test the next day. Really, I was drawing pictures of myself wearing the most spectacular prom dress ever. My first formal dress ever, for that matter. It was officially the best day of my life. Jeremy Gleason—an actual twelfth grader—stopped me on the way to health, waved me into a stairwell, and blurted out, "Wanna go to prom?"

It was the first time I'd been asked to go anywhere with a boy, let alone prom. I wasn't the type of girl Lundon guys even looked at, other than when they were flunking math and needed an afternoon of tutoring. Mom was going to die of excitement.

I looked up from my doodles and sniffed the air. Something wasn't right. The house should have been filled with the smell of my roasted chicken. You know, the kind of aroma that made you feel you were living in a real home, where sisters squabbled over bathroom time on school mornings and brothers thought the whoopee cushion was funny for the fifty-eighth time. Where a mother was there waiting for you when you got home from school with the best news ever.

But 67 Norma Jean Drive didn't smell like any of that. It smelled lethal, like chemical soup. I hurried down to the kitchen, stuffed my hands into oven mitts, and pulled the roasting pan out of the stove, praying the fumes weren't coming from the chicken I'd so carefully prepared to celebrate my news. As soon as I lifted the lid, it was pretty clear what I was dealing with. Toxic chicken.

I flipped through the recipe book to see where I'd messed up. I had washed the chicken, rubbed salt into the puckery skin. I stuffed a quartered onion into the revolting cavity—wait a minute. I touched my right index finger. No! Quickly, I spooned out what was left of the onion. Sure enough, twinkling from under the mashed onion was a hunk of blackened, once-gold metal sticking out of a melted pool of swirly black goo.

My mood ring.

Just then, a key jiggled in the front door. My parents were home. Quickly, I dumped my bejeweled stuffing into the trash and lifted the chicken onto a platter. I scattered a few handfuls of baby carrots onto the plate and placed it on the table I had set when I got home from school. Nothing, not even a baked mood ring, was going to ruin my big announcement.

It was pathetic to be so excited over a prom invitation. I was fairly sure other tenth-grade girls didn't rush home to cook a celebratory family dinner after being asked to prom.

Dad walked into the kitchen, kissed my cheek. Then he grinned and looked from oven to chicken to me. "Did you cook it in a rubber boot again?"

"Not funny. I *slaved* over a hot stove."

He sniffed the air. "Did you season it with erasers?"

"Rushed home from school . . ."

"Smells a bit like fertilizer."

"Plunged my hands into a raw chicken, risking salmonella poisoning, risking death by parasite . . ."

"Or is it toilet sanitizer?"

"All so I could announce to my adoring parents . . ."

"If anyone knows toilet sanitizer, it's me."

"That I got asked to prom!" I said with a squeal.

Dad's response wasn't exactly what I'd been hoping for. "Prom? You're only in tenth grade."

"Jeremy's a senior."

"I don't know. You've never even been to a school dance before."

"Rub it in, why don't you?"

"Sorry." He opened the cupboard and pulled out a bag of pretzels. "Are you—and this boy—going alone or with a group of kids? And does he drive? More importantly, does he drive well? Because I could drop you off and pick you up."

Oh, God. This was going to be a disaster. I needed my mother to intervene; she'd understand that having Dad peering at us from the front seat would be an absolute prom killer. I'd rather walk.

"When's Mom coming home?"

"Should be any minute now." He sat at the table and poked at my chicken with a butter knife. "Traffic is terrible out there."

The phone rang. Dad picked it up. "Hey. You might want to hurry home. Our girl has outdone herself in the department of Roasted Chickens Gone Wild." His face darkened slightly and he turned away, lowering his voice. "Seriously? Again? You worked late three nights last week."

I walked to the sink and pretended I wasn't listening. And while I was at it, I pretended it wasn't happening again. Pretended it wasn't killing me that my mother wasn't coming home to my meal. Didn't care to hear my . . . whatever.

It wouldn't matter. Not compared to what would follow.

"It's not me you're disappointing," said Charlie. A long pause, then, "All right. Don't wake us when you get in." He hung up and sat himself at the kitchen table in front of the noxious chicken. For a moment he said nothing. Then he picked up his knife and fork and smiled as if nothing had happened. "So, should we see if this bird tastes any better than it smells?"

chapter 10
cinnamon hearts

Worker ants are charged with the job of caring for the eggs, larvae, and pupae; protecting the nest; and foraging for food.

Other than the scrubbing of the frying pan, all was quiet on the OCD front over the weekend. I studied, Dad played with the van with no mention of door locks, and we shared a few games of Scrabble, most of which I lost to Dad's fussy vocabulary.

Monday morning Dad goes into "the office" early, so I get myself to school on a bus that takes forever to show up. For the first time, I step onto campus looking like a true Ant. With thick black socks that hug the backs of my knees. With bare thighs so cold they ache. With dark, sleepy, under-eye smudges that have puffed up into tiny pillows.

I have no idea what to expect today. What will Carling do now?

Trotting up Arlington Street, I realize I'm later than I thought. The sidewalk is completely empty of kids. A car pulls over and a boy dressed in jeans jumps out and races through the great carved doors. He might as well turn around and race home. From what I heard last week, forgetting your uniform is akin to showing up at school naked. They whisk you out of sight and place a swift and stern phone call to your parents.

The moment I walk through the doors, I spy two more kids in street clothes: a wannabe jock in cut-off sweats and a Red Sox T-shirt, and a tall girl in the Ant yoga pants and matching hoodie. On her feet are brown sheepskin boots. She looks me up and down and giggles as she passes. A sick feeling scrabbles down into my stomach.

Inside the classroom, no one is in uniform. I feel as if I'm in a bad dream. Guys are in ancient polo shirts, jeans, baggy shorts, sweatshirts, flip-flops. Girls are wearing blue, black, or colored jeans; jeweled ballerina flats or Vans slip-ons.

Some wear pastel Lacoste dresses with sheepskin boots. Willa, usually so buttoned-up and tucked in, wears a multipurpose sequined minidress that looks like a computer chip from afar. Isabella is ready for stripper pole or pop equestrian event in a plunging wraparound sweater, tan breeches, riding boots, and a velvet baseball cap. Poppy is even more versatile. In her grim reaper–colored taffeta dress, broken tiara, shredded fishnets, and knee-high combat boots, she's prepared for the exhuming of graves, the attending of brides, and the invading of unsuspecting countries. Sloane looks like she's just climbed out of bed in her thermal undershirt and plaid jammie bottoms tucked into sheepskin boots.

Hair, it seems, has exploded into ironic ratted, matted, teased, curled, pigtailed, or faux-hawked statements of rebellion; Willa's demure ponytail being the only exception.

I try to slip into my desk without anyone noticing. I fail.

Some people roll their eyes and turn away, bored by my unwillingness to participate in the fun. Others giggle and nudge their neighbors. But the worst is Isabella. She looks me up and down as if I just don't get it. As if I'm just too different to bother with.

I slide into the seat behind Carling, who is wearing a flaming orange fitted blazer, skintight faded jeans, navy ankle boots. It's pretty clear she's braless since the jacket buttons well below her breasts and she didn't waste any energy slipping on a camisole or a tee. Maybe her days-of-the-week panties got the day off as well. She turns around and looks right at me but I can't read the expression on her face.

Mr. Curtis turns from the board, where he was calculating an equation I just figured out in my head, and smiles. "Saint Sarah. Welcome. How befitting that you don't stoop to the wanton anarchy of your classmates. Your mythical parents would applaud you."

I start to explain, "I didn't know today was—"

He waves away my words. "Not only do I admire your extraordinary grooming, but I refuse to send you to the office for a late slip, on compassionate grounds." A ripple of giggles flows across the room.

I can feel my cheeks burn.

"I want you all to clear your desks. We're going to have a pop quiz so I can see how badly your brains were fried by the summer heat."

As soon as everyone turns around, groaning, I tug off my vest and tie, stuff them into my backpack, and pull out a pencil. Carling, I notice, slides her desk about an inch closer to Isabella's and gives her an appreciative smile.

Once the tests are passed out and Curtis gives the word, my mouth falls open. Carling Burnack is copying Isabella's answers onto her own paper.

We're let out of class a few minutes early because Mr Curtis has to take a phone call. Carling and Isabella head for their lockers in the near silence of the hallways, their heels ticking along the floor like cinnamon hearts clattering into a porcelain dish, while Sloane slides along behind them as if she's crossing a frozen pond. Knowing full well my locker is on a different level, I glide along in their wake and pretend I'm not listening to their mumbled chitchat.

They arrive at their lockers and Sloane dumps her books inside, then pauses to examine her fingernails. "Whenever I'm in Curtis's class, I fantasize about dropping out. I don't even know if I want a career. Sometimes I think my sole ambition is to fall in love and have babies."

Carling and Isabella stare at her, horrified. Then Carling bursts out laughing. "I totally thought you were serious." When Sloane doesn't react, Carling loses interest. "Thank God for Izzy's brain. If I didn't have *the* most brilliant eleventh grader as my bud, that class would destroy me."

Isabella's eyes widen. "I'd never let that happen. My brain is your brain."

"My brother said Curtis was an easy marker a few years back," says Carling. "I don't know what gives."

"That's what my cousin said," Sloane says. "The guy used to be a softie."

Without thinking, standing at a locker about four doors down, I blurt out, "Midlife crisis."

They're silent for a moment, staring at me as if a

homecoming poster has just sprung to life and dared to address them. Carling reacts first, tossing me a half nod. It's enough to make me bolder still. I say, "Teachers can't afford fancy convertibles or hot women. So what do they do when they realize they're falling apart, bit by bit? They lord their power over the very ones whose youth they covet."

Like a group of wild rabbits I'm trying to get close to with a handful of celery sticks, they're wary of me but don't quite shut me out. Sloane, digging through her locker now, actually says, "Yeah. And since Curtis has a full head of hair, it must mean his winkie is malfunctioning."

Just as I'm planning my next approach, Poppy strolls by, sucking on a mint.

"Hey, Poppy," says Carling. "Can I see your camera for a sec?"

Poppy wiggles her hand out of the camera strap and hands it over. "Be careful. It cost me a lot of money." Then Poppy notices me and flashes the peace sign. "Hey."

I smile. "Hey."

Carling flicks on the camera and pans around the hallway, slowing on Sloane, then me, then a pair of ninth graders walking by, then Isabella. She moves closer to her friend and, without taking her eye from the screen, starts unwrapping Isabella's sweater with her free hand.

Isabella grabs her sweater, clearly distressed. "What are you doing?"

Carling laughs. "Let's send Mrs. Middle-Aged Curtis a flesh tape and pretend it belongs to her husband. Then she'll dump him and he'll shut himself away with a bunch of cats and stop coming to work."

Isabella says, "Not with my flesh!"

"Give the camera back," wails Poppy. "You're going to drop it!"

Carling looks hopefully at Sloane, who flips her off, laughing. Carling shrugs. "Whatever, I'll film myself." She undoes her top buttons and angles the camera down her shirt, then sashays in a slow circle. Dropping her voice even deeper, she says, "Hey there, pop-quiz boy . . ."

"Gross!" Poppy snatches up the camera and wipes the lens on her sleeve. "You think I want my camera equipment touching your sweaty body parts, Burnack? You owe me a new lens."

"You're insane," Isabella says to her. "Your camera never had it so good."

"Yeah," says Carling, laughing. "I charge big bucks for peep shows like that."

"Exactly what I'm afraid of," Poppy says. "Your STDs on my lens."

Carling Burnack does not need a hero. She's a big girl. A wild girl. A girl who leaves people like me wishing I could spend five minutes *being* her, if only to truly understand what I'm missing. Still, I jump to her defense. "Don't trash-talk her," I snap at Poppy.

Poppy steps back as if I've pulled out a gun. "What?"

"She was just goofing around."

"Ohh, I get it." She starts nodding in recognition. "Right. How could I have been so stupid? You were never going to be friends with me. You wanted to be one of the Carlingettes."

I don't have to look to know the girls are staring—I can feel their curiosity crawling across my skin. Not wishing to appear as if I'm trying to be one of them, I spin around and busy myself trying my combination on someone else's locker. Though, even if this *were* my locker, my fingers are shaking too much to open it.

Isabella speaks first. "That's not your locker, London. It's Willa's."

I look around as if confused. "I might be on the wrong floor."

Carling walks over, glancing down at my uniform. "You're quite the spirited little Ant, aren't you?"

I shrug. "Number one rule about being the new kid. Be sure to make an ass of yourself." My voice echoes loudly in the long hallway. I hate the sound of it.

Sloane yawns into her hand, then runs her fingers through her hair, pushing it behind her ears. "The first Monday of every month is Grub Day. No uniforms. No dress code. No exceptions."

"That's cool. Thanks . . ."

But they're already walking away. Just before they disappear into the stairwell, Carling looks back. "Losing the tights was your first good move." And they're gone.

chapter 11
damsel in distress

The pheromones released by ants through scent glands signal any-thing from looming danger to food to an ant in heat.

It's official—I've survived two whole weeks. Now that we're into late September, autumn weather has settled in. Tuesday is unusually cold and windy, so after school I make an ill-fated attempt to study in the library so I can catch a ride home with Dad after five o'clock. In spite of its high ceilings, this is probably the coziest room in the school, with its ancient wooden shelving, tabletop task lighting, and chairs covered in nubbly fabric anyone's grandmother would adore. As soon as I step through the metal doors, I know coming here is a mistake. There doesn't seem to be a table or desk surface in the entire place that isn't six inches deep in textbooks, binders, graph paper, and—though I pretend not to notice—miniature cheat sheets.

Oddly, very few people are studying. They're mostly passed out atop their work in various stages of desperately needed sleep. Some have their faces buried in folded arms. Others are sprawled back in their seats, chins resting on books pressed to hunched chests like armor. But the best are the ones using their open textbooks as pillows, faces turned sideways, mouths agape, saliva pooling on defense-less paragraphs.

It's as if terrorists have pumped anthrax through the air vents and the librarian and I are the only survivors.

Eventually, I find an empty seat near the librarian's station and dump the contents of my backpack—about six hours of work—onto the table. My old school gave very little homework. If a high school's expectations of students' future accomplishments can be measured by the weight of their backpacks, it was fairly clear Finmory expected us to turn out pretty much like our parents—unfettered by the encumbrances of higher learning.

No such lighthearted attitude here. Anton's expectations could crumple a young girl's spinal column. I'm not even sure I'm still five foot six. Willa has been complaining school pressure is already so intense that even when she's done her homework, she can't sleep. I'm the opposite. With only four or five hours a night to sustain me, when not studying, walking, or talking, I'm having serious trouble staying awake. I fall asleep all over the place. During slide shows in history class. At the table eating cereal. I even dozed off on the escalator on the way to math yesterday. That'll teach me to skip my morning coffee.

After setting myself up with notepad, highlighter, and pens, I flip open my books and get to work. But not for long. Like the others, I'm way too sleep-deprived to resist this atmosphere. There's something too soothing about it—maybe it's the hum of overhead fans, or the *clickety-whir* of the photocopiers. Or maybe it's miasmic off-gassing from what smells like newly laid carpeting. Whatever the reason, it's impossible to fight off sleep. Just as I drop my head onto my arms for what I promise myself will be a ten-minute snooze, I hear the sound of labored breathing and look up to find myself being gawked at by none other than Griff Hogan.

His voice is husky as he holds out his wrist and says, "If you rub some of that perfume on me, I can tell my Scout leader I boned you."

"Little Man Hogan, you are disgusting." I fill up my backpack and head for the door.

I'm hit by a rush of wind the moment I step off the bus and onto the sidewalk. Blinking city grime from my eyes, I drop my chin and disappear behind two heavy blankets of hair, marching toward the safety of our building's front door. The wind is making it difficult, swirling overgrown bangs into my mouth and across my eyes.

Halfway across the sidewalk, still trying not to swallow my hair, I'm broadsided by a tangle of elbows, wheels, and handlebars and knocked down flat by a bicycle courier. The only thing stopping my skull from being mashed into the concrete is, of all things, my expectations-filled back-pack.

"Jesus Christ, kid, watch where you're going!" Catlike, the bicycle courier springs to his feet and lifts his vehicle off my chest. His delivery bag has burst open and packages and envelopes lie strewn across the sidewalk as if there's been an explosion. A few of his lighter deliveries take flight in the breeze and skitter along the sidewalk.

"Sorry, I . . ." I wince as I try to sit up. My shoulder feels like it's skinned, and I check my mother's sweater for holes. Thankfully, it's dusty but not shredded.

"You're gonna get yourself killed!" he spits.

Just then, I feel someone lifting me to my feet from behind. He's male, and from what I can see of him, navy-and-white-striped rugby shirt and gray shorts—plenty short enough to reveal mud smeared across the blond hairs of a well-muscled thigh it's pretty clear he goes to Anton High. Mortified, I scramble to get my feet beneath me and force myself to stand. Seriously, who wants to be picked off the ground by some guy from school? Too pathetic to fathom. Yet, some shameful part of me is swooning from the whole damsel-in-distress thing. I don't know whether it's that familiar trickle of musky cologne mixed with grass and sweat and mud that's wafting through the air, or the proximity of that seriously sculpted thigh, but I'm feeling kind of heady.

The moment I turn around, all swooning ends. This is no make-believe monarch, it's the senior I felt up in the dressing room last Friday. Stitched on his rugby shirt is *Leo*. Not sure which one of us is more shocked, I snatch my backpack and hold it against my chest like a shield, mumbling, "Thanks."

Leo looks sickened to discover I'm the damsel he peeled off the sidewalk. One big waste of princely valor, he's thinking, I can read it on his face. "You okay?" he asks.

"I'm fine." I turn away. "Seriously." He's less than three feet from the entrance to my building. Behind him, through the door, I can see the illiterate NO PET sign. Silently, I beg him to leave so I can be swallowed up by my foyer. There's no way on earth I can walk into that lobby in front of this guy.

"My bike's all messed up," rants the courier, glaring at me. "Look at the handlebars."

Leo scoops up the runaway packages, which the courier doesn't appear to care about, and stuffs them into a Lightning Courier carrier bag. "Relax," Leo says. "It was an accident. Anyway, shouldn't you be riding on the road?"

The courier snatches his sack and throws a Lycra-covered leg over his bike. He flashes me one final angry look before pedaling away. "Maybe your girlfriend should be on the road. On a leash."

I could die right here. Right now. If a lightning bolt would only strike anywhere on this sidewalk, I swear to God I'd wrap my body around it, stick out my tongue, and pray for the end. I wait for Leo to correct him as he pedals away. Shout, "She's not my girlfriend, dude!" But he doesn't. He holds up his middle finger and mutters, "Eff off, asshole."

Wow. Leo stood up for me. Flipped off the dragon. Maybe I misjudged him. I smile. "That was sweet. Thanks."

He reaches for my hand, examining the skinned heel of my palm. My skin tingles right down to my toes. Peering at me from beneath a fallen lock of sandy hair, he says, "You should clean this up. It could get infected."

I nod stupidly and he pulls a small zippered case from a bag. "I'm team captain in rugby," he explains. "Coach Hudson's favorite player gets to haul the first-aid kit to and from practice." He squirts disinfectant on his finger and rubs it on my wound, then holds up a Band-Aid as a question. Again, I nod, watching his face as he presses it to my skin.

In South America, army ants are actually used as sutures. Doctors squeeze the gaping wound shut and

89

deposit ants along the gash. In defense, each ant grabs hold of the edges of skin with its mandibles, or jaws, and locks it into place. Doctors then slice off the head, leaving the mandibles in place to secure the cut until healed. I'm not saying I'd lop off this guy's head, but if his squared-off jaw were to clamp down on my flesh, I'm pretty sure I'd heal in half the time.

"I'm Leo Reiser. I'm a senior. You're the new eleventh grader, aren't you?" he asks. "The one from England?"

If I stand here in the street and don't correct him, does that make me a liar? Because what's the alternative? Saying no, I'm the eleventh grader from *Lund*on, the only town in North America that doesn't track high-school graduates because the number would be too embarrassingly low?

For the first time in my life, I thank my dad for never allowing me to have a Web presence. With no Facebook page, no MySpace account, Sara Black from Lundon, Massachusetts, is virtually untraceable. I shrug. "I'm the one."

A storm front rolls across his face as he stuffs the medical kit in his bag. "My neighbor's British. He's a prick." Without so much as a backward glance, as if he'd never seen me or my bleeding palm, he spins around and strides away.

I'm wrecked by his remark and I'm not even British. I trudge up the stairs of our building, trying to think up the perfect comeback that I'll never use. As usual, I have nothing.

I trudge up the stairs and see Carling's dreadlocked chauffeur smoking a cigarette in his doorway, as if he's chilling on his sleepy suburban veranda, drinking a refreshing iced tea and watching the world go by. As it is, his refreshment of choice is a cigarette, and all he has to look at is me. He acknowledges me by raising his eyebrows as I pass. I wave and continue upstairs.

When I'm partway up, he calls out, "Hey, does your boyfriend drive that sky blue VW?"

Is he kidding? I stop and peer down at him. "That's not my boyfriend, it's my *dad.*"

He half laughs, half coughs. "Sorry. You never know these days. I'm Noah."

"Sara."

"Just let your dad know I used to have a van just like his and I miss it. If he needs someone to help out, hand him tools and all that, I'd love to have a look at that engine. I'll knock on your door later and introduce myself to him."

I nod.

Noah flicks ashes onto the landing and I continue up the stairs.

I hate the sound of human lips sucking on cigarettes—legal or otherwise. My mother smoked incessantly. Like most smokers, she was addicted. I always suspected, given the choice between her own daughter and a pack of smokes, that she'd take the Benson & Hedges. Like most things in life, it was a case of simple mathematical probability that was proven when she boarded that plane at Logan International Airport with only one of us on board.

She certainly chose other things over me. That night in early June, when the smell of toxic chicken had finally faded away—or annihilated my remaining nasal membranes—

I lay in my bed, stomach rumbling, pretending to reread my current favorite book, *What Every Girl (Except Me) Knows*, about a girl who grows up without a mother—how was I to know what would follow?—under the covers, with a flashlight whose batteries were growing weaker by the page. It was way past midnight, and if Dad caught me, he'd be furious. Getting Dad riled up that late at night could have sent him into a maniacal cleaning fit—one that may or may not have involved me scrubbing right alongside him.

It's not that I couldn't sleep. I wouldn't let myself. I had my window open wide so I could hear Mom's car the moment she pulled into the driveway. I thought she'd probably squeal with joy when she heard I was going to prom with Jeremy, and the sound would probably wake up Dad, but it would be worth it. Besides, Mom would stop him from pulling out the bleach and the mop.

Her cell phone had been off all night, but one more try couldn't hurt. Peeking out to make sure my door was fully closed—it was—I slid the phone under the covers and dialed her number one last time. Like the last zillion times, it rang. Unlike the last zillion times, she picked up.

"Hello?"

"Mom? Why are you whispering?"

I heard scratchy shuffling sounds. A man's voice. "I'm at work, Sarie. Is everything okay?"

"Yeah. I just have amazing news!"

"Really? What?"

"You know that guy I've been talking about?"

"Yes."

"You're not going to believe it! Today he—"

"Wait a second, honey." More shuffling, then, "I'll be right back." In the background, I could barely make out the sound of water running.

"Mom?"

"I'm here." The sound of an annoyingly long drag on a cigarette. "Can we talk in the morning, Sara?"

I lifted the sheet off my face just enough to see the clock. 1:40 a.m. "It is morning."

She let out a sigh, as if talking to me was the last thing on earth she felt like doing. "We're cleaning up from a party here. Believe me, I'd rather be in bed. Can this wait? I'd like to be able to really focus on you."

The flashlight faded to black and all I could see was the glow of the streetlamp out front. The light hit the wall above my desk, nowhere else, making the room look totally empty. "Doesn't matter. It's nothing."

Now, sitting at my desk in my new room, still wrapped in my green cardigan, I pull out my mother's cigarettes and light one, setting it on the windowsill so I can watch the smoke curl up toward the ceiling and disappear. The phone rings. Mandy. "Hey, you," I say.

"Ass in chair."

"What does sitting have to do with anything? I've never gotten that."

"Just do it."

"Done."

"I can't come this weekend."

"No! Don't do this to me. I'm desperate to see you."

"Eddie's family invited me to dinner. It's like they're sizing me up or something."

"You're a junior in high school. They're not sizing you up."

"He's almost twenty and the Wilcoxes reproduce early and reproduce big. Believe me, that mother of his wants a good look at my childbearing hips."

"She better look hard. You have no hips."

"I'm sorry. I can come next weekend instead."

"Perfect."

"I can't wait to go hang out at a big-city mall."

"There isn't really a mall near me. More like all these little shops."

"Then we'll hang out by the school and tease the smart boys. It'll make Eddie totally jealous. I just streaked my hair with pink stripes and I'm going to bring my tightest jeans."

I seriously doubt the new pink stripes in Mandy's overly bleached blonde spikes are going to be a hit with the male Ants. "Kids don't really hang out on street corners like they do in Lundon. It's different here."

"Then what do they do for fun?"

I don't know. I haven't had any yet. The prospect of Mandy coming in a week and a half should thrill me. It really should.

"Sara?"

Just then I smell smoke. The cigarette has rolled off the windowsill onto the carpet, and a fiery hole is spreading next to my desk. "Gotta go." I snatch up the burning cigarette and stomp on the smoking carpet with the sturdy sole of my black shoe.

Two bedroom fires in a week. I don't even recognize my life anymore.

chapter 12
the crowned princess
of calculus

After mating, the queen must leave her colony to form a new one, where she will produce offspring for up to twenty years from that one instance of mating.

The following Monday, I plop down behind Carling in math class. Just as I do, she crosses her legs and I can see the edge of her underwear. They definitely aren't Sunday's; this pair is blue. And I'd bet my mother's sweater they aren't Friday's, since today is Friday and conforming doesn't seem to be Carling Burnack's thing.

Is it pathetic to admit how badly I want to know what day of the week she's chosen today? It's not that I'm pervy. I'm just still baffled by the Sunday-on-Tuesday incident and want to know if she has a system or if her choice is random. Because I would totally have a system.

As I dig for a pen at the bottom of my backpack, there's a commotion to my left. A bunch of kids are huddled over Griff, who is holding up his iPhone for all to see. If I lean forward, I can peek past his shoulder to get a glimpse of Poppy's video for film class, which Griff took the liberty of secretly filming with his phone. I move close enough to see the tiny screen—it's a long shot of a female Ant from behind. She's in uniform, walking around the Store to the ominous music from the movie *Jaws*. Her face is never fully visible, but it's pretty obvious from the floaty hair and skinny calves that it's Isabella, and she's uncharacteristically feeding from a bag of Doritos.

Isabella stuffs a handful of chips in her mouth and the camera zooms in to catch her chewing. The kids in class roar with laughter when the word *Reduce* flashes on the screen and fades.

"Izzers, I've never actually seen you eat," squeals Carling.

"Give me that!" Pouting, Isabella grabs for the phone but Griff pulls it away, laughing.

"You've got some wicked appetite." Griff grins wide and I wonder if he has all his adult teeth yet. He wipes his dripping nose with his sleeve. "It's making me hot."

"Shut up, you sicko perv. You're a miniature freak of nature."

Poppy walks into the room, sees what's going on, and right away her face crumples. "That film's copyrighted, Hogan! You can't just air my work."

"I'm *so* gonna be your manager one day," he says.

Isabella says, "You aren't allowed to just film me without my permission, Poppy! That's not even legal."

Someone says, "Like that's ever stopped her."

Poppy drops into the seat beside me, her breath coming in torrid little puffs. "Mr. Curtis is going to confiscate your phone if he sees it."

Sloane asks, "What day was this filmed, Izz? And why didn't you share?"

Video Isabella continues, picking up textbooks with

greasy orange fingers. Everyone groans, deliciously disgusted, when Isabella turns to see if anyone is watching, then wipes her oily digits on the arm of a white shirt hanging on a rack. Seconds later, an unknowing younger girl takes the shirt, holds it up, and admires herself in a mirror. She doesn't notice the orange streaks on the sleeve. The word *Reuse* pops up. Fades.

"That's Griff's big sister!" says a guy. "She's tainted now."

"Come on," says Sloane. "She lives with Griff. You think she's not tainted already?"

"Izz, this is so gross!" Carling says, laughing so hard she can barely get the words out.

"I'm going to get you, Poppy," says Isabella.

Poppy squints at her. "Yeah? I have twenty-five witnesses."

After stuffing a few more chips in her mouth, video Isabella mashes up the bag and drops it on the floor in front of the dressing rooms. The camera pans down, zooms in on the crumpled bag. The word *Recycle* flashes for a moment before the screen goes black.

Kids crumple over their laps, hysterical with laughter, while Isabella pouts. She swats at her friends, jutting out her lower jaw. It's fairly clear, however, she doesn't mind being the center of attention.

Willa, her hair in its usual slick black ponytail, leans over Griff. "Wait, rewind a bit."

Griff fiddles with his phone. "What Patel Hotels wants, Patel Hotels gets. Isn't that your family motto?"

"Just to where Isabella inhales that last fistful," Willa says with a giggle. "Before she drops the bag."

"Ugh, once was enough," says Carling. "I'll retch if I see it again."

Isabella looks crushed by the rebuff.

"No, it's the background," says Willa. "I saw a flash of something in the dressing rooms behind her."

I can no longer see the phone—too many kids have swarmed it—but I hear the *Jaws* music again. Whatever. I flip open my binder and write today's date across the top. Then Willa shouts, "There. See? It's Leo Reiser and . . ."

The class goes silent and, to my horror, everyone turns to stare at me, mouths agape. Carling is the worst. She's so angry she crackles.

Griff shoves his phone close enough for me to see the frozen image on the small screen. I nearly inhale my tongue. There I am entering a dressing room in the yoga pants. In front of me is Leo's bare chest, his scars too tiny to register on the phone screen. "So Poppy does porn after all," Griff says with a whistle.

"Any particular reason you were in a dressing room with Carling Burnack's boyfriend, London?" asks Isabella.

Heart pounding, I stammer, "It—it was an accident. I was half asleep. I stumbled into the wrong room while he was changing."

"Yeah, right," someone mumbles.

Sloane, to my surprise, says, "Chill, people. It's obvious nothing happened."

"It didn't, I swear." After shooting a grateful look at Sloane, I look at Carling. "Didn't he tell you about the spazz who walked into his chest? The one who got hit by a bicycle courier the next week?"

Carling looks me over like I'm no better than the

98

crinkled-up Doritos bag left on the floor. She is silent for a moment, then says, smiling, "I guess he didn't think you were worth mentioning."

I guess he didn't.

"By the way, those yoga pants looked good on you." She twirls a strand of hair around her finger and tilts her head. "Did you buy them?"

I don't say a word.

The phone disappears when Mr. Curtis breezes in. He holds up a stack of papers. "You'll all be pleased to learn I cancelled my date with Mrs. Honors Math last night in order to finally grade your pop quiz. It's the kind of guy I am. You can all thank me by coughing up better results on the next test. With very few exceptions, your grades are nothing short of abysmal. Only two students scored above ninety-five. The rest of you averaged a B-plus."

Back at Finmory, such a statement would have been met with a chorus of cheers. Here, the kids whimper and lick themselves in near-silent misery.

Mr. Curtis sets the test on the desk of a tall boy with wiry hair and motions for him to pass them back to us. "This is *Honors* Math and I don't have the reputation of being the toughest prof in the school for nothing," says Mr. Curtis. "If you do not work your pampered tails off this semester, you will not see the perfect scores your parents believe you to be capable of. This quiz was nothing compared to the next test. Are we all clear?"

No one has the strength to nod.

In the next row, Griff gets his test back. His fist shoots into the air. "Yes!" I take it he was one of the top scorers.

99

Carling crumples her test in a ball and mutters to Isabella, "Lot of good that did me."

"Sorry!" Isabella squeaks in self-defense.

My test appears on my desk. "I guess you guys have better schools in England," says the wiry haired boy. He nods toward Isabella, who, along with Sloane and Carling, has perked up and is listening. "Latini's been replaced. We have a new Princess of Calculus in our midst."

It's as if Isabella has just taken a fist to the gut. Her face falls and her shoulders hunch forward. Her chin tilts toward the sky as she gulps in air. Then, when Carling turns to laugh at her, she straightens up and does a spectacular job of feigning nonchalance. The only thing that gives her away, and I'm likely the only one who has noticed, is the way her fingernails are boring into her thighs.

There's a tidy "98.89%" in the upper right-hand corner of my quiz. I flip through the pages to see where I went wrong—I'd been fairly confident about my answers. After a few moments I can feel someone reading over my shoulder and I look up.

Carling is leaning close to me, staring at my test, her eyebrows leaping like dolphins. I brace myself for a bitchy remark, but she says, "Nice work."

After a grueling fifty minutes of working through brain-bending equations on the chalkboard, the bell rings and we all wander out into the hall in a mathematical daze. As I head toward the door, Poppy sidles up beside me.

"Was that film some kind of punishment for me?" I ask.

"Oh, believe me, I'm not the one who's into punishment.

Your good buddy Carling is Ant's resident expert on getting even. She once threw an ex-boyfriend's laptop into the deep end of the pool because he didn't notice she'd had her hair trimmed."

"She's not my good buddy. I barely know her."

This makes Poppy smile a little. "I swear it was an accident. I wasn't focused on the background."

"Whatever," I say. "Doesn't matter."

She holds out her hand. "Want another peppermint?"

I don't think I can get mixed up with her. She might be acting normally right now, but who knows what histrionics are around the bend. "I'm actually more of a spearmint kind of girl."

"Okay. Cool. I'll see you in pre-law, okay?"

"Sure."

As Poppy wanders off, Carling appears beside me, followed by Isabella, then Sloane, who appears so bored she could be asleep. "You did great on the quiz," Carling says to me, her voice unusually high-pitched and sunshiny.

"Thanks." I search her body language for any sign that I should flee.

"Curtis is such an ass," says Carling. Isabella tugs on her sleeve as if to pull her away, but Carling shrugs her off.

Aware of their stares, I search fruitlessly for something witty to say. "Yeah."

Carling plunks her books in Sloane's arms, pulls a rubber band from her pocket, and wraps her hair in a messy bun. One thick strand falls away and nudges her cheekbone. "So, where do you hang at lunch?"

Where do I hang? Let's see . . . there was that bus shelter the first week. And I sat in the girls' locker room with the lights off once last week. Not exactly a pattern I'd like to brag about. I shrug. "I don't know. Wherever."

"Well, if you're around, come sit with us. We'll save a spot for you at the Petting Pool. Heard of it?"

"Yeah. But I'm not really sure where or what it is."

Sloane drops Carling's books to the floor and says, "You won't know it from the surface, but it's the tangle of body parts on the second-floor landing."

"Where? Right there on that big sofa? There's tangling of parts right out in the open?"

"Not as far as the teachers know. They're pretty certain it's an urban legend," says Isabella. "The good stuff happens down below. The kids on the surface are more of a shield."

"Yes," Carling says. "Better not be late or you'll have to sit on the floor. Miss out on all the fun."

Without waiting for my answer, she floats away with Sloane and Isabella being sucked along in her wake. As they trot up the stairs, I get a flash of Carling's lime green panties. In light pink type, they read WEDNESDAY I'VE GOT JUICY ON MY MIND.

I nod to myself. Mathematical formulas never fail me.

Before the girls disappear into the crowd, Isabella glances back at me, her face completely devoid of expression.

It's been a while since I've been invited to lunch. And I've learned that lunch dates, once made, are easily broken. Like the time Mom took me shopping for my prom dress. It was the night after the toxic chicken, and her motherly guilt for not having been home to hear my news was peaking. Right after breakfast, she announced it was time for Girls' Day Out.

Dad drove us to the mall in the van and, after a quick stop for an Orange Julius, walked us to the balloon- and prom-dress-filled windows of Wanted, the teen shop on the second floor. Inside, music thumped from speakers and teenage girls and their mothers swarmed the displays. Near the front, two girls argued about which one picked up a tangerine minidress first.

"I'm afraid this is as far as I go," Dad said. "I will be of no use to anyone in this estrogen-rich emporium."

"Don't worry, Dad," I said. "As badly as you don't want to go in, we don't want you even more."

"Now that hurts," he said, pointing his straw at me. He ruffled my hair and kissed Mom. "Off you go, then. Call me on my cell if you need me to break up any brawls."

"We can take these girls, can't we, Sara?" said Mom, guiding me inside. She called back, "Don't buy too many car magazines, Charlie. We're already heading toward an intervention. Two or three more *Road and Track* magazines in that rec room and I'll start calling your long-lost family members."

"One," he said. "I'll keep it to one this time, I promise. And don't be too long. I want to work on the VW this afternoon."

About ten minutes later I was in the changing room. Mom knocked on the door and yanked it open before I could answer. Standing in my bra and underwear, I grabbed my jeans from the floor and covered myself so strangers wouldn't get an unexpected eyeful of my shivery white flesh. *"Mom,"* I whispered. "I'm practically naked."

"Try this one, sweetie," she said, holding up a strapless dark green gown. "It'll look terrific with your eyes."

I snatched it from the hanger and slammed the door.

"It's simple, don't you think?" she called to me. "And elegant. Like something Jennifer Aniston would wear to the Oscars."

The zipper got caught and I wiggled it free before stepping into the dress and sliding it over my hips. I wished my mother would lower her voice. I saw a couple of girls from school on the other side of the store.

"Sara, did you hear me? Don't you think it's something Jennifer Aniston would wear?"

The price tag said $99.99. I kind of doubted it.

"Hon?"

"Sure."

I shuffled out of the changing room, tripping over the long hem.

The saleslady, Ruth, pulled off her glasses and set them on a ledge, then she took my hand and led me to a wide step at the trio of angled full-length mirrors. "Don't worry, we'll take up the hem and nip in the waist," she assured me. I stepped onto the platform and spun around, and I don't know who went more crazy, my mother or Ruth.

"Oh, Sara," said Mom, moving closer and tugging the dress out from under my heels. "You look beautiful."

Ruth nodded. "Just like Miss Aniston."

I stared in the mirror. Mom was right, green did match my eyes. I never would have picked this dress off the rack, but I had to admit, it looked pretty decent on me. Made me look older, at least twenty, I thought. I pulled my hair off my shoulders and held it up in a sexy kind of half-up/half-down bun.

Holding my shoulders from behind, Mom stared at my reflection. "Have I mentioned how proud I am of my girl? You're growing into such a lady." She laughed and wiped a tear from her cheek. "Look at me. Getting all weepy in the Lundon Olde Towne Mall."

I reached up to touch her hand. I didn't mind her getting weepy over me. Not one bit.

Ruth folded up the fabric at the hem, then looked up at me. "How high will your heels be?"

I looked at my mom. "I guess I'll wear my black flats? The ones I wore to Grandpa's funeral?"

"No flats," said Ruth, glowering as if I'd insulted her. "Go with black patent. They have gorgeous slingbacks in the shoe store next door, with a three-inch heel. Just in from Europe."

Sounded expensive. Sounded like something Rebecca Morgan's mom would buy her, not like something I would dare hope for. "That's okay. My flats are fine."

"Absolutely not," said Mom. "If my daughter needs patent slingbacks for her first prom, she's going to have them. We'll stop at the shoe store on our way out. What do you say to chicken fingers and shakes at the Foggy Dog—just you and me, since Dad wants to work on the van? He can drop us off and we'll take the bus home."

I nodded, scarcely able to believe it. "Sounds great!"

Tori Nathan, my science teacher's daughter, walked into the changing area carrying an armload of dresses, followed by her mother in her wheelchair. Mrs. Nathan was the school guidance counselor, adored by everyone

for what kids called her Friday Night Bitch sessions—
a weekly gathering where any student was welcome to
drop by and discuss problems they were having at home.
She even let one girl stay for an entire weekend when her
parents split. And after Mrs. Nathan's paragliding accident . . . well, the students of Finmory only loved her
more.

"Hi," said Tori. "You look great in that dress." She
reluctantly pulled a green dress from her arms and hung it
on a hook. "Guess I'm not trying *that* one on."

Mrs. Nathan rolled closer, taking my hand and beam-
ing. "Oh, Sara. You do look glamorous. This dress was
made for you."

"Thanks."

"Hello, Tina," Mrs. Nathan said to my mother.

Mom, usually so friendly and talkative, friend of all
people who interrupt her mother-daughter time, shot Mrs.
Nathan a quick smile and took a step backward. Her voice
was frosty. "Gloria. You're looking well."

I just thought Mom was guarding our mother-daughter
moment. That she wasn't going to allow even the greeting
of an acquaintance to break up our fun. Her rudeness gave
me a private thrill.

I wouldn't find out the truth for another seven days.

Mom's cell phone rang. As she moved away to talk,
Mrs. Nathan and her daughter disappeared into the corner
changing room, and Ruth pulled pins from a puffy, heart-
shaped cushion and began taking in the side of my dress.
The velvet of the heart was blood-red in the creases but
had otherwise faded to a sick, fleshy pink. About a hundred
pins pierced the little pillow's surface. It was eerie. Like the

heart of a floppy doll had been torn out and stabbed with tiny daggers.

The day was turning out to be better than I'd imagined. The perfect dress. New shoes. The Foggy Dog. My glorious mother all to myself.

When my mother returned from her phone call, her expression had changed. She seemed exhilarated, and I hoped it had something to do with finding me a bag to match my new gown.

It didn't.

"Slight problem, sweetie. Turns out I *do* have to go into work. So we'll come back for the shoes one night after school. We have two and a half weeks until prom; we're not in a big rush. Does that sound okay?"

I flinched from the prick of one of Ruth's daggers. "Are we still going to go for lunch?"

"Oh, I don't think so. Not today. Let's make it a dinner the night we get the shoes. It's not a big deal." She didn't look me in the eye, just bent over to gather up our purses.

It's impossible to focus in pre-law with the Petting Pool looming less than an hour away. I'm equally torn between excitement and dread. But mostly I'm still reeling from Carling Burnack's sudden interest in me.

Mr. Kazinski stands at the front of the class, his sneer so prominent it nearly cripples his entire left side—from his bent leg and cocked hip all the way up to his sunken shoulder and hooked mouth. He dabs at his nose with a balled-up tissue as Carling, from where she sits in the front row with Sloane, looks on. "Today we'll be discussing an area of law I happen to be very familiar with—divorce. You've probably heard by now that more than half of marriages end in divorce; I'm sure more than half of you are living it. Each case is different, but many follow this timeworn pattern. Boy meets Girl. There's so much lust in the air no one can think straight. Girl convinces Boy what he's inhaling is actually love, and Boy pops the question he will ultimately live to regret."

Bored, I flip open my notebook, pull out a pencil, and start scrawling my name in long, sausagelike letters. If there's one subject that will ruin me, it's this one. We had a quiz last week and I might have gotten the lowest mark in the class, B-minus. When the girl who sits beside me caught sight of my test, she inched her desk farther away from me as if mediocrity were a disease and she was determined to stay clear of the aura of contagion.

"Wedding plans and square footage of starter homes keep everyone nicely preoccupied for a few years and then the babies arrive—and let me tell you, the babies arrive squalling and bawling like nothing you've ever heard. What is shocking is how much you love them in spite of it. A few years pass, then a few more, and one day you notice the air has grown too thin. Both love and lust are gone for Boy and Girl. So is most of Boy's lush head of hair, but that's another lawsuit for another day." The class laughs as Mr. Kazinski rubs his shiny head.

Carling, seated way up front, puts up her hand. "Did either Boy or Girl sign a prenup? Because as long as both parties had independent legal advice, the divorce should be fairly straightforward."

The teacher grins, pointing at her. "Ahh, at least one of you is going into this life prepared. Miss Burnack, you scored higher than anyone in the class on our quiz last week."

It's as if she's climbed into another body and zipped herself in, the way she blushes, sits up tall, and squeezes her mouth into a confident smile. This class is good for her. Not only are there no escalator handrails to tempt her, but her intellect actually shines here and it's pretty clear she is proud of herself.

"Tell us," says Mr. Kazinski, "do you see yourself choosing law as a profession?"

The sweetness drains from her face and she slides down in her seat. "No."

If Mr. Kazinski is surprised, he doesn't show it. He folds his arms and leans against the dusty chalkboard. "So now our pair is ready to divorce. Boy and Girl are both teachers. Prenup or no prenup, they started broke and will end broke. What we're going to discuss here is something not help up in prenuptial agreements—custody of the wailing wee ones. And this is where the law gets good and discriminatory. The mother, in this case, Girl, usually gets more rights when it comes to the children. What the courts call 'shared custody' really means Boy sees his babies Tuesday and Thursday evenings and every other weekend."

I look away from him. Divorce and custody are not things I want to think about today or any other day. I was born in the wrong era. The nineteenth century must have rocked. Most people parked themselves in a marriage and stayed there, no matter what. I stare at the clouds piling up outside the window and wonder if it's too late to transfer to European history.

Mr. Kazinski continues, "In other words, no matter

how God-fearing, law-abiding, carpool-committed, or willing to battle nightly bogeymen the father may be, the mother gets dibs when it comes to the kids. The courts never really consider the umbilical cord to be fully severed, and, as such, are extremely reluctant to separate a mother from her child. It is the belief of the Commonwealth of Massachusetts that a child needs her mother, and so, mother and child should rarely be apart."

My pen clatters to the floor and I make no move to pick it up. I can't. This information has thumped me so hard in the stomach I can barely catch my breath. A child needing a mother is so basic, so natural, so crucial there are state-manufactured laws to ensure it. Lawyers and judges and government workers and teachers—and now even students in this class—know it. Why doesn't my own mother?

"I assume you've all read your required chapters," he says, walking to the blackboard to pick up a piece of chalk. "Miss Black, can you tell the class how long Boy and Girl have to be separated before the state will grant them their divorce?"

I open my mouth and answer with absolutely no idea what I'm saying.

chapter 13
the petting pool

The spine-waisted ant boasts two sharp spines on its thorax, likely to ward off attacks on the vulnerable pedicel, or waist.

I'm not in the best frame of mind after pre-law. My legs have that same bendy-straw feeling they had the day after my mom left, and there's a greenish-blackish stink wrapped around my shoulders that snaps and growls to let people know they should keep their distance. If my own mother can't be near me, why should anyone else?

I think about skipping this Petting Pool thing at lunch. My mood could be damaging to my social life. But once I get caught in the flow of bodies pushing toward the stairwell, it seems to be easier to lose myself in the current than dream up the right hiding place where I can eat my lunch. Besides, I really don't have much to lose right now.

In the few times I've passed by the second-floor landing between classes, I've never witnessed anything unusual. Then again, the landings in this stairway are enormous, more like long observation areas or sunrooms, and all four landings are identical. Huge leaded glass windows on three sides, a seriously ancient tufted-leather sofa, and a small forest of tropical plants in tarnished brass urns. Maybe a student or two squatting down to reorganize a binder or tie a shoe, but nothing pool-like. And other than a girl smoothing her hair in a tiny mirror, no petting.

As I make my way up the first flight of stairs, I'm relieved to see clusters of kids squatting on the steps eating lunch. It means that no matter what Curling and Company are up to on the couch, at least there will be plenty of witnesses.

I pass through several layers of social stratum. To actually reach the leather sofa, I first pass the anime girls with their pigtails and platform Mary Janes; the Benadryl kids, whose complexions look all at once rashy and translucent, painful and allergic; and a slew of boys wearing ANTON MATHATHON caps and buttons in support of this afternoon's Numerical Analysis showdown in the gym. Sad but true—Anton mathletes actually have groupies.

Pushing on—could approaching the Petting Pool really be any worse than sitting with one of these other groups?— I move through the echelons, certain the air is getting thinner as I rise. Like climbing Mount Kilimanjaro. By the time I spy the summit—a gap on the couch between Carling and Sloane—I'm light-headed.

Everyone at the Petting Pool oozes a quiet sort of comfort. Like they've known each other forever and have never, not once, felt a hairy ball of yarn in their stomachs on the Sunday night before another long week at school. I've never had a Sunday night without it, not even in the summer. That ratted ball of wool is programmed to prickle and chafe, my weekly reminder that people like me should probably not make ourselves too comfortable. Anywhere.

So far, things look reasonably tame in terms of roving body parts. Seven or eight kids sitting on a sofa eating lunch. All hands and feet in plain view. Other than Carling, Sloane, and Isabella, I recognize a few faces. Willa, Little Man Griff. Leo Reiser, which does not help my nerves. He seems relaxed, lounging between Carling and Willa. Carling looks up as I approach, smiles, and pats the empty spot between her and Sloane. "There you are. Everybody, this is London. London, this is everybody."

Hating that my cheeks are probably searing red, I squeeze in next to her. "Hey, everybody."

A few people mumble hello, clearly surprised. They look from Leo to Carling to me, as if poison darts are about to shoot from someone's eyes. Isabella leans forward and squints at me. "I've wondered for weeks now, London. Where's your British accent?"

I've been preparing for this question ever since Leo picked me up off the sidewalk. "I was born here. It didn't seem cool to go all Madonna and adopt the accent later in life."

She doesn't look convinced. "But how long did you live there?"

"I don't know. Since about third grade."

"That's a long time. You'd think living there"—she pauses to calculate—"eight years would give you *some* sort of accent."

I'm about to reply, say something idiotic about my parents correcting it, when Carling swats Isabella in the arm. "What are you, the accent police? Shut up and give me something out of your lunch bag. I forgot mine at home."

Isabella frowns and digs through her paper sack.

Carling nudges me. "Leo, you've met London, haven't

you?" Her voice stretches into a piece of wire at the end, pulled so tight tiny threads of metal snap and fray and crackle. A fresh crop of kids have arrived. Some perch on the sofa arms, others stretch out along the back of the sofa behind our heads or on the rug by our feet. Another three spread themselves across our laps, creating a second layer of humanity. I have a set of male ankles on my lunch bag. At the far end of the couch, someone starts giggling. My stomach starts flipping again.

Leo barely looks up from his pasta. "Hey."

"Hey," I say back to Leo. The moment I pull a milk carton out of my rumpled lunch bag, a guy on the floor leans back against Carling and me and stretches his arms across our laps, crushing the rest of my lunch.

Carling leans close. "You're just in time to make first layer. It can get a bit intense at the bottom, but your body parts are much safer if you're underneath the others."

I think I know the answer, but I ask anyway. "Safe from what?"

Sloane opens a bottle of sparkling water. "Wandering hands. Someone undid my bra the first day of school—I barely felt it happen."

"Don't scare London, Sloaney," says Carling. "And anyway, it's only the girls who can undo your bra without you knowing. The guys are way less nimble."

"A girl undid your bra?" I ask. "Why?"

Sloane shrugs. "It's pretty relaxed up here. Some kids are straight. Some aren't. Some bend both ways. Some are multi—doesn't matter. No one cares."

A small anteater-shaped robot lurches past my feet, sucking french fries off the floor like a vacuum while making clickety chewing sounds. It's chased by two sopho-more boys who snatch it up just before it tumbles, metallic snout over tail, down the stairs.

"Enough sex talk, it's so boring," whines Isabella.

"Sloaney just started a game," explains Carling. "We're all going to spill a junior-year secret. What will you be doing this year that you don't want anyone to know about? Willa, you go first."

Willa Patel lifts long, elegant fingers to her cheeks in mock embarrassment, though I can't imagine what a girl like this could possibly fear. Even with her bare face and her hair pulled back into her trademark ponytail, she could easily grace the cover of *Vogue*. If I pulled my hair back like that, with my colorless lashes and total lack of bone structure, I'd look like an egg.

"Okay," says Willa. "Thanksgiving weekend I'm flying straight to Dr. Raj in Beverly Hills for a *procedure*."

"What kind?" says Carling. She glances to her right to make sure Leo is looking in Willa's direction, then shifts her weight to allow some guy's hand to wander down behind her back.

Willa leans forward to show her flawless profile. "Isn't it obvious?"

"Willa's like a computer. Her flaws aren't detectable by the naked eye," says Sloane with a yawn.

A few laughs. Willa reddens. "Hey, none of you was born to my motherboard. Until you've passed through her rock-hard loins and had your peripherals examined for flaws before anyone's had a chance to check your breathing, don't mock my quest for highly integrated perfection."

Griff Hogan, with a mouthful of animal crackers,

snorts, "Willa, have I not been begging to get between your motherboard's loins?"

"Shut up, Griff," says Willa with a sigh. *Tu es un petit cochon.*

Carling says, "Isabella, how about you? Junior year secret?"

"My cousin's family is coming to stay next week," she says, raising her eyebrows as if everyone will get the inference. "For two nights in our teeny-tiny apartment . . ."

"Ah," says Sloane. "Is this Utterly Beddable Benjamin?"

"I see where this is going and I, for one, am going to puke," says Leo.

"I've seen Cousin Benjamin," says Carling. "Illegal union or not, the boy is utterly beddable. Besides"—she winks—"the British royalty did it all the time, didn't they, London?"

Someone's limb is snaking around behind my left hip. I tuck my skirt under my thighs and press my legs together. "What . . . incest?"

"I prefer to think of it as promoting from within," Carling says, "but, yes, incest."

"Might explain why my grandfather makes me call him Mumsy," I say. "The mind's the first to go with inbreeding."

A few kids look amused and, for a moment, the shaggy yarn ball in my stomach disappears. I try not to smile too wide and blow it by looking as though I actually tried to be funny. Better to appear inadvertently witty.

Leo's eyes are on me and hot flames lick my neck. When I finally risk a quick peek, I find him grinning. Either he approves, or he thinks incest explains a few things about me.

"Okay," says Carling, "Willa's going to get even more perfect, Isabella's going to do her cousin—"

"Not *do* him!" Isabella giggles. "But I might do a hell of a lot of spying and fantasizing."

Willa looks around. "Nice one, Isabella. Next? Sloane?"

"I'm going to drop out," Sloane says.

The air grows quiet. "Seriously?" says Willa.

"Nah." Sloane slumps lower on the sofa. "My parents threaten to split all the time as it is. Me quitting Ant would drive them to murder. But a girl can dream."

"You're the one person who doesn't need to be here," says Carling. "You can go to any law school you want and you'll still go work in your dad's firm."

"My point exactly," says Sloane, staring up at the ceiling. "So why work this hard? Anyway, being a lawyer will be a stepping-stone for me."

"Our little Sloaney wants to be barefoot and preggers," Carling says. "So quaint."

"I do. When I come back to our ten-year reunion, I swear I'll have four kids."

"Better get on it then."

"You should take my place at my dad's firm, Carling," Sloane says. "You're the one who rocks at law."

Carling says nothing, just roots through Isabella's lunch again, pulls out some grapes, and starts eating.

Leo leans back and stretches. "I don't have any school-year secrets. I'll be studying. Eating. Trying to fix the clicking sound in the Aston's engine."

With her mouth full, Carling says to me, "Leo has a big thing for European convertibles that don't run. He looks hotter than hell driving around in them, but he spends an awful lot of time on the side of the road waving down blondes."

"Relax." Leo grins lazily. "That girl was old enough to be my mother."

After flicking her grape stems to the floor, Carling snuggles into Leo's chest and tugs his shirt out of his pants, which he doesn't seem to mind one bit. Sliding her hand onto his stomach, she says, "As long as she knows that *you*"—she pauses and pushes his shirt farther up— "belong to *me*."

Leo's relaxed demeanor vanishes. His face darkens and in one sweeping motion, he knocks her hand from his chest and pulls down his shirt. "What the hell? Cut it out!" He lifts his hips and pushes the wrinkled white cotton back into his pants.

A hush falls over the couch. No one moves. No one speaks. Carling, red-faced now, turns away from him and folds her arms across her chest. "Jesus. You don't have to freak on my ass."

It's like witnessing a wineglass-hitting-the-wall fight between your parents. The unspoken friction is terrifying. Even the Benadryl girls stop talking.

The scars. His anger. It all makes sense. Leo Reiser doesn't hate me. He hates what I've seen. And from his reaction today, I'd be willing to bet even the great Carling Burnack has no idea her boyfriend's chest and shoulders are covered in the painful mystery of his past.

Sloane breaks the prickly stillness. "Your turn, Sara. Junior-year secret?"

All eyes fall on me and the yarn ball springs to life in my abdomen like it's being swatted by an angry kitten. Let's see. I've stolen a pair of pants. I walk around every day in other students' lost clothing. I've set my room on fire. Twice. "I'm not very exciting. My dad'll probably make me clean the grout on the bathroom floor every weekend with that industrial foam cleanser they use in the locker room showers. You know, the pink stuff that stinks of gasoline? Does that count?"

People eye each other with confusion and I realize my mistake. Regular kids aren't familiar with janitorial elixirs. Griff speaks first, with a yawn. "Call us if you need some help. I'd show up just for the fumes."

"My dad's just a clean freak," I say, hoping to muddy up the conversation. The urn-burying incident pops into my mind—Charlie out in the rain, knee-deep in sludge and murdered flowers and slain shrubbery, completely unaware of the people around him—and I regret using the word *freak*. Now I feel disloyal and filthy. The anonymous hand moves around to my waist and I jam my elbow against my side to block it.

"What do your parents do?" asks Isabella with a nervous edge to her voice. "We have a little theory about that kind of thing, don't we, Carling?"

Carling shrugs and bites into a cookie.

"My mother is a chef," I say. "In Paris." I don't mention she's there on a two-year work–learn program and is living for free in a friend's flat.

Sloane brightens up. "Tell her to send Izz something fattening."

"Shut up, Montauk," Isabella snaps. "For your information, fasting makes you live longer. It cuts the risk of clogged arteries by forty percent."

"Not this again." Carling lets her head drop backward as if she's unspeakably tired. "Tell them who was in the study, Izz."

"Mormons."

Everybody laughs, which only irritates Isabella further. So who does she turn on? Me. "What about your dad, London? What does he do?"

On cue, my uniformed father strolls along the third landing and down the steps, scooping up lunch litter and stuffing it into a huge trash bag, which is practically overflowing with waste. Faced the other way, Dad crushes the garbage down with his foot, and sets about tying the top of the bag together.

What does my father do?

He continues to make knot upon knot in the big black bag until there are eight, ten, maybe fifteen knots. A tornado full of cats couldn't get out of that sack.

Worse still is what this means. I was stupid to think his OCD might remain safely tucked away at an ugly little apartment building in Brighton. That it would behave itself until he gets home from work. That I could count on it like $E = mc^2$. It was only getting warmed up, perfecting itself, and preparing for its ultimate audience—the most perceptive, precocious, intelligent teenagers in the country: the students of Anton High School.

"Speaking of freaks," says someone.

What does my father do?

He doesn't stop his knot-tying until every last flap of plastic has been fastened together and the top of the bag stands up like a drunken bunny ear. He stares at it a moment as if debating undoing the whole thing and starting from scratch and I realize this isn't really new behavior for him—it's just the green plastic bag version of the VW's locks.

"Can anyone spell O-C-D?" says Isabella.

Carling whispers, "Someone should tell him there's a rehab center down the block."

"Whacked," says Griff.

Dad looks up and smiles when he catches my eye. My heart pounds as he starts down the steps and straight toward me with a great green sack of social annihilation bobbing against his leg. This can't be happening. I'm finally making friends, I'm actually being accepted by these genetically enhanced beings—being treated as one of their own—in this insanely elite school my dad is forcing me to attend, and with this one action, he's going to snatch it all away.

This OCD is grotesque in its greed. It doesn't rest until it seeps into every part of our lives and rots it from the inside out. I'm tired of fighting my dad's condition all by myself. I love my father, but he has no interest in managing his problem. He's happy to let it pummel him from every which way. Wherever. Whenever. With no real concern what it's doing to him.

Or me.

I watch, terrified, as Dad waves to me, moving ever closer. Then a well-timed herd of thundering seniors blocks him from my view. Which gives me a moment to compose my thoughts. Only I can't. All I see is Rascal in the grotty café just after he saw the old pawnbroker for the first time. He sat there drinking tea and was astonished to overhear two guys at the next table discussing the pawnbroker and how terribly she abused her sister. Treating her like a servant and nearly biting off her finger to the point of amputation. One guy threw up his hands and exclaimed a woman like that was better off dead and there was nothing to be done. What will be will be. It was nature. But the other said nature is to be "shaped and directed."

Or else.

And I have about three seconds to shape and direct this situation before "or else" happens to me.

Feeling I might be killing more than just the OCD, I drop my granola bar down behind the others just before the cloud of jocks thins out, and vanish from view, fussing around beneath the cushions as I pretend to search for it.

Only when I'm sure my beloved, stubborn father has decided he was mistaken and gone on his way do I resurface, granola bar in hand, fully aware of the shift that has just taken place inside me. I am now, officially, a wretch of a daughter.

Sloane repeats Isabella's question. "So what does your super-clean father do, Sara?"

I tread water for a moment, sputter on the traitorous grime that's settled in my lungs, before telling the ugliest lie of my life. "Brain surgeon. My dad likes things clean because he's a neurosurgeon."

"That's how you squeaked in here as a junior? Because your dad's a surgeon?"

I force a sly grin. "Well, it's all confidential, but let's just say he's tinkered under some very fancy hoods in the Ant community." Not a total lie. Noah let him help tune up the Bentley last week.

A few kids nod and the conversation shifts away from me.

I can't believe how easy it was to lose my reality. Ironic, really. I swam down a no-hoper from a town pockmarked with liquor stores and pawnshops, nothing more than the janitor's daughter, and emerged something else entirely. A girl sparking and flashing with the very finest in genetic material.

A girl completely unworthy of the man who raised her.

"Are you going to grow up to be just like Daddy?" asks Isabella.

"Nah. I'm more of a math nerd."

With the still-unforgiven Leo turned toward Griff, Carling tips her head back and lets some guy with long bangs snake the inside of her mouth with his tongue. The ultimate punishment. Then she pulls away, checks that Leo didn't see, and turns to me. "That reminds me, London," she says. "A few of us are getting together Saturday afternoon to work on our calculus. You're welcome to come . . . if you want."

Saturday afternoon. Mandy arrives Saturday morning. But our weekend together can be rearranged, can't it? Carling, however, cannot.

I knock the roving hand off my rib cage and hoist myself out of the bobbing heap of anonysexuality. "I want."

chapter 14
need-blind

Leafcutter ants are nicknamed fungus ants, because they don't actually eat the leaves they cut; rather, they grow fungus on the leaves.

"You're cooking dinner for Charlie? Dude. I beg you to reconsider and let the man live," Mandy says into the phone that night.

"Hilarious." I lean across the stovetop to adjust the burner flame. "He's not feeling great these days. I'm just trying to be a . . ." The words get caught in my teeth and I have to sweep them out with my tongue. "A good daughter."

I've decided to step up and make Charlie's life easier in ways that go far beyond the odd game of Scrabble. I'm going to make all our meals. Tonight's dinner is more like breakfast: cheese-and-spinach omelets, sliced tomatoes, toasted bagels. I slide the spatula under one side of the egg mixture and prepare to fold it over.

"Just don't threaten to do the same for me Saturday night," warns Mandy. "I'd like to live to see my birthday because I'm pretty sure Eddie's going to propose."

"And then what? You'll have a two-year engagement?"

"A year and a half. And he'll be roped up good until I graduate."

Mandy has been my best friend since third grade. When the teacher had us make paper chains to decorate the classroom for Christmas, Mandy poured white glue on her palm, spread it around, and peeled it off like a second layer of skin after it dried. I was fascinated enough to invite her over after school. So Mandy stuffed the glue bottle in her pocket and we peeled our palms until her mother picked her up and took her to swimming lessons at four thirty.

I've never wanted to spend a day apart from her. Not until today.

"I kind of have bad news about that." I'm keenly aware I'm the worst friend ever. A true friend doesn't drop her pal just to spend a couple of hours with some girl she barely knows, no matter how fascinating her gravelly voice and billboard undies. But somehow I find the strength to go from lousy friend to dirty rotten liar. "I know it's last minute and everything, but I have to hole up and study all weekend."

There's a long pause. "You're cancelling our weekend to study? That is just wrong."

My omelet folding, like my dependability, has failed. I overshoot and slop wet egg and melted cheese over the side of the skillet and onto the stovetop, which I'll have to clean up before Dad gets any manic scrubbing ideas. "This school is different, I told you that. I'm in Honors Math, and if I don't keep my grades up, I'm screwed."

"You've always been in Honors Math." I can hear the pout in her voice. "It never stopped you from hanging with me."

"I know. The workload here is completely ill."

"I got someone else to ride Bo for me, plus Eddie has to work."

125

Which makes me feel worse. While I'm bettering my social life at Carling's under the guise of teaching her calculus, Mandy will be stuck at home staring at her yellow-flowered bedroom walls and listening to her parents fight. "I'm sorry, I don't have a choice. There aren't that many spots at Ivy League schools. Even fewer if you're going for the Baxter scholarship."

She groans. "Do I even want to know?"

"It's a Harvard scholarship that gives preference to Ant grads. But it's 'need-blind,' meaning anyone can apply, rich or poor. So my complete lack of fundage won't even help me. Only perfect grades will."

Mandy doesn't say anything for a long while. I hear a bit of crunching, then, "Seriously, Sara. People like you and me don't go to Harvard."

Irritation rockets through my veins and I realize that, for the first time in my life, having a lid on my potential has been suffocating me. Even with top grades, my future used to look something like the ramshackle bungalows back on Norma Jean Drive: homely, with ceilings so low I could touch them on my tiptoes. But it's as if a quake has taken place. The pressure on the earth's plates has caused a huge seismic burp, temporarily allowing me to scrabble to higher ground, groomed Ivy League turf I never had access to in the past. But, as with all seismic activity, further shifts can change things again, so the smart girl climbs while she can. "Hey," I say. "I'm not even seventeen. Don't squash my future just yet."

"You want to go to Boston U and become a principal at Finmory, remember?"

"I still might. The Ants wouldn't even expect *that*

much from me if they knew I was the janitor's kid."

"Sara . . . how can they not know?"

"I haven't told them."

"You mean, as far as these bug people know, your dad is not your dad?"

"Kind of. I said something about my dad being some kind of doctor. These kids are different, Mandy. It's not acceptable to come from nothing. Believe me; you'd have done the same thing in my position."

Mandy is silent and I hear a flicking sound in the background. I don't have to see her to know she's picking at the bottom of her shoe. It's been her nervous habit since we were kids. "See, that's where *we're* different," she says. "I may be the daughter of a cable repairman and a receptionist, and I may live in the lamest town on the planet, but not for *one second* have I ever thought I come from nothing."

"That's not what I meant. It's not a class thing. It's—"

I don't get the chance to explain. She's already hung up. That I deserved it makes it worse.

Dad comes in and sits at the table. "Who was on the phone?"

I drop the phone into its cradle and set Dad's dinner on the table. Over-toasted bagels and crippled omelets. "Mandy. She can't come this weekend."

"That's too bad. You could have used a little fun."

"Yeah, well. Now I can study."

He doesn't comment. As he eats, he lines up the salt and pepper shakers in front of his plate. Then pushes them slightly to the left. Then the right. Then moves them closer to his juice glass, where his folded napkin, glass, and the shakers now form the letter *L*. Wait a second, not quite perfect, because he's adjusting the napkin now, making it straighter. There. Now the L is as flawless as a glass/napkin/salt and pepper shaker L could possibly be.

I watch as he dismantles the L, then lines it all up again. This time the napkin and the shakers make up the long arm of the L, and the juice glass becomes the short part. Lining things up like this is not a good thing. It's not a sign of neatness or boredom or an extreme fondness for the middle section of the alphabet. It's a sign his OCD is spreading into the tiniest corners of his life.

"You used to take pills for it, right?"

"For what?"

"You know, lining things up and stuff."

"Dr. Harris put me on an antidepressant for a while. But the side effects were overwhelming. My concentration was off."

"Why don't you see Dr. Harris anymore?"

He stabs a piece of egg and stuffs it into his mouth. "What for? I'm managing quite well now."

His denial feels like food poisoning, piercing my stomach wall. I wonder if he believes himself. "But did he ever give you any guidelines? Like, how to tell if your OCD has gone from being just an annoyance to being something more?"

He takes a long sip of juice, sets down the empty glass, and wipes his mouth. "He said as long as my behavior remains within about twenty degrees of the spectrum of normal daily functioning, I am fine to manage on my own."

God. We've sailed way past that one. "It's good we have his number. You know, just in case."

Dad shakes his head. "I suspect that number wouldn't do us much good. Harris died about a year and a half ago."

My math brain starts clicking and whirring as it tries—and fails—to find a solution it can live with.

(my unhappy father × tabletop items becoming letters of the alphabet) − normal daily functioning + one dead doctor = one Russian pawnbroker coming back from the dead

Early Saturday morning I wake to Dad shaking my shoulder and asking me to run to the corner market for milk for his coffee. Seeing as today is his birthday, I have no choice but to peel my bones from the warm, squishy mattress and step out onto the icy floor. Still half-asleep, I gather my hair into a ponytail and pull on a pair of paint-splattered gray sweats and fleecy boots. By the time I reach the foyer, I'm at least alert enough to take the back door to the alley to eliminate any chance encounters with early-morning Ants who might wander into Brighton. It's happened before.

It's even colder than I imagined outside. I step into the alley and shiver in the weak sunlight, pulling my sleeves down over my hands. In the parking area, heaving a trash bag into the Dumpster, is Noah, wearing nothing but wrinkled shorts and a torn undershirt that looks like he's been living in it for days—stained, with a collar so stretched out it's falling off one shoulder. His dreads are glued together in long, wormy tufts, like licorice ropes that've frozen together.

"*Geez*, it's cold," he says when I wave.

"Yeah."

He hurls a couple of pizza boxes into the recycling bin, then reaches into his pocket for his cigarettes. After lighting up he tosses a spent match on the roadway. "You're Charlie's kid, right?"

I nod.

"He's a pretty cool guy. I helped him with the van the other day."

"You're the one who drives the Bentley?" I point at the shiny black car.

He nods. "You a friend of Carling's?"

Simple question, really. All I have to say is yes or no. But the answer isn't that clear. What he should have asked is, do I sit behind Carling in math class and analyze her lineup of underpants? Did I go through a half tube of gel trying to style my hair like hers before school this morning? Have I ever grabbed hold of her boyfriend's chest? Worn her skirt? To any of those questions, I could squeak out a definitive yes. But as it is, I can only mumble, "Kind of. You work for her family all the time?"

"Kind of." He laughs to himself. "Not a bad job, riding around in a fancy car. Hanging out with a fancy family. I don't have much in the way of relatives myself, so this kind of works for me." He sucks on his cigarette, exhales, and analyzes my face. "I worry about that girl, though. She's like a kid sister to me. But I can't be around all the time, you know?"

"What do you mean?"

"I'm not just her driver." Another drag on his smoke. "I keep her safe."

"Keep her safe from what?"

130

"Mostly herself." He tosses his cigarette onto the pavement and flicks it away with his bare foot. "Carling Burnack is none too stable. Haven't you noticed?"

"Kind of."

"Her father's nuts, and Carling . . . I adore her, but she's capable of just about anything. You'd be wise to avoid her."

He's right. I should stay away from Carling.

Trouble is, I can't.

chapter 15
slush snooker

The yellow crazy ant is blond, leggy, and impulsive, and emits a protective acid that is potentially blinding.

Carling Burnack's house is like no other house I've seen. Perched on the edge of a hill, tangled up in zillions of tree branches, it's a big white brick box that is seriously confused with itself. It's all at once ancient and modern, obnoxious and impressive, beautiful and repulsive. The three-car garage tucked beneath the house appears to be dug straight into the hillside, the open doors revealing wide-eyed cars peeking out like worried moles, watching as I park my rusted ten-speed against dead cedar hedge and walk around the property in search of the front door.

Following a leaf-strewn path down one side of the house, I eventually find a door toward the back. Windows on either side of the door flaunt hanging mobiles made of glass discs in reds, purples, golds, and blues. They look like kindergarten art projects of Carling's that nobody ever thought to take down. Slinging my book bag over one shoulder, I suck in a big breath and ring the bell.

The air is filled with the smell of Sunday-night dinner. Like beef and gravy and mothers who wear aprons. Looking around, I notice a brown paper bag by my feet, folded neatly at the top, and a large aluminum tray. There's a note taped to the foil lid of the tray, and I bend down to read it.

Grace,
Heat the roast for one hour at 350. Potatoes for 20
min. Better times ahead, darling.
Ted sends his love.
xoxox, Barbara

Just as I stand up, the door swings open. A tiny woman in a gray dress and running shoes steps out from behind it. "You come for Miss Carling?" she says in a troubled whisper.

I nod.

She steps to one side and motions for me to enter. Before she closes the door, I say, "There's some kind of food out there."

"No," she says, refusing to look. "No food."

"There is, see?" I point.

The door thumps shut. She says nothing, just waits while I take off my boots, then motions for me to follow, leaving Barbara's roast and Ted's love to rot on the porch with the autumn leaves.

The hallway is wide enough to allow for busloads of tourists, and the walls are smothered in art of all sizes. Tiny architectural drawings in plain black frames are squashed between massive canvases splashed with hallucinogenic blotches of what looks like dried vomit. And speckled between these are African masks and photos of a big, hairy man, probably Carling's dad, shaking hands with

Tom Hanks, Matthew Broderick, and a blonde woman with cropped bangs and huge black glasses.

I slow in front of a drawing framed in copper. The frame and the surrounding white mat are enormous, but the pencil drawing in the center is no bigger than my palm. It's a badly done sketch, scribble, really, of a bus and a couple of stick people holding guitars. I peer at the signature—Elton John. Wow. The guy's clearly no artist, but I'm guessing this little doodle is worth a fortune.

The old wooden floorboards are so warped it feels like we're walking over hills. The housekeeper's spongy shoes are completely silent—between her soundless footsteps and the way she refuses to look me in the eye, it's as if she barely exists.

We pass dark, cavernous rooms full of building-block furniture that seems uncomfortable as hell. Everywhere are messy stacks of magazines, journals, and humungous books—piled high on coffee tables, pushed under spare chairs and deep into corners. I slow at the door of what must be Mr. Burnack's recording studio. Double glass doors etched with sunburst patterns lead into a black room covered floor to ceiling on one side with buttons, dials, flashing red lights, and knobs. Other than the enormous keyboard at the base, the whole right side of the room looks like the cockpit of a plane. The desk is nearly empty but for a row of silver disc trophies—Tony awards, I assume—the ultimate prize for anyone working in theater.

The dining room has three walls lined floor to ceiling in books stacked as haphazardly as the others, most threatening to tumble over the edge and onto the floor. The fourth wall is a floor-to-ceiling window looking out on the patch-work of autumn leaves outside, as if to remind the owners that there's a world beyond these walls. The table is made entirely of glass, with cone-shaped stools of every color tucked underneath

The maid stops and presses a button on a panel, and I realize we're standing in front of an elevator. Our four-story apartment building doesn't even have an elevator, and Carling has one in her house. I must appear shocked because the woman smiles to herself. Stainless-steel doors slide open, and it takes every ounce of control I can muster to pretend this is all normal.

Inside, she presses a button marked B, the elevator lurches, and we begin to descend. Then she looks at me. "You are from Ant School?"

I nod. "I'm new."

"Too nice friend for Miss Carling."

I'm confused. Did she mean I'm *too* nice to be friends with Carling or that it's nice that I'm friends with Car-ling? Her tone was so flat I can't tell. Then the doors slide open and we're in the basement, in a caramel-colored rec room with a pool table, a roaring fire in a double-sided stone fireplace, retro-looking pinball machines, and music thumping from floor speakers. Isabella and Carling have pool cues in their hands, and Sloane fiddles with an enormous machine on a bar counter. Willa, perched on the edge of a cushy chair, pecks away on a laptop. Everywhere, spread across the butterscotch carpeting, are calculus textbooks, binders, calculators, pencils.

They look up.

"Hey, London," Carling says. Then she waits. Maybe

for my reaction to the room, which is the most incredible basement I've ever seen. Back home, our cellar had a cement floor, cheap paneling, and a TV with an antenna made from a coat hanger. Stained acoustic tiles lined the ceiling, and the only entertainment was a couple of puzzles with missing pieces and a Twister game with a spinner held together by gum.

"Hey," I say, as if bored.

"We're taking a study break to cheer up Carling," says Sloane. "She's bummed that Leo won't do her."

"I didn't say that," squeaks Carling. "I said he gets all weird about things. It's fine for me to take off my shirt, but when it comes to him, he gets all hostile. How are we ever going to have sex?"

Sloane sips from a paper cup and squints in disgust. "How long have you been dating now? A year?"

"Eight months."

Sloane considers this. "That's a long time. I bet he has extra nipples."

"Maybe he's a virgin. Or a dieting Mormon who has no energy," says Willa, grinning at Izz, "but really clean veins."

"Oh, that's hilarious," snaps Isabella.

"Can we get back to me?" Carling says. "It's not like Leo's pure. Believe me, the guy's no Mormon. It's more like, I don't know, he's not into me or something."

I cross the room and drop my backpack, fully aware I should keep my mouth shut. "Not everyone's right for each other," I say. "Maybe Leo's just being realistic. I mean, it's not as if he's going to marry some girl he started seeing when he was in eleventh grade, right? That would be right up there with dating your cousin."

"Maybe that's where he got the extra nipples," Sloane says from behind the sink. "His parents are first cousins."

"Supernumerary nipples are not a joke," Isabella says hotly. "Lots of people have them. They usually occur along the abdominal part of the milk line, like with animals. Though sometimes they present as high as the neck or face. One woman even had one on the sole of her foot."

Carling bends over in disgust and groans. "Stop! Now when I *do* get him naked, I'm going to be thinking of nipple feet."

Sloane just stares at Izzy, shaking her head. "Just when I think you can't possibly come up with anything more disgusting, you always manage to top yourself. That's it, ladies. We cleanse our minds by playing Slush Snooker." She starts setting out small paper cups. "You miss your shot, you drink."

"Drink what?" I ask.

Carling leans over the table and lines up her shot. The ball bullets into a corner pocket. "Who knows?" she says. "Sloane's slushie shots are one of life's great unsolved mysteries." An ice machine whirs.

"Carling's right," says Isabella, placing a pool cue in my hand. "It could contain soy milk, yogurt, extract of pumpkin seed, chocolate sauce, whatever."

"Maybe we'll do mashed Doritos today, in honor of Izzy's film debut this week in math class," says Sloane with a sly grin.

"Don't be cruel, Sloane," says Isabella. "It's unbecoming."

"Now, now, children," says Carling. "I say we let Sloane spike her slushies with the contents of whatever liquid she doesn't have to get up for." She waves toward the huge mirrored bar, which is groaning with liquor bottles of every size, shape, and color.

"Hmm," Sloane says. "I just got back from yoga class, so I'm feeling a little Zen. We'll only drink pure, uncolored spirits." She points to various bottles. "White rum, vodka, gin, and, if you sink the white ball, anise."

"What's anise?" I ask.

"Liquid licorice," says Willa, leaning closer to her screen and squinting. "But don't get excited. By the time she mixes it with her health food, it'll taste about as yummy as Isabella's foot nipples."

Carling shrieks. "No more nipple talk."

Other than the odd sip from Mom's wineglass, I've never had a real drink. To be honest, I hate the flavor and I hate the way it makes me feel all floaty and flu-ish. "I thought we were going to study."

"So bookish is our London." Carling positions her cue in front of the white ball and takes her shot, sending the solid blue ball ricocheting around the table, eventually smacking back into the white ball, which narrowly misses the side pocket.

Sloane does a little pouring and mixing, then sets a squishy cuplet on the edge of the table, where Carling picks it up and inspects it. "This isn't white, it's pus green."

Sloane holds up a narrow bottle. "Spirulina. The Russians say it cures radiation poisoning. You'll thank me if you ever have to eat rice grown at the ruins of Chernobyl. Hey, that's an Izzy-type fact." She sticks out her tongue at Isabella.

Carling downs it and grimaces. "Tastes like you scooped it out of a dirty fish tank." She crumples the cup, tosses it behind the bar and looks at me. "Your turn, London. Pray like hell you're a good shot."

I've never played snooker in my life. I set myself up behind the white ball and shoot, missing the striped ball and grazing the red felt of the tabletop instead. I lean over and inspect the damage. "I scratched it. Sorry."

The little cuplet of green icy slop is passed by Sloane to Isabella (who sniffs it and feigns gagging), then to Carling and finally to me. With no other choice, I tilt back my head and let the rancid slush slide down my throat, nearly retching it back up onto the table.

After a few more rounds of Slush Snooker, Willa has gone back to her laptop, Carling and Isabella are giggling drunk, and I feel like I have the plague. My head hurts, I'm shaky and nauseated, and I want to go to bed. The last snooker shot is mine, and it surprises no one—least of all me—that I sink the white ball. So this time Sloane passes me the licorice-spirulina mixture. I sip, but the slop is so vile I choke, sputtering the terrible green slush all over the carpet.

"No worries," says Carling before I can speak. "It's why we have a Molly." She presses a button on the wall and calls into the speaker, "Molly, cleanup on aisle four."

Molly's voice answers, "Coming, Miss Carling."

"Don't bother her. I'll clean it up." I head behind the bar and find a rag and some seltzer water, then return to dab at the spot.

Molly arrives with a cleaning basket full of supplies and

looks shocked to find me on my hands and knees. "No, no," she says, shooing me away.

"It's okay. I'm good at this."

Sloane peers over my shoulder. "Actually, she is."

Isabella laughs. "God, London. That's impressive. Scrubbing the floor comes so naturally to you."

I drop my rag as if it's burning my hand.

Carling giggles, pulling me to my feet so Molly can get down on the floor and finish the job. "I wonder what the Genius Theory would say about our London's future?"

I allow myself to be led away, suddenly more nauseated than ever. I know exactly what the Genius Theory would say and it terrifies me. My mother's a cook and my father's a janitor. It's well documented that I can't cook. So guess what's left?

When Carling's mother, Gracie, insisted I stay for dinner, my first instinct was to dig my bike out of the bushes and pedal home fast. The thought of sitting in a big edgy space between Carling and her parents filled me with dread. So I told Gracie no. Said it was my dad's birthday and I had to get home. Which is true.

Then Carling smiled at me and asked if my new yoga pants can go in the dryer. I turned to Gracie and told her I'd love to stay.

Isabella, Sloane, and Willa were picked up a few minutes later by Isabella's mother. It wasn't until they were heading out the door that Isabella realized I was staying. She actually slithered back into the foyer and offered to stay a bit longer, but her mother wouldn't allow it, complaining she'd given up enough writing time to carpool;

she wasn't leaving the house again. As Mrs. Latini headed down the darkened walkway, Isabella muttered, "Leave, bitch." Whether she was talking to me or her mother, I can't say.

One thing is certain. Isabella's usefulness to Carling is being shaken and she doesn't like it one little bit.

We sit at the see-through table surrounded by teetering books, Carling and I along the sides, Gracie at one end. With Barbra Streisand playing in the background, Gracie hums tunelessly to the music. "What did you say your last name was, Sara?"

"Black."

She thinks for a moment, going through her mental Rolodex of families in her social circle. "The Back Bay Blacks? Or the Charleston Blacks?"

"Mom, you're sounding embarrassingly old lady," says Carling.

"Carling tells me you had the highest grade in your math class yesterday."

I smile. "I'm kind of math obsessed. Birth defect, I guess."

"Really? Carling's older brother is gifted in math and science. He's at Harvard Medical School. Where Carling is meant to go." She glances at her daughter. "*If* she can pull off grades like yours."

"I will, Mom," says Carling. "London's my new study partner."

Gracie smiles. Her eyebrows drift skyward and she sizes me up anew. "Well. I hope you have better luck with her than her last tutor did."

The room goes silent and I struggle to break the tension with a cute remark. All I come up with is, "That's cool you're going to be a doctor, Carling."

Carling mutters, "I don't have a freaking choice, do I?" Then she raises her voice and winks at Gracie. "My mother didn't get into med school, did you, Mom? Things didn't go so well at Ant. So now every one of her offspring has to pay for it."

"Carling," says Gracie with a frown. "We've had this discussion. Lawyers only bide their time until something better comes along. You become a doctor and you're set up for life."

Molly comes in with a tall pitcher and fills our water glasses, and, at Gracie's insistence, our wineglasses. Carling's imposing father, with hair that rises toward the ceiling like angry black flames, at least six feet tall and as broad as the doorframe he passes through, walks in wearing nothing but a faded-to-pink Harvard sweatshirt and baggy paisley boxers.

There's something arresting about seeing an award-winning composer in his underwear, even if his career is teetering on the brink. It makes him seem far crazier and far more dangerous than the drunken vagrant that might flash you in the park. The guy in the park is underfed, weak, probably psychologically unsound. Right off the bat, he's at a disadvantage. The composer with his bad reviews and hairy knees parked under the glass table is different. He's well fed, pampered, and annoyed. His exposure is part of his power. Like a 450-pound Bengal tiger, he cannot be forced into a pair of corduroys or jeans in the name of social acceptance. Like the tiger, he'd like to see you try.

Gracie sighs and drops her forehead into one hand, rubbing her temples. "Honestly, Brice, we have company. Put on a pair of pants."

"My house. My rules." He narrows his eyes and looks at me. "Who are you?"

"Sara."

"You drink, Sara?"

Does he know about the Slush Snooker? My spill on the carpet? I have no idea what to say. He's the scariest-looking man I've ever met. Under the table, Carling gives me a kick, which, of course, everyone can see. "Not really," I say.

He nods toward my glass. "That wine costs about seven hundred and fifty bucks a glass."

"*Brice*," says Gracie.

He looks surprised. "What? I'm just saying she should enjoy it, that's all."

"We were saving that bottle. It was the last—"

"There'll be more bottles like it. Young girls should grow up enjoying the finer things in life. Wine and"—he waves toward his hairy legs—"absolute comfort." He looks at Carling. "Right, Ladybug?"

Carling picks at her bamboo placemat.

"I hear from Griff Hogan's father that you got your math tests back," Brice says.

Gracie sets her wineglass down too hard and, barely perceptibly, nods toward me. "Don't start up, Brice. You and I have already discussed Carling's mark."

"But I haven't discussed it with *her*." He stares at Carling. "Sweetheart, how did you do?"

"Seventy-nine."

He's silent for a moment, and from the way he sits back and half smiles, I can tell he's enjoying this moment like the tiger enjoys watching a wounded deer bleed to death. "Seventy-nine . . . seventy-nine. Not quite up to Harvard standards now, is it?"

"But London, I mean Sara, is my new study partner and she got the highest mark in the class. We'll be *so* ready for the next test."

"Still means you're going to do without your cell phone for a week." He holds out his hand and waits while Carling blinks back tears of humiliation, then yanks it out of her pocket and slaps it into his palm.

He sets it beside his plate and looks at me. "So Sara has a talent for math, does she?"

"Yeah," says Carling. A sly grin spreads across her face. "Sara's dad is a neurosurgeon. So she must have grown up surrounded by the right sort of brilliance. And *education*."

The ultimate slur against a man whose claim to fame, I've heard in the halls, is that he learned to compose music by ear, with no formal training whatsoever. He graduated from a small Boston public school and scrabbled to songwriting success without the benefit of the prestigious musical training of his peers. Brice's hair seems to blacken and smolder under his daughter's implication, and the air around us grows pungent and charred. Hard to breathe. He raps his clenched fist against the table softly, saying nothing.

Gracie comes to the rescue. "To Carling, our future pediatric surgeon. And to Sara, our future . . . what is it you want to do with your life, Sara?"

My wineglass shakes in my hand. "Um, I'm not quite sure yet."

She grins. "And to Sara, who'd better decide soon."

Everybody drinks, so, despite the fact that my stomach feels like a rusty metal can, I drink too.

Just then, Molly backs through the swinging door from the kitchen. In her hands is the roast beef whose existence she'd denied a few hours earlier. Gracie stands up to clear space on the table for the enormous silver platter.

Brice inhales. "Your roast smells delicious, Gracie."

She blushes and spoons teensy roasted potatoes onto my plate. "Just something I threw together. Nothing special." Just like that, Barbara and Ted's generosity is squashed flat. I guess all the x's and o's in the world can't buy a little gratitude.

Carling rolls her eyes and picks a sprig of parsley from the tray, stuffing it into her mouth.

Gracie looks at me. "Is your father at Massachusetts General, Sara?"

Shit.

I drop my fork. I'm the very worst daughter on earth. I forgot all about my father's birthday. This, his thirty-fifth birthday, his first since she moved out. He's home alone . . . sort of. Just Charlie and his obsessive-compulsive disorder watching TV side by side in the dark.

chapter 16
hungry man dinner

Trophallaxis is the sharing of food between ant colony residents and is accomplished through regurgitation or defecation.

Pedaling across the bustling city in the cool night air blows the suffocating Burnack-family atmosphere—like a noxious gas—out of my system.

With no reflectors on my bike, I'm not willing to risk death by riding on the road, gliding in and out of the Saturday-evening traffic. Instead, I guide my bike through the unhurried pedestrians on the well-lit sidewalks, making my journey home twice as long as it should be but mathematically doubling my odds of survival.

It's ten thirty by the time I creep through the front door. Just as I thought, other than the flicker of the TV coming from the living room, the apartment is unlit. I follow the eerie glow to find Dad hunched over a TV dinner, watching the History Channel. No sign of his twisted partner. He looks up, smiles. "There you are. How was the studying?"

I rush forward and wrap my arms around his neck, kiss his stubbly cheek. "I'm sorry I'm late. I wanted to make you a special birthday dinner."

He points down at his microwavable food tray and says,

with his mouth full, "Don't terrorize me while I'm swallowing."

Still has his sense of humor.

I'm a terrible person. While my broken father's been in here ingesting frozen turkey, I've been at Carling's house sipping from a three-thousand-dollar bottle of wine. "What have you been doing all day? Anything fun?"

"Had a superb day. Noah assisted me with the VW's engine in the morning. The guy really knows what he's doing. Then I did a bit of purging."

"You threw up?"

"I cleaned out my sock drawer. Disposed of my unmatched socks."

"Oh. Cool. While you finish your Hungry Man special, I'm going to make you horrifically ugly brownies with lumpy icing. So prepare to be astonished by my culinary skill."

"I'm always astonished by your culinary dexterity, Sarie-bear. Mood-ring chicken, tumbled omelets . . ."

I walk into the kitchen, pulling off my backpack and dumping it on the floor. "You ain't seen nothin' yet."

Reaching into the cupboards, I pull out a brownie mix, eggs, canola oil. There's a swimming pool smell in the kitchen and it isn't until I pull a 9" × 9" Pyrex pan from the drawer under the oven that I realize what it means.

Dad's been into the bleach.

I peek into the cupboard and examine the mop Dad bought the day we moved in, exactly two weeks ago. The spongy mop head is worn down to almost nothing.

About half an hour later, I emerge from the kitchen with a plate of brownies in hand. They aren't quite cooked to perfection, being somewhat soggy in the center, but the twelve colored candles look great.

Walking slowly, so as not to blow out the candles, I start to sing "Happy Birthday" and then stop.

Dad is asleep, his unfinished dinner still on his lap. After setting the brownies on the table and blowing out the candles, I remove his tray and cover his legs and chest with a blanket. I watch him breathe for a minute, then notice his hands. They're so dry and cracked they look like they've been slashed by razors. His day wasn't spent doing a bit of straightening up. His day was spent scrubbing out the memory of my mother.

Charlie's problem is spreading too fast. It's a problem way too complicated for a sixteen-year-old math brain to compute. No amount of joking, game playing, or home-cooked meals is going to help. With no one but a dead doctor to help me, I need to take the most drastic step yet. I need to call my mother and ask for help.

Careful not to wake him, I creep into Dad's room and close the door. His black address book is lying open on his desk, so I flip to the section marked *T* and find the last entry on the page. Tina Black. The phone number is weird and long and foreign.

As soon as I pick up the phone and start to dial, a thick brown envelope slides off the desk and topples onto the seat of Dad's chair. Holding the phone to my ear, I pick up the package and turn it over. It's from, of all places, Mallory, Mallory, and Montauk—Sloane's father's law firm. With buttery fingers, I reach inside and pull out a neat stack of papers bound together with a rubber band. As I scan the top sheet, the real reason behind Dad's knuckle-grazing, birthday-boy cleaning frenzy hits me in the stomach like a dripping mop.

My mother wants a divorce.

Through the phone receiver, I hear a faint, buzzing ring. Then a faraway voice, my mother's voice, says, "*Allo.*"

I don't speak. Somehow I never imagined her speaking French.

"*Allo? Qui est-il?*"

She's changed so much it takes my voice away. As quietly as I can, I lower the receiver and drop it into the cradle.

chapter 17
nobody

Researcher E. O. Wilson discovered that when ants find a single drop of water near the nest entryway, they alarm other colony members, and the nest can be cleared in half a minute.

It's Friday morning and Mandy still hasn't taken my calls or answered my messages. My slip-up was bad, but did it really warrant complete and total exclusion from her life? Seriously. And now I'm stuck with my mom's smoky French accent running through my brain like the clunking pipes in the wall behind my bed. But instead of wanting an extra pillow to put over my head, I want someone to remind me that experimenting with foreign languages is good, nothing at all like a textbook mother who lives on a different page from her unborn baby.

I try Mandy's number one more time on the way to class. When she doesn't pick up, again, I head inside.

Mr. Curtis, we're all quickly discovering, is a huge fan of pop quizzes. He strolls in cradling a stainless-steel Starbucks travel mug and waves a stack of light blue papers up in the air. "I hope you've all been following my advice and spending your spare time studying. Today's quiz differs from our first in three ways." He sets his things on his desk and removes his blazer. "It's longer.

It encompasses everything we've learned in the last two weeks, plus the material you'll all remember fondly from our first quiz." He rolls up his sleeves. "And it will comprise *ten percent* of your mark in my class." He sets his hands on his hips and winks. "Enjoy. Saint Sarah, can I call upon you to pass out these tests?"

I make my way to the front of the class, aware I'm one of the few in the room who isn't wrecked with anxiety about the quiz. Carling leans forward like she might throw up, and Little Man Griff is flung back in his seat, looking as if he needs life support. Or maybe the comfort of his teddy. The joke of this being, he'll ace it no matter what. Isabella isn't concerned at all. She continues to pick at a muffin on her desk as if worried she might find a dead mouse inside.

Up goes Sloane's hand. "Mr. Curtis, will all of our quizzes be surprises? Because most of us do much better with a bit of warning."

"You're meant to be learning as we go along, Miss Montauk. I thought I made that point clear after the last quiz. Life, I can assure you, will not come at you with an appropriate period of warning, so you might want to consider putting a little more effort into it."

Isabella and Carling burst into peals of laughter, and Mr. Curtis shushes them and turns back to Sloane. "The more time you spend preparing yourself now, the better you'll do on my tests, it's as simple as that. You could learn a thing or two from your friend Sara. I'm willing to bet she's ready for this, am I right?"

I look up from where I'm setting tests in front of Carling, Sloane, and Izzy. "I don't know. I guess."

He leans on his desk and grins, twisting the lid off his coffee. "Perhaps you were able to see all this coming. There is a theory that Saint Sarah was entirely unrelated to Jesus, but that she was of noble birth and was chief of her tribe on the banks of the Rhone. Some say she had visions that the saints who'd been present at Jesus's death would come to the shore where her tribe went every year to receive benediction. Sure enough, the Three Marys arrived by boat."

A few people snicker and I force a weak smile.

To my horror, he continues. "Of course some have very opposite beliefs. In other accounts, Saint Sarah is a native of Upper Egypt and only appears in theological history as the Egyptian domestic of one of the Three Marys."

Griff snorts. "I don't get it. Saint Sarah is an Egyptian domestic . . . a domestic what?"

Carling rolls her eyes. "A domestic is a maid, you Neanderthal. He's saying Saint Sarah was nothing more than a common maid."

My nervous system goes gummy, then melts and runs down my legs to where it pools in my feet, seeping out between my toes and into my shoes. Now that my feet are too heavy to move and my Lost and Found oxford shoes have glued themselves to the floor, I stumble. The tests slide out of my hands and flutter around the room, over to the blackboard, under Mr. Curtis's desk, and beneath the feet of the kids in the front row. Mr. Curtis gets up to help, accidentally knocking his lidless travel mug across the floor. He stares at the spreading pool of brown liquid and shakes his head. "Five dollars' worth of caffeine gone to waste."

"Sorry," I say.

Sloane pulls her book bag away and squeals. "Ugh! It's headed right for me."

"Somebody call a Molly," sings Carling.

Thankful for any reason to delay the quiz, a few of the boys at the back of the class begin pounding their desks and chanting, "Mol-ly. Mol-ly. Mol-ly."

I'm hit by a revolting realization. Carling's housekeeper isn't named Molly at all. Carling just considers the woman so beneath her, such a lower form of humanity, that she's tagged her with the generic label—Molly Maid.

Isabella crumbles what's left of her muffin into the mess. I must look shocked because she says, "What? It's getting cleaned up anyway."

"Now who's the pig?" squeaks Griff.

"A bit disrespectful," says Mr. Curtis, looking appalled. "Miss Latini, you can head down and request a custodian to come to the class. Walk back to class with him or her and try to imagine yourself in the janitor's shoes, cleaning up after a student's inconsiderate actions."

"Whatever." Isabella heads out of the room as I reach under her desk and sort out the pile of fallen papers.

In my haze of humiliation at having gone from the daughter of the most infamous icon in religious history, to a noblewoman who can see into the future, to a "common" maid; in my anxiousness to undo my giant fumble that has caused Mr. Curtis to lose his coffee and us to lose valuable test-taking time; in my disgust at Carling's disrespect for her housekeeper; I didn't anticipate right away what could happen next.

The call for a custodian might bring my father.

I don't have to fret for long. Not five minutes later, Charlie strolls into the room.

Spinning on my heel, I rush along the far row, passing out quizzes with my head lowered. At the back, I step behind the open door of a storage cupboard and tuck my hair behind my ears, hunching over and praying Mr. Curtis won't call for death by social stoning by ordering me to my seat.

I watch as my dad wheels his big red bucket closer to the mess, then pulls out the great, dripping string mop and wrings it out on the strainer attached to the pail. He glances up at the kids watching and laughs. "Feels like being onstage."

A few sympathetic giggles. Charlie mops up the coffee and muffin crumbs fairly quickly, rinsing the mop in the bucket. But he doesn't stop there. He wrings, scrubs, and rinses two more times, seemingly unaware of the curious looks he's getting from the class. Even Mr. Curtis, defender of the custodian, looks confused. As the class's reaction grows, I, from my hidey-hole behind the cupboard door, die a thousand deaths for my father.

Then it gets much, much worse.

Charlie removes a plastic spray bottle from his belt. Then he lowers himself down on his knees and starts spraying the shit out of the floor, which is already spotless. He sprays and scrubs, sprays and scrubs, and soon the air is heavy with the overpowering smell of bleach.

Kids in the front rows begin to cough, some of them getting up and joining me at the back. Groans and snorts pop up from all over the classroom and I hear murmurings, like, "Guy's messed up!" and "Someone needs to call for help" and "One crazy Molly."

Willa stands up coughing a tight, high-pitched cough, holding her vest over her mouth. She pulls a puffer from her bag and mumbles through the woolen vest, "Mr. Curtis, I have asthma. . . ."

He guides her from the room, calls another girl over, and tells them to go straight to the infirmary. The girls disappear.

The scrubbing isn't going to end anytime soon, so eventually Mr. Curtis lightens the mood by clapping his hands. "Well, now I understand why the school is so sparkling clean this term." He pats Charlie's back and pulls him to his feet. "It's the work of our new custodian, Mr. . . . what is your name, sir?"

No. Please, no. Please, Dad, don't say "Black," not to Mr. Curtis. He'll haul me out of the cupboard and start making comparisons that will only end with the entire school knowing who I really am. A liar.

But Dad just smiles, nods his head at the class, and points to his name tag. "You can address me as Charlie."

For a moment, it looks like Dad is going to drop to the floor again to keep scrubbing, but Mr. Curtis leads him to the door. "You've done us a wonderful service, Charlie. I can assure you our floor has never been so hygienic."

Just before Dad disappears, he waves back to the kids. The moment the door clicks shut, the room explodes into animated whispers and giggles, and I make a run for my seat.

"Okay, that's enough," says Mr. Curtis as I slip into my chair. "The excitement is over. Thank you for your assistance, Saint Sarah. Remind me never to call on you for help passing out tests again."

I'm safe. For now.

"Pick up your pencils, people." He settles himself in his chair, sets his feet on his desk, cracks open a math journal, and reaches for his reading glasses. "You now have only forty-one minutes to impress me."

I scratch my name at the top of the quiz and start on the first problem. The solution is obvious and after I've written down my calculations, I scrawl $X = 37$ and move to the next question. Beside me, a chair shifts. I look up to see Isabella has slid her desk slightly closer to Carling's and moved her paper to the edge of her desktop, giving her friend easy access to her work. But Carling turns away from Isabella and turns to face me. She raises her eyebrows. I know what she wants. And I have no freaking choice but to give it to her.

I slide my paper toward the edge of my desk and watch as she copies $X = 37$ onto her quiz.

chapter 18
private caller

The average ant lives about a year, but the queen lives fifteen to twenty years. Her death will mean the death of the colony.

I have a test in pre-law coming up. It's mid-October now; I've been at Ant long enough to see this class is going to be my toughest. Law is nebulous, floaty, and gray, completely unlike the dependable sturdiness of math or science. There is a solid certainty to polynomials—they simply are what they are and always will be. But a law is never just a law. If you're in a fistfight and happen to knock over your opponent to the ground and he hits his head on a parking meter, you may or may not be charged with assault, depending upon how angry the guy rubbing his cranium might be. And if that person happens to have an eggshell for a skull and dies after the exact same scuffle, suddenly you're facing a manslaughter charge even though you could never have known the man was born to a chicken. It's called the Thin Skull rule.

All of which means tonight will be a caffeine-and-chocolate-fueled, flashlight-under-the-covers, pray-Dad-doesn't-wake-up, all-night cram session.

We've been studying *Vosburg v. Putney*, a case where an eleven-year-old kicked a fourteen-year-old in the shin at school. The older kid was recovering from a previous injury and, as a result of his miniature assailant's anger, lost the use of his leg permanently. No one could have predicted such a thing would happen, but the little boy was still held liable. The Thin Skull rule in action and good reason to keep your feet to yourself.

Speaking of keeping body parts to oneself, Carling, Sloane, Isabella, and I all have a spare second period, and my plans to study are torpedoed by Carling dragging me back to the groper-infested tides of the Petting Pool. At least, without the encumbrance of my lunch bag, I'll have both hands available to block the flesh-eaters.

As I follow them into the stairwell, my cell phone vibrates from the bottom of my backpack. I dig it out to see a jumble of numbers I don't recognize. Since the only two people in the world who know this phone number are Dad and Mandy, I figure Mandy must have a new phone. "Hey," I say, shielding the phone from any teachers that might walk by.

"Sara? Sweetheart, it's Mom."

I say nothing, just stop dead and reach for the handrail to steady myself. I haven't heard her say my name in months. I'd forgotten how smooth it sounds. How comforting. I think about hanging up.

"I've been desperate to talk to you," she says. "Are you at school?"

"Yeah."

"Darling, I miss you *so* much. How do you like it there? Have you made any friends?"

Carling and the girls have stopped at the landing and are waving me to hurry up. "Sort of."

"That's wonderful. Sweetie, I love you so much. You know that, don't you?"

"Yeah."

"I want you to fly out here and visit."

"I don't know. School's pretty tough."

"I've been a little worried about your dad. Is he managing okay?"

No. He's a total mess and so am I. You need to come back right this minute and erase what you've done, I don't say. *It might take away his need to pour bleach on the whole world. Might stop his downward spiral.* But somehow I can't give her the satisfaction of knowing she hurt us so badly we don't recognize ourselves anymore. "Yeah."

"No return of his problem? No signs of scrubbing or checking things over and over?"

"Nope. Dad's fine."

"Oh. I'm so relieved. I was going to ask Aunt Jodie to fly in from Chicago to check on you. Just to be sure you're not struggling—"

"Mom? I've got to go now. Talk to you later."

"Wait, honey. What about—?"

I snap the phone shut. Then, when I'm certain the connection has been severed, I open the phone up, press a few buttons, and hit Block Caller.

The sofa is already layered with bodies, in some spots two students deep. Carling and Sloane are happy to fling themselves on top of the heap, and I settle myself on the leather arm beside Griff and Leo. I'm shaking after my mother's call and not sure it's a good idea to be within verbal striking range of Leo Reiser—you never know what will come out of his mouth—but I'm not willing to plunk myself down on a pile of squirming half strangers in the name of sexual enlightenment.

"That was brutal," says Griff as we sit. "Curtis is such an A-hole with his pop quizzes."

"Agreed," says Sloane, kicking off her worn shoes and closing her eyes. "I totally bombed that one."

Isabella looks at Carling and says, with a voice so thin and glassy it could shatter, "I think I did exceptionally well. How about you, Carling?"

Carling lets herself fall backward across Leo and Griff's laps. Then she grins at me. "Fantastic. Maybe even perfect."

"I hope so," says Sloane, picking her teeth. "Or Brice and Gracie will implode."

Carling's skirt is hiked up high enough for me to see today's panties are yellow. I won't be able to tell unless she rolls over, but I'm guessing these are Saturday's. "True. It's Harvard med school or death for me."

I can't stand this anymore. Carling loves law, she's the darling of our class. We did a mock trial the other day and not only did she win for our team, she made her points with such passion and humor. What judge, male or female, could resist her? This electricity that surrounds her isn't always channeled into crazy, I can see that now. When Carling Burnack feels good about herself, she's the most charming girl in the school. "I don't get it," I say. "Why don't you tell your parents you want to be a lawyer?"

She's still for a moment, then says robotically, "Because law is for hiring. Medicine is for aspiring."

Mrs. Pelletier heads down the stairs, eyeing the Petting Pool with mock reproof. Anything that might have been going on beneath the surface stops as she pauses on the landing and leans down to adjust Carling's errant skirt. "Are we keeping it clean here today?"

"Just a bunch of honor students swapping biological theories," says Carling, "It's all very innocent."

"Hmm," she says with a sarcastic nod. She starts to walk away. "I rather doubt that. Just remember where you are, people. You wouldn't want to come to school next week and find your favorite sofa has been moved into the teachers' lounge. Because that can be arranged."

"You're the coolest, Mrs. P.," calls Griff. "If only I were a few years older, I'd give your husband a reason to step up his game."

She stops and looks back, dumbfounded that this randy suggestion came from Anton's famed wunderkind, then hurries off as if it never happened.

"I adore Mrs. Pelletier," says Isabella.

"Forget her," says Sloane. "If something doesn't change, Mr. Curtis is going to screw me for Yale."

"Don't worry, princess." Griff pulls a tissue from his pocket and stuffs a corner of it up his nose. "I'll screw you either way."

Sloane stares at him. "Say it for me, Griff. I'm too tired."

He pinches up his face. *"Griff, you're such a pig."*

"Got that right," says Carling.

"Hey, you guys know anyone who might want to buy the Aston?" asks Leo. "I need the down payment to buy something that actually—I don't know—runs."

Carling pokes him. "A down payment—are you kidding me? You think none of us saw that *Times* article about Reiser Industries last week?"

"Yeah, Reiser," says Sloane. "You and your brother are inheriting practically the entire Eastern seaboard."

"What does Reiser Industries do?" I ask.

"Biggest car-parts manufacturer in the country," says Carling. "And my boyfriend's going to run it one day." She turns to Leo. "Tell Papa you need an advance on your allowance."

"Yeah, right," says Leo. "My dad's old school."

"Daddy Warbucks wants Leo to learn about life the hard way," says Griff.

"Since when?" asks Carling. "You're always sufficiently loaded when we go out."

"Why do you think I work summers at the Manhattan office?" says Leo.

"I don't know," she says with a dramatic pout. "I figured you were using that as an excuse to meet New York skanks. Which makes me lie in bed and cry."

Griff boffs Leo in the head. "See? Leo's parents are smart. They're not going to raise him all spoiled and lazy like Carling."

Carling pinches him. He shoves her off and says, "Seriously, you can't sell the car, Reiser. She's a legend. I plan to lose my virginity in the backseat. Just me, a six-pack of beer, Micheline Farber's dim-witted sister, and a piece of shoestring licorice that will be framed after what she'll do to it with her tongue. I've already stashed a few pieces under the seat."

Okay, even I can't stand this one. "You're going to feed a girl candy that's been festering on the dirty carpet with the grimy quarters and rotting french fries? You really are porcine, Little Man."

Griff stares up at me, his mouth hanging open. "I do think our little Brit is settling in." He slides his hand up my knee. "You're some feisty kind of mystery chick, aren't you, London?"

I swat away his stubby fingers.

What comes next shocks me to my socks. Leo grins wickedly, puts one arm around Griff's neck, and yanks him away from me, grinding his knuckles into Griff's wild hair. He says, "Leave her alone, asshole. She's miles too good for you."

I have to bite down on my lips to keep my face from splitting into a big, dorky grin. It means nothing, I'm sure of it. He probably meant it as an insult to Griff rather than a compliment to me. Leo Reiser is wholly connected to Carling Burnack. She's lying across his lap playing with his shirt buttons, and all I can think about are the scars on his chest. I wonder if Carling has touched them. Counted them. Kissed them. It's clear these two are solid. It's clear he's hers. So why is my heart beating so fast?

The moment that meant everything to me clearly means nothing to the others, and passes without a blip in the conversation, with Griff pulling away saying, "If you're lucky, you might lose your own virginity in there one day, Reiser."

"Yeah, well. Not all of us can be as classy as you."

"Come on, don't sell her," says Griff, smoothing out his hair. "The girls *love* guys in Astons."

Carling, twirling Leo's tie in her fingers, snorts. "All the more reason to ditch it. No one gets her hands on my guy." She kisses her fingertips and presses them to Leo's mouth. "No one."

It sounds like a threat.

chapter 19
by invitation only

Red ants milk the honeydew from aphids by stroking them with their antennae while the aphids eat.

The following Thursday morning before school, Mandy finally calls me back. She's sobbing so hard I barely recognize her voice.

"He dumped me," she says, taking in great hiccupping gulps of air.

"Seriously?"

"Yup. He found 'real love.'"

"Shit, Mand. Who is it?"

"Some twenty-two-year-old wretch who works with him at the video store. But wait—it gets even better. Kristy Vance heard they're engaged. He gave her a ring!"

"What an asshole."

"It's a sign that I am brainless. I really did think he'd wait for me."

"A year and a half. That's a long time for an asshole to wait."

"And forget my birthday. He was going to take me out to the Terrace for steak and to a hotel room he booked. I bought a teddy with skulls on it."

I can't help but laugh. "And still, he left?"

"Shut up." I can hear a tiny smile in her voice.

"I'm kidding. It's just so you."

"Now I get to lie in bed and bawl my eyes out while he takes *her* to *my* hotel room."

"You're miles too good for him. Don't you know that? It sucks that this happened, but one day you're going to look back on this and think, *Thank God I escaped.*"

"I won't."

"You will. You'll see. Now that you're single, every guy in Lundon will be banging on your door."

"Dude, that just isn't going to happen."

"You know what? My dad got me this free long-distance thing for my cell."

"So?"

"We'll spend your birthday together. We'll stay on the phone and watch a movie together. Just like we used to do when you were grounded."

"Come for the weekend instead."

"I don't know. Midterms are coming up. We'll do the movie things, though. It'll be fun, I promise."

"Okay, I guess."

"Perfect. Forget Eddie. I would never have let you marry a guy who looks like an animated baby."

"He doesn't look like an animated baby." Mandy blows her nose, then chokes out a laugh. "Okay, maybe he does a little. Geez, now I can never watch cartoons again." She's quiet for a moment and I can hear her drumming her fingers on her desk.

"Mandy? I'm sorry about what I said before. It's not what I meant."

"I know. No more battles. I need you in my life."

"Me too. From this moment forward I'm the model best friend."

"Honestly? I won't be able to handle anything less."

Our math quizzes come back to us at school that morning. The results aren't quite as abysmal as the first time, but there's enough slumping and sighing in the room to make it clear that people are beginning to panic about what this class will do to their averages, their Ivy League dreams, and their futures, in that order.

"The class average was disappointing," says Mr. Curtis. "And I don't mind telling you it would have been lower if not for three students. Mr. Hogan, Miss Burnack, and Miss Black, would you mind standing up?"

Carling is up before the words tumble from his mouth. I stand up next, then Griff, but who can tell if he's standing, really?

"Mr. Hogan, your score was ninety-eight point-eight percent. A solid achievement. You may sit." Griff sits but not before doing a pixie-sized touchdown dance with his arms in the air and his eyes closed.

"Sara, your test was clean and completely error-free. An accomplishment never achieved on any pop quiz in my class, not in fourteen years at the school. You've restored my faith in your generation. Congratulations, you may sit."

I drop into my seat and bury my flushed face in my collar.

The displeasure in the room is palpable. Vexation bounces about the room, ricochets off ceiling, blackboard, and walls, pinging me in the flushed cheeks. Isabella looks particularly miffed, as this comes awfully close to confirmation that she's been replaced as top in the class. Here's the thing about gifted kids. They're territorial about their smarts and don't like to be beaten. I've overstepped newbie laws, that much is clear, by having the audacity to come in here and, for the second time, beat their gifted faces off.

"Miss Burnack," says Mr. Curtis. "Your case is a bit more complicated."

Carling's eyes widen. She shoots a look of terror my way. She's thinking he knows. That he saw our identical answers, considered her lousy mark from the first quiz, and is about to call her a cheater in front of the entire class. I'm not sure what they do to cheaters in this school, but at Finmory it would mean an automatic zero, a meeting with your parents, and suspension. And from what I now know about Big Bad Brice, a meeting like this would mean serious clawing apart. Even if Carling pulled off straight As for the rest of the term, she could never land an A in the class. Bye-bye, Harvard.

Carling knows exactly what is at stake. I can see from the way the edge of her skirt is shaking.

Mr. Curtis stares her down. "Due to the illegibility of your penmanship, I was unable to make out some of your answers. They may have been one hundred percent correct, but the world will never know. You wound up with a ninety-five out of sheer messiness."

Sloane and Willa shriek, both jumping up to hug Carling as if she's just been crowned Miss Massachusetts. I'm surprised no one is crying. Once she's been sufficiently embraced, Carling slides down into her seat. She scrawls something on a piece of paper, and when Mr. Curtis turns around to write a long formula on the board, she passes it back to me.

Thx, u saved my sorry ass. Are u going to the party on Saturday?

I look up. Party?

Mr. Curtis clears his throat and I see he's staring at me. "It's not even nine thirty a.m., and already I've caught more people texting and passing notes than the whole of last term. In the halls, in the office, and now in class. I won't embarrass you girls by confiscating the note and reading it out loud, but in the interest of furthering our collective mathematical educations, I'll give Sara all the information I've gleaned so far about 'the best party ever.'"

He knows?

He continues with a smirk. "It's called Crush and it's by invitation only. It's held on a Saturday night around Halloween in some undisclosed warehouse in the Central Square area. If there's one sane person anywhere who knows where it is, they've chosen not to tell. It doesn't usually end until the sun comes up Sunday morning. Lindsay Lohan had to be carried out of a bathroom stall last year. It promises to be the social event of your young lives. And, what our social hummingbird, Carling Burnack, is no doubt about to ask you is"—he raises his voice to a girly squeak—"'Like, are you going?'"

The entire class bursts out laughing. I look from Mr. Curtis to Carling and back again. Then I grin and say, "Like, totally."

I get to Ms. Solange's class too early. The class before ours ran late and the kids take their time filing out. Poppy doesn't seem to mind; she's sitting on the floor across from the door, filming the students' feet as they leave. The double standard works on her behalf. She's a girl, so no one really cares. She's just being artsy and weird. If she were male, she'd probably be hauled down to the office and accused of inappropriate camera angles.

The class is doubly crowded with clusters of seniors lingering around desks juniors are trying to slip into, so I detour all the way around the back chairs to avoid the whole tangle. It isn't until I'm almost upon it that I realize my desk is still occupied.

By Leo Reiser.

He gathers up his books and looks up, grinning right away. "Hey!"

Thank God for the pile of books I have mashed against my chest. Gives me something to hide behind. I shift my weight onto my back foot and rock side to side. "Leo. Hi."

"Sorry, our class went a bit long." He slips his books into an open backpack on the floor. "What class is this—American lit?"

I shake my head. "Nineteenth century."

"Ah, right. I loved that class. Raskolnikov and his half-baked soul. Great book."

"We're not that far along yet." I bump my books against my chin. "Rascal's soul could pretty much go either way at this point."

He looks surprised. "Wait, you call him Rascal?"

I nod.

"Me too. I mean, I did. Last year. When I was reading the book." For a moment we stare at each other, smiley and dumb, then he breaks the spell of stupidity by standing up and stepping aside, motioning for me to sit. I slip past him and drop into my chair. It's still warm and I try not to imagine I'm sitting on his lap.

"Will you be at the party Saturday night?"

Before I get the chance to answer, Poppy appears and pokes Leo in the back. "Uh, excuse me? I can't exactly get to my seat."

"Oh, right. Sorry." He backs up against another desk to allow her to pass, and as she does, she looks at me and rolls her eyes as if he's a major annoyance.

Slumping down into her chair, she mumbles, "Get a classroom."

Leo backs away with his head tilted to one side like a little boy who's hiding a broken teacup behind his back. He raises two fingers in a wave. "Bye, Sara."

He's forgotten his question about Saturday, and it takes everything I have not to jump out of my seat and tell him I'll be there. Instead, I say, "Bye, Leo."

Ms. Solange claps her hands. "Clear your desks, ladies and gentlemen. All you need is a pen and one sheet of paper. We're going to do an in-class essay on Raskolnikov's dream about the old mare in part one of the novel. I want you to tell me what you believe is the dream's significance to the story."

Willa's hand shoots up into the air. "It's to illustrate Raskolnikov actually has a heart before the murder. To show his personality is split. Between this cold-hearted guy who is able to plan out a murder, and the kind of human who feels something for an innocent creature who is being brutalized by a society full of heathens. It shows him to be extraordinary amongst all these lesser people."

I feel my pulse race. I didn't see that at all. Just read the entire passage as a dream without any analysis whatsoever. And I thought I understood the book; how did I miss such a blatant metaphor? This unnerves me. I do well in lit classes. When my family isn't falling apart, that is.

Willa adds, "Is that the kind of thing you want to see, Ms. Solange?"

Ms. Solange gulps down what's left of her coffee. She's getting used to us. There's no sign of fingers in her hair and no more pacing when she loses her place. These days she just looks at me, and I tell her. It's a good system. She nods in Willa's direction. "Well, it was until you gave everyone your analysis. Now we'll need a different topic." She looks out the window at the rain slapping against the glass, then back at us. "Okay, how about this? How does Raskolnikov's tiny room, a room described as a cupboard, influence his actions? You have thirty minutes to make your point. Go."

Raskolnikov is influenced by his room? He should come on over to Brighton. Take a good look at mine. He'd probably take an ax to *himself*.

chapter 20
the beaded sweater

The black carpenter ant does not eat wood like the termite; rather, he tunnels inside it, causing great damage.

Standing in front of my closet Saturday evening, wearing nothing but bra and panties, I'm faced with the ugly truth. Nothing I own is worthy of a party called Crush where Lindsay Lohan might pass out in a bathroom stall. Nothing. I'm keenly aware of this as I shower, dry my hair with a swooping side part, and flick on mascara and lip gloss. Eventually I settle on black boots, my denim mini, and a lacy black camisole under my mom's green sweater.

Carling calls on my cell. "Hey. So here's the deal. There's a party before the party and ours starts a bit earlier. In the back of the limo with a fully stocked bar."

Not good. With Carling's car comes Carling's driver. And Carling's driver has no idea he lives one floor below the daughter of a brain surgeon. "You're going in the Bentley?"

"Are you kidding? My car doesn't have liquor. Anyway, Noah has the weekend off to party in Manhattan. I swear my dad pays that guy way too much. Brice's driver will take us."

"Cool. But won't he tell your parents about Crush?"

"Did I say he's dropping us *at* the warehouse? Horace is dropping us at the Four Seasons, where we'll head inside to attend the party Samantha Ross *isn't* throwing in the ballroom, and wait until the car drives away. Then we'll cross the Common and hop on the Red Line to get away from the party that isn't and get ourselves to the party that is. Are your parents home?"

"No."

"Perfect. We're all coming to your place to get ready so we can have a little drinkipoo before Horace picks us up. Sloaney's bringing wine, Izzy's bringing makeup, and I'm bringing clothes. Where do you live?"

Horrified, I picture the Carlingettes standing on the sidewalk in front of the hardware store and thinking the address must be a mistake because there's nothing but paint cans and leaf blowers in the window. I see them stepping into our lobby with the chipped floor and the misspelled signage and the cobwebby chandelier. Walking up the groaning staircase and worrying they'll get dust on their ballerina flats. Coming into my room to see my faded comforter. The tinfoil bits on my window. The stain on my ceiling. Oh God—the photo of Dad and me on my desk.

"That would be great, but . . ." Glancing around my room, a small unpacked box catches my eye. "Our place is still revolting with boxes. Cartons and packing crap every-where. I don't mind coming to you in the interest of saving us from being forced to unpack the good china."

"Such a selfless little soldier. Then get your tail over here pronto."

I load up my purse with lip gloss, cash, and cell phone and rush down the hall to find Dad arrived home while I was changing and is now sitting at the dining room table flipping through the newspaper. "The VW broke down again," he grunts when he sees me. "I had to leave her at the side of the road and walk home. I'm starting to believe she's a lemon."

"No kidding." I've been taking the bus in to school every day. There were only so many floor-level shoe situations I could fake.

"That's the last time. I cannot afford the parts needed to recondition her, even if Noah and I could get her running again. We're getting a new vehicle."

Great news. Fantastic news. To be able to ride with Dad to school without the worry of metallic gunshots and hollow burps to give me away? Sublime. Especially during the winter months, when the only other option, traipsing to the bus through the snow with frostbitten thighs, might just kill me.

"Cool," I say. Could this day get any better? Perfect grade in math, we're getting a new car, and I'm headed to the social event of the year with the coolest kids in school. "An actual *new* car?"

He laughs. "Not in my lifetime. We'll buy another vintage vehicle. But this one will be in better shape."

"Whatever. As long as I don't have to car shop."

"You don't have to car shop."

"Good. I'm going out tonight, Dad. To a party at a hotel by the park."

He looks up. "I can't drive you."

"It's okay. I'll get a ride with a friend."

"Her parents?"

"No. Her driver."

"Should be enjoyable. Do me a favor, sweetheart. Take the garbage out when you go."

"No problem."

He picks up the paper again and I notice his enormous hands are road-mapped with thickened skin so raw and red they're nearly violet. He's bandaged them in places, but what skin remains visible is cracked so deep at the knuckles his fingers could crumble and fall right off. I leave the room and return with hand cream from the bathroom.

"You should wear gloves, Dad."

"Hard to clean properly with gloves on."

I press a kiss onto the top of his head, then drop into the chair beside him, pick up one of his hands, and work cream into his devastated skin. "I saw the lawyers' papers."

He looks up at me, smiles sadly. "I figured you might have when I found them on the chair. But I was hoping they'd slipped." Neither of us speaks for a bit. Outside, a police siren grows louder, then fades into nothing. Dad reaches into his pocket and pulls out a long envelope. He removes a large ticket and slides it in front of me. American Airlines. Roundtrip. Boston to Paris. Logan International Airport to Charles de Gaulle. I laugh angrily. Just like that, the umbilical cord can be reattached without any surgery at all.

"She wants you to come out and see her," Dad says, slipping the ticket into my purse.

"Yeah, right. That's happening."

"I don't think there's a whole lot of choice involved. Her lawyer wants to make it part of the custody agreement—that you spend school holidays with your mother."

"Tough for her lawyer. I'm staying with you."

"You can't. It'll cost me a fortune to fight."

"I won't go. She's the reason . . ." I stare at his palms, which are shiny from wear, and rub the cream in harder, hating my mother more than ever. "I won't go."

"Sweetheart, the law is the law."

Something in me snaps. I stand up, grab my purse. "That's where you're wrong. The law is not the freaking law. The law can be bent and twisted and wrapped around your neck, did you know that? And I'm going to find some kind of Thin Skull rule that will get me out of it."

His eyebrows squeeze together in a deep fissure. "I've never heard of any Thin Skull—"

"Of course you haven't. You never took pre-law. You never took anything." I grab the trash bag from the kitchen and stomp toward the front door. "No matter what Mom said about your career, you never did anything but read about cars. Which is why we're in this gigantic mess to start with!" The door slams behind me, blotting out my father's stricken face.

Outside in the back alley, I pull the plane ticket from my purse and drop it into the trash bag. With a mighty heave, I swing it into one of the garbage cans and walk away.

chapter 21
dress your tiger
in corduroy and denim

Army ants perform swarming raids, fanning out as far as twenty-five feet in width to kill leaf-litter invertebrates.

Brice opens the door and, right away, I'm grateful he's wearing pants. He looks at me, says hello with his eyebrows, then growls to the air behind him, "Gracie, they're picking us up in seven minutes!"

I step inside. "You're going out, Mr. Burnack?" If it's at all possible, the man looks even scarier dressed up in black trousers, brownish blazer, and black mock turtleneck than he did in his hairy legs and boxers.

He's restless tonight. Distracted. For a minute I'm not sure he remembers me. "Dinner with the lawyer. I can break any law I want tonight. He's got my ass covered."

"Yeah, well, someone's got to cover it." As soon as it's out of my mouth, I regret it. It sounds like I was referring to his pants. Or, rather, his lack of pants. Which, of course, I was. It just wasn't meant to sound so horribly obvious.

There's a terrible moment where he doesn't move, doesn't speak. Sweat dampens my chest and underarms. I've offended Carling Burnack's father—a man so powerful he can walk around undressed—and I can no longer breathe.

His face cracks and he coughs out a deep laugh, setting his paw on my shoulder and leading me into the house. "You're all right, kid."

I follow him past the messy living room and down the hall toward the back of the house, slowing when I realize something is missing. It's the Elton John drawing. It's gone. All that's left in its place is a hook on a wall. If Brice were any less Brice-ish, I might have asked if he moved it to another room, just to make conversation with him.

As we pass his recording studio—so completely strewn with papers this time I suspect he might have had a temper tantrum in there—Brice bellows through my ear, through my brain, through my soul, "Gracie, you're down to five and a half!"

Feminine shrieking from the back of the house grows louder as we approach the den. "The girls are back here," he says. "No doubt trying to figure out how to pour my good scotch into their purses."

"So, your musical opens next week," I say.

"It does. We're expecting a full house. Actually having trouble with scalpers buying up huge blocks of tickets in anticipation of cashing in on all the hype."

"Wow."

"Wow is right. My manager tells me it's a better indicator of a show's success than a great review." He winks at me. "These scalpers are like wolves. They have superior instincts."

"Good luck. Or maybe I should say break a leg."

He glances down at me and half smiles.

We walk into the den, a comfy-looking room with light brown leather sofas, wooden tables and wall unit, and old brass lamps. The bar along the far wall is lined with cut-crystal canisters filled with liquids ranging in color from pale yellow to deep brownish amber, and shallow glass bowls brimming with cashews and Jujubes.

Carling looks up from the longer sofa where she, Isabella, and Sloane are watching MTV. Sloane waves me over with the controller and I lower myself down into the cold leather chair next to them.

"Love your sweater," says Carling.

Isabella grunts and turns back to the TV. "Every vintage shop in New York carries those."

At the bar, Mr. Burnack pulls out a gleaming crystal bottle and pours himself a hefty drink. "A little toast to my girl, who scored the third highest grade in Honors Math this week. Ninety-five percent." He drinks hungrily, then gives Carling a cuff to the chin that is intended to be gentle. "I am so proud of my Ladybug."

With a jerk of her shoulders she backs away from his touch, then forces a grin that's too wide to be real. "All thanks to my new study buddy."

He looks at me. "What have we done without you all these years, Sara?"

"Yes." Isabella's head snaps around. "What would we have done?"

The inside of Brice's limo smells like rich leather, woodsy cologne, and Sloane's cinnamon Tic Tacs. As soon as the car pulls onto the bumpy cobblestones of Sycamore Street, the driver, Horace, an older man with gray beard and laughing eyes, calls out to us, "The Four Seasons is a grand hotel, ladies. I stayed there on my wedding night. You should fit right in with all the glitterati."

"Thanks, Horace," says Sloane, who is sitting beside me while Carling and Isabella look on from the seat facing us.

Something about the way the girls ignore his attempt to make nice makes me hurt for Horace. I spin around in my seat and say to him, "When did you get married?"

"Centuries ago," he says with a laugh. "My brother works the front door. If you see a short guy named Arthur, tell him I'll be over for dessert after his shift. And tell him this time I want the good stuff. None of those animal cookies he keeps for the kids."

"Arthur. No animal cookies. Got it."

"He'll be easy to spot. A bit less gray hair than me, but not nearly as good looking."

Before I can answer, Carling leans forward and presses a button. The barrier rises up from behind my seat and shuts him out. "No more small talk, London. It's irritating as hell."

"God, Carling. I was talking to him."

"It's time to start the party." She pulls out a small funnel, a bottle of Evian water, and a handful of small plastic vials with colored lids, and dumps them onto one of the seats. She pulls the lid from the closest decanter. "Grab yourselves a glass, girlfriends. Tonight we drink the good stuff."

"But your dad marked the bottles," says Isabella. She moves closer and whispers. "Seriously. You don't want to get him mad."

Carling shrugs her away. "Shut up and pass me your glasses." She sets the glasses on a ledge and fills each about halfway. "This shit's expensive, so no sipping until we hit smooth pavement." Once four glasses are filled, the decanter is nearly empty. Carling sets the funnel into the neck of the decanter and pours in the water. Then she holds up the plastic vials. "Food coloring," she says. "I've become something of an expert on re-creating the exact hues of the world's finest scotches. Two drops of yellow. One drop of red, which we'll neutralize with a splash of green. . . ."

We watch as the two colors explode into colorful clouds inside the decanter. Eventually, the shaking of the car mixes them together. "I don't know. Doesn't look much like the color of the scotch," I say.

"Watch and learn." She holds up a bottle of soy sauce and lets two drops plop into the funnel. About sixty seconds later, we're staring at some fine-quality scotch.

"Loser," says Sloane, tying her tangled hair into a knot. "It's not going to taste like scotch. You're still going to get murdered and I'm *so* not getting my hands bloody as we pick up your severed limbs."

Carling feigns shock and hands us our drinks. "I didn't touch Daddy's booze. If my father's ever sober enough to notice, Horace did it. We all saw him, didn't we?"

Isabella giggles into her drink.

I say nothing. There's no way on earth I'll rat on that man. "Why does your dad have a driver anyway? Why not drive himself?"

"Small matter of a DUI," says Carling. "In case you haven't noticed, Brice is something of a career drinker. Helps him forget he was once famous."

Isabella nudges her. "But his new musical will do it for him."

"Yeah. This is it for him. If the reviews are good, he's made his comeback. If reviews suck, he'll implode. He's totally freaked out. Yells at everyone, fired his manager."

"The reviews will be amazing. You'll see," says Isabella.

"Whatever." Carling peers down at her pumps and taps her toes together. "So, ladies. Tonight's the night. I'm going to have sex with Leo."

Is it too much to ask not to hear about this? I'm aware things must be going on between Carling and Leo, physical things, but I try to wipe these images out as soon as they form in my head. I cough out an unconvincing laugh. "Where? In the car?"

"Wherever. Maybe I'll sneak him into my bedroom later, who knows?"

"What about us?" says Isabella, looking alarmed. "*We're* sleeping in your bedroom."

"You'll just vacate until I'm done with him. God, Izz. I thought you'd be happy for me."

"I am," she says quickly. "Of course I am. You and Leo are perfect together."

The car goes quiet, no sounds but the hum of the engine and the sipping of scotch. To break the uncomfortable silence, Sloane shrieks, "One-two-three, swap to the right!" Drinks move to the floor and all three girls yank off their tops and pass them to the girl on their right. Carling's sweater goes to Isabella, Isabella's blouse goes to Sloane, and Sloane's silver sequined top lands on my lap. Carling shivers in her white camisole and tugs on my sweater. "Hurry up, London, I'm freezing here."

"What? You want my sweater?"

"Rules, London," says Carling. "When someone calls a swap, you swap."

"Seriously? But I'll be freezing."

"Swap," snaps Isabella.

I pull my sweater off, pass it to Carling, and tug the sequins over my head.

Carling buttons up and admires herself. "I *love* this sweater. It's so ironic, like you'd see on a drive-in ho from the fifties."

Isabella nods and narrows her eyes at me. "And so versatile. Just the kind of piece to take the poodle-skirted town slag from backseat to abortion clinic."

I try not to react, but fail. "It's not slutty," I snap, feeling an angry flush thump across my chest. My mother was no town slag even if she did get herself into an affair that would rock the entire Finmory High School community.

I never meant to listen in on my mother's phone call. There I was, lying on the sofa watching some skater-dufus on *Judge Judy* get nailed for paintballing his landlord's new truck, when Mom's car pulled up. It was hot for June, so hot that the living room windows were pushed all the way up and the breeze that drifted in smelled like a sunburn.

I sat up and watched her. She was talking on her cell phone and was insanely slow gathering her purse and walking to the front door. Only she didn't come in. She lit a cigarette, leaned against the porch railing, and kept right on talking.

Her voice was what caught my suspicion. It wasn't her usual voice at all. This voice was all flirty and sexy. As if she weren't someone's mother. Someone's wife. As if she were somebody's girlfriend, or wanted to be.

It was wrong to silence *Judge Judy* and listen. But that's exactly what I did.

"I do not!" Mom said, laughing. I could hear her suck on her cigarette, then a long stream of smoke curled up past the half-moon-shaped window in the door. "I have never in my life eaten like a bird on a first date. I like to think I'm a bit more modern than that."

A long pause, followed by a softer voice. "That's because you made me nervous back then. I was afraid I'd choke or get a piece of broccoli stuck between my teeth. You'd never have spoken to me again, much less gone out with me."

She couldn't be talking to my dad. Charlie was definitely not the kind of guy to get offended by a sprig of broccoli between someone's teeth. On the floor, maybe, but not in the teeth.

Her purse dropped to her feet. "Well, I guess we all can't be as unself-conscious as you, baby. You're used to being stared at all day long."

Baby.

She laughed. "That's why you're a teacher and I whip up purées in the back of a restaurant where I can't be seen." A short pause and her voice dropped to a near whisper. "I know, babe. I'm counting the seconds. Why don't you meet me earlier Friday? Cancel your last class. It'll be the ultimate gift for a bunch of high-school students desperate to start summer holidays."

There was only one high school in Lundon. Mine.

"I love you too, Michael."

And only one teacher named Michael. Mr. Nathan, my science teacher.

chapter 22
the carling burnack who cares

Although the queen lays the eggs and is fussed over and fed by the workers, she is by no means the ruler of the colony.

Carling blows a drunken kiss to the limo from behind the great glass doors of the Four Seasons Hotel. Then she leans against the glass and grins at us through the wavy net of streaked hair lying across her face. "Ladies, we are free."

"Couldn't you have faked that Samantha's party was closer to the actual party?" Sloane pouts and tilts her head to the side. "The T is such a hassle. So much walking."

Isabella swipes her lips with blue-pink gloss. "I don't mind. I walk everywhere. Makes me feel like a New Yorker."

"It's only a few stops," says Carling. "The boys are meeting us on the platform. Anyway, we'll stink of Brice's finest scotch. Which, when combined with T exhaust, should make us smell like we took a private jet over from Rome."

Not me. I took one sip of my drink and felt my throat catch fire. I fake-sipped the whole way here and when the girls stupidly stuck their heads out the windows to howl at boys at a red light, I dumped my scotch into their empty glasses. No one seemed to notice the gift from the alcohol gods when Horace forced them back inside.

"Anyway, I like the T," says Carling. "Remember when we were in kindergarten, Sloaney? Throwing fishy crackers at the third rail during field trips was the best part."

"Why? Can you see it spark?" I ask.

"*Je sus.*" Curling looks at me, shocked. "Don't they have subways in London?"

Before I come up with an answer, I'm saved by Sloane. "I heard a story," she says, "where this college guy stood on the platform and peed on the third rail and the electrical current raced back up his urine stream and killed him."

"Impossible," says Isabella with great authority. "But you can die a urinary death by candiru. If you pee in a South American river, this little heat-seeking fish can follow the urine stream and swim into your body. Once inside, it flares its barbed fins and gets lodged in your flesh. Has to be surgically removed."

Sloane says, "Once again, Latini, you make me retch."

I watch Isabella push her lip gloss into a flowered container and slip it into a special lip-gloss-shaped pocket in her purse—so nonchalant, so assured of her superiority. But the way she labors over her possessions, her lopsided friendship with Carling, her tales of revulsion, expose her as anything but. I'm still incensed by her abortion-clinic remark about my mother's sweater, and something inside me splinters. "It's a sign of insecurity, you know," I say.

"What does that mean?" she says, shifting her weight.

"Dropping these sensational facts like tiny conversation-busting bombs to make yourself sound superior. It's a sign of insecurity."

Isabella doesn't answer right away. Two splotches of color bruise her cheeks.

Sloane bursts out laughing. "Go, London!"

Isabella sweeps through the doors, which are being held open by a man in a uniform with gleaming brass buttons. She calls back. "I'm not even going to acknowledge that remark with an answer."

Of course not. Because you don't have one.

I follow her through the door and slow to check if the doorman's name tag says ARTHUR. It does, so I stop to tell him his brother is coming over for dessert. Arthur is thrilled and tries to chat with me but Carling yanks me away. Out on the busy—and freezing cold—sidewalk, she puts her arm around me. I don't mind one bit; it gives me a chance to be warmed by my mother's sweater. "Our London is a real friend of the people, have you noticed, girls? She brings a certain groundedness to our little group. Makes me feel like a better person. Like, at any moment, I might go dig a well in Sierra Leone or bottle-feed a goat in Belize."

Sloane snorts. "Knowing you, you'd probably hand the poor goat to your Molly and tell her to duct-tape its noisy parts. You're better off adopting Izz. She's starving just as bad as any goat."

"Why is everybody picking on me?" asks Isabella, folding her arms across her chest. "I'm going home."

"Leave Izzy alone, girlies," says Carling. "She's the only person on earth who's got my back. Right, Izz?"

Isabella stares out into traffic. "I guess."

"I'm being serious about this charity thing," Carling continues. "My boyfriend's going to work at his dad's office and pay for his own car, which doesn't make me look good. So what if I give back to society? Donate money or something?"

"Easier than getting a job, that's for sure," says Sloane, peeling brown polish from her chewed-up thumbnail and dropping the curled shards to the ground.

"You read my mind, Sloaney. Tomorrow I'm going to get up early and sponsor one of those kids in a third world country. You know, where you give up one coffee per day and it pays for, like, rancid milk and pencil stubs for a kid in Ethiopia."

"This is seriously impressive," says Isabella, tucking Carling's hair behind her ears. "You're like a really hot Mother Teresa."

I look at Carling's platform sandals, her skintight jeans, her long blondish hair and peach-kissed lips, the way she glances at her reflection in the windows we pass. "I can barely tell them apart," I say.

Carling grins and blows a kiss to a couple of tourists.

The Park Street station was the first subway station in the country. Built about a hundred years ago, the entrance looks like a grand old mansion, only shrunken down to the size of a freestanding public restroom. It's getting dark outside, so the lights from within cast a pretty green glow on the sidewalk as we approach. The girls skip nonchalantly inside and down under the ground, but I slow down, taking it all in. The gum-spotted steps, the gust of heated wind that rises from below and lifts my hair. The disappearance of street sounds—no more honking, car engines, bus motors. The stale, pungent, earthy smell of soot. Filth. Microscopic particles of metal that fill my lungs.

I've never been on the T before. While the others might be bored by the thought of traveling underground, it's a shameful thrill for me. We buy tickets at the glass booth, stuff them into the fare box, and push through the turnstile. More rushing air. The faraway metal-on-metal screech of a train slowing down.

As planned, waiting for us down on the platform are Griff, Leo, and two guys I've seen around school but never met. Carling rushes up to Leo, who gives her a self-conscious hug, and Griff moves close to Isabella to be swatted by her purse. The other boys are introduced as Jeffie and Mike.

With Carling still hanging from his neck, Leo glances at me. "You came."

I nod and turn away from Carling's eyes.

Sloane ruffles Griff's gelled hair. "And how are you going to get into Crush, Little Man?"

He flashes a California driver's license. His photo is badly Scotch-taped over the original, which belonged to someone named Aaron Zitzer, born in 1985. "I'm twenty-four, with a very serious growth-stunting condition called focal segmental glomerulosclerosis. Don't tell me you've never heard of it."

"I have," says Isabella. "The actor from *Diff'rent Strokes* has that. But where's your proof?"

Griff holds up a fifty-dollar bill and grins. "Here's my proof."

A hopeful voice comes from behind us. "You kids have a few dollars for an old geezer?"

We all turn around to see a life-worn man sitting on the bench by the tracks with a huge bottle of wine on his lap. All around him is evidence of his vagabond existence: ripped sleeping bag blackened with city grime, sacks full of rotted cardboard and bits of cloth, a rickety stroller stuffed with filthy jackets and plastic bags filled with plastic bags.

"Good thing you ladies have us around," says Griff. His nose is so stuffed tonight it sounds like he's underwater. "If only to stop Slummy from falling in love with the locals."

I sneak another glance at the homeless man, paying particular attention to the layers of T-shirts under his shirt. The hero wrapper making his pocket bulge. The battered ladies' purse strapped across his chest.

"London has inspired me," says Carling. She fishes through her tiny patent bag and pulls out a twenty. "You people are looking at the new Carling Burnack. The Carling Burnack who cares." She turns to face the man and flashes him a smile.

"Leave him alone, Carling," says Leo.

With a flirty wink, she spins around and sashays toward the man, swinging her hips as though she's headed down a fashion runway. It's pretty clear her actions have little to do with philanthropy and everything to do with being the center of attention.

The blackened tunnel behind us starts to rumble, then roar, with an oncoming train. The money in Carling's hand flutters, then flaps in the rushing wind. When the silver train whooshes into the station on our left, the fierce wind gust snaps the bill out of Carling's hand and sends it bucking and darting through the air until it loses force somewhere over the empty tracks on the other side, and somersaults down to the ground below the platform.

"Aw, hell," wails Carling. "You try to be charitable one goddamned time . . ."

The homeless man waves his hand, looking resigned to what is probably only a minor disappointment in the lousy scheme of his life. "Thanks anyway, princess," he says. "God will remember you."

Carling ignores him and hands her purse to Leo. "I'm going after it."

"You are not," says Leo. "You'll get yourself killed."

She looks at him as if he's crazy. "It's only about eight feet down. I've jumped off boathouses higher than that."

"Yes," says Isabella, "into lakes. The Red Line is filled with rats. Plus there's the third rail. And a train could come at any moment. Don't do it, Carling."

"There's a ladder right there." Carling points to a spot near the mouth of the tunnel where a thin black ladder leads down to the tracks. "I'll be back up in ten seconds." She presses herself against Leo. "If I get hurt, will you save me?"

"Me? I'm not jumping onto the train tracks."

She slithers her arms around his neck and plays with the curls at his collar. "What if I got pushed? Would you save me then?"

"No way."

Griff snorts. "Why should the boy ruin a perfectly good pair of jeans? It's not like it was me who needed saving. Now *that* would be worth wasting some denim."

Leo laughs. "Not quite. But I would point out the girls who pushed you to the cops."

Carling pulls away from him and wanders to the edge of the empty tracks. Behind us, the other train closes its doors and pulls away. For a moment, it looks as if she's just waiting for a train like anyone else.

"Don't do it," says Isabella.

"She won't," Griff says. "You know Carling, she's just gunning for attention."

Carling looks back at us. She doesn't belong down here. With her wild, sunstreaked waves flung across her right shoulder and dewy olive skin, it's as if someone has lassoed the perfect summer day, sculpted it into female perfection, and set it up against a backdrop of soot-stained billboards and blackened exit signs to show just how depressing it is down here. It's pretty clear Leo has noticed. His eyes are drinking her in as if parched. She blows him a kiss, which makes his mouth twitch to one side. Then, without any warning, she jumps.

We gasp and rush to the edge of the platform. Leo, Sloane, and I get there first, along with the homeless man, to find her sitting in a giggling, inebriated heap between the tracks, the rumpled twenty in her hand.

"Carling, get up here now!" I plead.

"I think I'm drunk," she says. "But I got my money back."

"Now, Carling," says Leo. "Straight to the ladder and climb up."

"You're so cranky, Leo," she says. She points at all of us, laughing. "Hey, it's like you guys are my audience." With that, she stands, starts humming and fake stripping, pulling off my mother's sweater and twirling it on a finger above her head while she swings her hips.

"Carling," says Leo. "Cut it out. Climb up now!"

She giggles, dropping my sweater into the grime. "Look. The third rail. Should I pee on it?"

We all shout, "No!"

I feel a faint rumble beneath my feet. "A train's coming! Please climb up, Carling!"

"I don't hear it."

"Carling, now," shouts Leo. "Up the ladder this minute!"

She crosses her arms and looks at me, an evil smile spreading across her face. We can hear the train now; the sound inside the tunnel changes from a distant hum to a roar. "Hey, London. Why don't you come down here and get me? Doesn't that sound fun?"

She wouldn't. No way. Even Carling Burnack wouldn't resort to this kind of blackmail. "Me?" I squeak. "I'm not climbing down there."

"No? If I were you I'd rethink it. Because you never know. All this danger just might force me to start doing yoga."

You sick and twisted little bitch. You freak-of-the-earth sicko. You scab on the flesh of humanity. I should stand perfectly still. Ignore her. But I can't. My heart clashes against my ribs as I step closer to the ledge and squat down. "Carling, this is crazy talk."

"Jesus Christ, Carling," says Leo. "Get the hell up here!"

"No." She juts out her chin like a stubborn toddler. "Not until London comes down."

A faint reflection of headlights illuminates the tunnel walls but I have to go. I don't even care if she tells on me. She's drunk, she's insane, and she'll be killed if I stand here any longer. Tears sting my eyes and my body is shaking so hard I think I might pass out. The roar of the train is getting louder; the headlights are now in full view. A horn blares. Carling looks straight at me. "You better hurry, London. I don't want to die."

I spin around backward and step on the ladder. It's greasy with soot and one foot slips. I right myself and start down.

People at the other end of the station race to the mouth of the tunnel, waving their arms, coats, briefcases, anything to get the driver's attention. The horn blares again and the brakes screech so hard I think my ears will split. Everyone, everywhere is screaming. It's all for nothing. The driver is doing everything he can, but a high-speed train needs a certain distance to stop and Carling isn't twenty feet from the mouth of the tunnel.

In one motion, Leo yanks me up to the platform and jumps off the ledge. I fall hard and roll over to see him down on the tracks, where he barrels into Carling with his shoulder, stands, and heads for the ladder. He races up the rungs and dives up and onto the platform. They both hit the ground seconds before the face of the train bursts into the station.

We all drop to our knees around Carling, who is only mildly shaken by what happened. The train inches into position and the doors open. Strangers pour out of the back end of the train and step around us. Train employees crowd our little heap, looking down at us, reprimanding. The conductor arrives and shouts something I'll never remember. Everything has become too blurry to be real.

Leo crawls over to me; his face is smeared with soot and he looks angry. "What were you thinking?"

Wait—he's mad at me? I'm shivering now and wrap my arms around myself, hunched over my knees. "She was going to be killed!"

He squeezes his lips together and stands up, pulling

me to my feet. I guess that's it. I'm back on his naughty list.

The stationmaster arrives and now we're being led to an office under threats of police arrest. As we trudge along, still in our own personal bubbles of shock, Carling flirts with him, explaining she lost her balance and just tipped over the edge. Whoopsie. She looks back at us and giggles. "You should have seen your faces, guys. You were, like, so freaked."

No one answers. Sloane catches my eye. Her expression is flat. Worn out. As if she might be feeling, as I am, that Carling's friendship just isn't worth it. Then Carling turns to Leo, who by some miracle is holding my dirty sweater. "Leo, you saved me. You totally rock as a boyfriend."

"Save it," he says, his face flushed. "You and I were done the moment you stepped off the platform."

Carling grins, sticks out her tongue at him, snatches up my sweater, and follows the stationmaster into an inner office where two policemen are waiting. I have absolutely no worries about either her freedom or her relationship.

(What Carling Burnack Gets = What Carling Burnack Wants)[2]

chapter 23
the kiss after the kiss

In spring, colonies of pavement ants attack nearby nests, resulting in enormous battles that leave countless warriors lying dead on the sidewalk.

Other than the crowd outside the Central Square warehouse—a dirty, low brick building with boarded-up windows wedged between enormous buildings with signs that could be a hundred years old—you'd never guess there was a massive party going on inside. The place is packed with teenagers, probably from every part of Boston, maybe even beyond. But even with all these people, I spot tons of kids from Ant: the Benadryl girls, the kid from pre-law who has the neck of a giraffe, some of the girls who'd been in line behind me the day I didn't pay for my yoga pants.

The fun was over for me before we arrived. The flashing strobe lights, the throbbing bodies on the dance floor, the stench of alcohol and puke—they have no magic for me. All I want is to go home and make sure Dad put more lotion on his hands.

As expected, Carling sweet-talked her way out of trouble with the police. Smiled, flirted, swayed her slender hips, and convinced them her tumble was the fault of her new Italian shoes, the towering heels of which seemed a bit wobbly. Before she left the office, she practically had the cops ready to fly to Milan and apprehend the designer himself.

I can't say as much for her relationship with Leo. He disappeared the moment we arrived at Crush and I haven't seen him since. Griff's fictitious disease didn't fool anyone at the door, but a few of the guys from school snuck him up the fire escape and through some upstairs window. He won't last long in here. Even if he's kept in dark corners, it's a matter of minutes before either his puniness or his obnoxiousness gives him away. As it is now, he's surrounded by a half dozen model-type girls, who must have been dazzled enough by his celebrity disease and his fake California address to bump and grind with him from north, south, east, and west on the dance floor.

As soon as we got here, Carling, Izz, and Sloane met up with Willa and a few others from school and headed upstairs to some really dark room they call the Cave. The entire floor is built up to about waist level—making the ceiling so low you can only crawl inside—and covered in scratchy industrial carpet. The only light in the room comes from the hall or the plasma TV at the far end that no one is watching. Kids lie strewn about, propped up against pillows and walls.

Willa leads the way inside, climbing up onto the platform and slithering on hands and knees to a clearing in the back corner. The other girls follow.

"I think I'm going to have my room built up like this," says Isabella as I approach. "Who needs furniture?"

Sloane points to a blond guy posing against the opposite

wall. He's wearing a tuxedo, with the tie and shirt collar undone, and from the way his head is bobbing, he looks hammered. "He's cute in a rich-boy-just-gambled-away-his-fortune kind of way."

Carling nods and pulls a small bottle of vodka from her purse. She takes a long gulp from the bottle and squeezes her eyes shut with disgust before passing the bottle to Izz. "I agree. Go talk to him."

Sloane grabs the bottle and sips, still eyeing the guy. Vodka spills down her throat and soaks the neck of Isabella's blouse. She wipes her collarbone and smiles. "Nah. He's wasted."

"So are you." Carling snorts, pointing at Sloane's wet shirt.

"I'm not wasted. I'm clumsy."

The bottle is pushed into my hand. I sip, swishing the vodka around my mouth as if it can wash away this entire evening, but all it does is burn the inside of my cheeks like Dad's mouthwash.

Carling says to Sloane, "I'll give you ten bucks to crawl over to him and retie his tie. But you have to talk dirty to him while you do it."

Sloane shrieks with amused disgust. "I'm not talking *dirty* to him!"

"Then just do up his tie." Izz places a crisp ten on the carpet in front of her feet. "Go."

"I'll do it for fifty."

"No way!"

Carling pulls out two twenties. "That's fifty. Now go."

Sloane grins and crawls across the floor. The guy pushes his shaggy hair out of his eyes and perks up when she settles herself beside him. It's too noisy to hear what they're saying, but Sloane is doing an awful lot of blushing and hair flipping. At one point she touches his dangling tie but doesn't tie it. Carling stomps her foot and waves the little pile of money, but Sloane clearly likes this guy. Without looking away from him, she shoots Carling the finger.

"How dull," Carling says with a pout. She hands the ten back to Isabella. "Sloaney went and fell in love."

"I'm glad," I say. "It shows she has a soul."

Isabella eyes me. "God, London. You're so predictable."

I just shrug.

Sloane comes crawling back to us. "Okay, guys. I'm totally into this guy. You know who he is? His mom is Astrid Saatchi, the—"

"The interior designer?" Carling pushes hair off her eyes. "She did my aunt's penthouse in Paris. She's huge."

"Anyway, his name is Ned."

"Ned?" Isabella squeals.

"It's nerdy cool," I say. "I like it."

"Big surprise," says Izz.

Sloane slaps my hand. "See? London knows what's what. I have our whole lives planned out. A house on the Cape. Four kids in six years, born in the following order: boy, girl, boy, girl. All of their names will start with *N*. I'm going to pee, so think of some names while I'm gone. And keep an eye on him, girlies. You're sitting across from my future, and I don't want some tramp to come by and snag it." She crawls away.

Without missing a beat, Carling says, "Watch this.

I'm going to go mess with his head. I'm going to tell him Sloaney's a dude."

I grab her arm. "Don't. Sloane really likes this guy."

"Oh, please," she says. "Sloane likes every guy." She pulls away, slinks across the room, and folds herself up next to Ned, playing with her sunny streaks. They chat for a few moments, then Ned's expression changes. He glances toward the door a few times, then settles in to talk to Carling. Just when I can't believe what a bitch she is, she takes it one step further. She grabs both ends of Ned's tie, pulls him close, and starts making out with him.

I look at Isabella, horrified, but Izz just sips from the bottle and grins. "Go, Carling," she says, holding the bottle up in a toast.

Of course Isabella would support this, even if it hurt Sloane. Like any good cult member, Isabella is so Carling-infatuated she'd probably shave her head and drink poison for her leader. I can't take these people anymore. I have to leave the room. Crawling across legs and purses to the door, I bump heads with someone climbing in.

Leo.

From where he is, I'm certain he cannot see Carling deep-tonguing the interior designer's son. He sits back and rubs his forehead, stares at me.

"Told you I was spastic."

"You weren't kidding."

"Leo, about the T thing. I didn't thank you—"

"Forget it. We all just reacted."

"Still. Could've been ugly."

He laughs a bit. "I'd say we reached ugly the moment she jumped. You having fun in here?"

"Not really."

"I lost Griff. I think he got carried off by a herd of blind females." He sits up taller and looks around the room. "Is he in here?"

"No."

Leo stops. His mouth settles into a hard line. He's seen Carling.

"It's not what it looks like," I say, tugging on his white shirt. "She's just goofing around, playing a joke on Sloane. . . ."

He turns to face me again, leaning over his knees and releasing a long breath. His hair is growing shaggy, so long in the front it flicks upward in front of his eyes. Up close, his lashes are long and curly. Lashes every girl wishes for but that usually get doled out to boys. Shaking his head, he lets out a sound so tired it makes me sad. "You can't do it, Sara."

"Do what?"

"Make Carling Burnack a decent person."

I try to hide my shock, looking down at the carpet and picking at the fibers. "I don't know, she doesn't have it all that easy. . . ."

"You don't have to make excuses for her. She's a big girl who makes big decisions."

"But she's your girlfriend."

"Was." He glances over to where she's sitting with Ned. They've stopped kissing now, and she's writing something on his hand with a pen. Her number, no doubt. As she writes, Ned massages her shoulder with his free hand.

"I wish he wouldn't do that," I say, watching.

"Carling can take care of herself."

"No. That's my sweater. The threading on the beadwork can't take much stress."

Leo grins. "Want me to go strip it off her?"

The thought of Leo removing any of Carling's clothing makes my stomach juices curdle. I shake my head.

"Want to get out of here?" he asks.

Fighting back a smile, I follow him into the crowded corridor, where we snake through wall-to-wall bodies in the near dark. It isn't easy keeping up, and I lose him before we even reach the dance floor. On my tiptoes, I pause beside enormous speakers and try to peer over the sea of throbbing arms, legs, heads, hips, but it's too crowded. I can't find him.

The room goes pitch-black before a strobe light starts flashing. On. Off. On. Off. It's nausea-inducing and makes me want to leave. Out of the violet shadows, Poppy appears. "Hey!" She's clearly overjoyed to see me and pulls out her camera to zoom in on my face. "I was hoping you'd be here. You look really great."

"So do you."

"Who were you looking for?"

I see him now. Leo. He's weaving through a crowd of girls wearing pink wigs, making his way back to me, looking sheepish and mouthing, *I'm sorry.*

Poppy repeats herself. "Were you meeting someone? Because it would be cool to hang out. I'm making a mini documentary about underground parties and people are getting all whacked backward when I film them. Even the bouncer threatened to kick me out, which is insane. I could totally tell he didn't like me, because some guy peed on the bathroom door and even *he* didn't get kicked out."

A trio of Goths pass between us and flip her off when she points her camera at them. It makes me feel sorry for her, actually. She's just doing her thing. Can she help it if that turns off the rest of the world?

Leo is getting close now and I have to make my exit. "Maybe later, Poppy. I have to take care of something right now."

"Cool," she says. "I'll look for you."

There's a little-known bathroom in this place. Leo found it. Probably meant for staff only, it's down a long, drafty passageway, past the locked office. Just outside the men's room, between a time clock and an ancient payphone, sits a padded bench. Leo sits down beside me and we both stretch out our legs at the same time. The music is muffled in here, making it sound as if we're underwater. I don't know if it's Leo, the atmosphere, or Carling's vodka, but my heart is racing and my head feels swimmy. I shiver.

"You okay?" he asks.

"Yes."

"I'd offer to drive you home but I have no wheels."

"It's all right. I'm meant to be sleeping over at Carling's."

He grunts. "That would go well. Me dropping you off."

Yeah. Considering Carling's big plans for him. "She'd implode. Or else Isabella would implode for her."

He laughs and leans forward, resting his forearms on his thighs and poking at the ground with his boot. "I've been rotten to you."

I giggle. "I guess I should lie and say you haven't."

"No, you shouldn't. I'm sorry."

"It's okay."

"It had nothing to do with you. It's just that you got a firsthand look at my dirty little secret." He glances down again. "You can probably tell, I'm not good at talking about this kind of thing."

"So don't."

He sits up, surprised.

"You don't owe me an explanation," I say. "You don't owe *anyone* an explanation. Your past is your past just like my past is mine." I laugh softly and tuck my hair behind my ears. "I have a few secrets myself."

Leo is so still he can't possibly be breathing. His eyes travel across my face—from my forehead to my mouth to the stray hairs that are blowing against my cheek. Blinking softly, he moves closer. So close I can smell the soapy shower he had before he left home, the greasy iron rails of the ladder from the train tracks. Then, just when I think I'll pass out from anticipation, Leo Reiser kisses me, and everything else vanishes. His soft lips, his probing tongue, erase my mother's packed suitcases. My father's peeling hands. My faraway best friend. Gone are the never-ending nights studying, my lopsided bedroom, and my mother's Parisian postmarks. All that exists for that moment is me, Leo, and the faintest whisper of Carling Burnack's musky perfume.

Our moment doesn't last. About twenty minutes later, Leo's phone goes crazy with desperate text messages from Griff. Turns out the girls grew tired of his perv-child advances and reported him. Leo doesn't want to send the tot home alone on the T, so he apologizes, kisses me one last time, and heads outside to where Griff waits with a bouncer.

Which leaves me to return to Carling and Company, my eyes swimmy with happiness. And guilt.

Once Leo is gone, Carling sees no point in staying, so we head to the door. Out on the street, in the cold night air, we shiver and pool our money to determine whether we have enough cash to take a cab all the way home or whether we're heading back underground. Carling sends an emergency plea for transport. Ten minutes later, a black car flashes its high beams from down the block. Noah. I keep my head turned the other way as he pulls up, then stand behind the others so he doesn't see me.

Sloane says, "What's he doing here? I thought he was in New York."

Carling yanks open the back door. "Guess he got dumped. No big surprise. Would you date a guy whose scalp hadn't been scrubbed in, like, five years?"

Poor Noah. We pile into the back of the car. There's no way he knows who I am right now. And if I can exit the car as inconspicuously as I get in—head down, hair pouring over my face—he won't have a clue I was ever here.

The Bentley isn't as pristine on the inside as it is on the outside. The leather seats are creased flat from wear, and the carpeting is so thin in spots you can see the metal flooring. Not only does the car look depressed, it feels it. Gone is the excitement of a forbidden party. Gone is the feeling it was the four of us against the strobe-lit, adolescent underworld.

Once the car pulls into traffic and Noah is safely separated from us by the divider, Sloane turns on Carling. "You had no right to make out with Ned."

Carling cracks up. "Ned! I had to make out, just once in my life, with a guy named Ned. Anyway, I was being funny. Wasn't I being funny, Izz?"

"Funniest ever."

"He actually believed you were a guy," Carling explains to Sloane. "I totally had him going."

"Maybe I don't want my future boyfriends thinking I'm a guy—not for a single second," says Sloane. "Call me crazy, but picturing the girl you have the hots for with chest hair and chin stubble is a *slight* turnoff."

Carling laughs so hard she collapses sideways on the seat, her head landing in Isabella's lap. "I didn't tell him about your chest hair, Sloaney. It's important to leave some things to the imagination."

Isabella joins in the laughter. "It was pure genius."

Sloane crosses her arms and stares out the window.

"Come on," says Carling, nudging Sloane's leg. "I gave him *your* number, not mine."

"Why would he call? He thinks I'm a man!"

"He'll call because he thinks he's calling me. Then"—Carling holds out her hands as if performing magic—"ta-da, it's you he's talking to. You tell him I'm a bitch who goes after all your boyfriends, that I'm mentally unstable, and everyone's happy. Feel free to trash me as much as you want. I can take it."

"Tell Noah to take me home," says Sloane. "I'm not in the mood to stay over."

"You have to," pleads Carling. "Leo was a total jerk to

206

me tonight. Didn't come near me once at the party. I think he wants to break up with me."

"He did break up with you," I mumble, tracing my lower lip with my finger and watching the city lights race by.

"What?" says Carling.

I sit up taller. "I just said he kind of broke up with you, didn't he?"

"He was just cranky because of the T thing. I swear, the guy is so sensitive. He's like a girl. Doesn't matter. I'll call him when we get to my place. He'll come over, I'll seduce him, and all will be well."

I can feel the anger rise up from my gut and spread across my chest and down my arms, where it curls my fingers into fists. The thought of Leo in Carling's bedroom tonight makes me sick. I squeeze my hands shut tighter, if only to curb my instinct to slap her. "I don't know about that," I say. "He's pretty angry."

Isabella stares at me. "How would you know, London? Are you and Leo trading secrets in the changing room again?"

He won't go to Carling. Not after our kiss. "No. I just meant he seemed upset, that's all."

Carling yawns, completely indifferent to what Leo might or might not be feeling, thoroughly confident that if she wants him later, he'll be there. I've never had that kind of confidence in my life. "Even with Leo coming, I still need you guys. I'll need someone to talk to after."

"Can't," says Sloane.

"Actually, I'm tired too," says Isabella in a shocking and unprecedented lack of Carling support. Though, from the circles under her eyes, I'm guessing she's telling the truth.

"London?" asks Carling.

"No!" Isabella says quickly. Her eyes dart back and forth between me and Carling. "If we all don't stay over, no one stays over. Right, Carling?"

"Whatever," says Carling. "It won't be any fun without Sloaney and Izz anyway. Let's all go home and we'll do the sleepover next weekend. I'll tell the Dreaded One to drop you guys off at home instead."

Bad plan. I can't be dropped off at my apartment. I can't let the girls watch me walk through the cracked glass door of my building and wonder why my neurosurgeon father works for no pay. In the next few seconds, I need to come up with a proper home. Someplace befitting the daughter of a brain surgeon.

There's a cul-de-sac in a leafy area at the edge of Brookline not far from my building. I've seen it while out walking. It's full of homes so massive several families could live in them. The driveways are always littered with expensive cars and most of the properties have either indoor pools or tennis courts. One has both. It's set back from the road, nearly obscured by overgrown bushes out front. An old woman lives there, alone, from what I've seen. The street is called Hemlock Crescent and the house is number 151. I know this because the little address sign out by the road keeps falling over and I've watched the owner set it straight on several occasions.

I'll give Carling the address, hop out of the car, and disappear behind the bushes. Noah will never see my face. Then, once the Bentley pulls out of sight, I'll walk to Brighton in the dark. Should take about half an hour if I'm not kidnapped by a passing sex fiend who stuffs me into his van, has his way with me, and kills me before chopping me up into tiny pieces, setting my hands and feet and kneecaps in cement, and dropping them one by one into the Boston Harbor. As long as that doesn't happen, it's the perfect plan.

"Where did you say you live, London?" asks Carling.

"Right in town," I say, trying to sound bored. "One fifty-one Hemlock Crescent."

Carling raps against the partition. "Noah?"

What happens next may blow my plan into smithereens.

The Bentley speeds toward a yellow light and the glass partition lowers behind Carling's seat. At the same time, the light turns red and the car lurches to a stop, pitching us out of our seats. Noah says, "Sorry, girls!" and looks back just as I right myself. For a moment we stare at each other, then his eyes widen with recognition and he smiles. "Hey, there . . ."

"It's freezing cold back here," I say quickly, giving Noah a slight shake of my head that's meant to say *Please don't blow my cover.* "Do you think you can blast the heat?"

He looks confused. "Aren't you . . . ?"

"Noah!" snaps Carling, obviously irritated by his attempt to communicate with the humans. For once I'm thankful for her bitchy condescension. "Change of plans," she says. "The girls are going to their own places tonight, so we'll drop them off in this order: London, Sloaney, then Izz."

He looks right at me, amused. "London?"

I nod, hoping I don't throw up. "Sara. But the girls call me London because I moved here from England."

"England, huh?"

"Yup."

Noah doesn't react. His eyes travel from me to Carling, to Izz and Sloane, and back to me. A disbelieving smile crowds his face, then, with a small laugh, he shrugs and turns around. The light turns green and he calls back, "And what would your address be, Miss London?"

"One fifty-one Hemlock Crescent."

As the glass partition starts to rise, I can see Noah shake his head from side to side. Then he disappears from view.

The closer we get, the more I realize my plan is full of splinters and worm holes. What if the old lady in Brookline is an insomniac, peering through her front window at two in the morning? Worse, what if she forgot to let the cat in and is wandering around in her yard, calling, "Here, Puss Puss," when we arrive? Or what if her nosy next-door neighbor sees me squatting in her bushes and calls 911? Worse still, what if the old lady drops dead, tonight of all nights, and we find the driveway bustling with emergency vehicles and weeping grandchildren? From the look of her veiny hands and sunken cheeks, it could happen at any moment.

The car coasts into the cul-de-sac and we're engulfed in trees. Suddenly the street is so thick with fallen leaves it's as if we're driving on carpeting. Noah pulls the Bentley to a stop in front of number 151 and I breathe a sigh of relief. The house is dark and the driveway free of paramedics.

Noah comes around to open the door and as I step out into the frigid night air in Sloane's thin sequined top, Sloane and Isabella peer through the doorway. Sloane nods, looking around the property. "Nice place, London. Though it looks like you could use a good gardener."

"Yeah, well"—I glance back at the cedars that will hide me from the road—"we're not quite settled in yet. You know how moving is."

Isabella is strangely silent, examining the house with great interest. Then, "When did you say you moved in?"

I start walking backward. "Right before school started." I hold up my hand in a stationary wave. "Bye, guys. See you at school. And thanks . . . Noah, is it?"

Noah rolls his eyes and climbs back into the car.

As I make my way up the driveway, I realize hiding in the bushes is not going to work. Too many leaves have fallen; the girls are certain to see me crouching behind the branches. So I follow the driveway along the side of the house until I find a door, which, by some sort of miracle, is set in from the wall. With a final wave, I press my body into the doorway and hold my breath until the car pulls out of the street.

I completely misjudged the distance home. Hemlock Crescent is farther away than I imagined—two miles at least. At this rate, I won't be home until well after two thirty, and if one of the crackling or rustling sounds I keep hearing from the blackened bushes I pass by doesn't morph into a murderer and kill me, my father might.

Even the main streets are dark—the streetlamps are placed so far apart and throw off so little light they're practically useless. Then, just when I'm walking through an extra-longish dark patch in front of the dry cleaner and a bank, a dark car pulls up to the side of the road and stops.

It takes me a moment to realize it's the Bentley.

The tinted front window slides down and Noah peers out at me. He's taken off his cap and has a serious case of crooked dreads. "I've dropped everyone off. Get in."

I climb into the seat beside him. "Thanks. It's a long way home."

He smiles. "Longer than you think, I bet." He looks sideways at me and shakes his head. "You're in deep, little sis."

I shrug.

"Eventually they'll find out."

"Maybe. Maybe not."

"What about Charlie? I'm guessing these girls don't know who he is."

I say nothing.

He whistles silently. "Your dad's a good guy, you know. Pretty much lives for his daughter."

"I know."

"He'd be devastated if he knew she'd erased him."

I don't have an argument, so we ride through the shadows of Brighton in silence. Finally Noah pulls up in front of the building and stops, waiting for me to get out. "Were you really supposed to be in New York for the weekend?"

"New York? Brice told me I wasn't needed."

So Carling lied. Or Brice did. Noah doesn't turn off the car as I climb out. I peer back at him from the sidewalk. "You're not coming in?"

"I have to be back at Logan for a VIP in a couple of hours. Took a little job on the side. Don't tell Carling."

"What about sleep?"

"I'll catch a nap in the airport parking lot."

"Pretty messed-up way to live."

"I guess you'd be the expert on messed-up ways to live."

Good point. "Why do you take on other jobs when you already work for the Burnacks?"

"Need the cash."

"I thought Brice pays you tons of money."

He reaches for a cigarette but doesn't light up, just shakes his head, confused. "Who told you that?"

"Brice."

Laughing softly, he stares out into the dim glow of the streetlamp. "Yeah, well. Brice lied." I must look confused, because he adds, "That's what people do when they get desperate. But then, I don't have to tell you that, do I, Little Miss London?" He looks at me with a wink. "I think, once people have been swimming in money, they feel the need to look that way, no matter what."

"They don't have money anymore?"

"You didn't hear it from me. Not until they've coughed up my last few paychecks."

"And Horace?"

"Also working for free. We all are until Brice's big show opens and, hopefully, takes off."

I think back to the trays of food. The missing piece of art. The fight over serving the expensive bottle of wine. I've been watching them in awe and the whole time, the Burnacks have been putting on a show.

Noah pulls a rumpled envelope from his pocket and places it on the seat beside me. "By the way, an animal got into the trash. I found this on the ground beside a ripped-up garbage bag."

It's smeared with pizza sauce and one corner has been chewed away, but there's no mistaking what it is. It's my airline ticket to Paris.

chapter 24
what she needs

Amazon ants take other ant species as slaves. The Amazon worker ants lie idle as these slaves do all the work—even feeding the slave masters by regurgitating into the Amazon ants' mouths.

I spend all day Sunday in my pj's pretending to do my homework while Dad searches the paper for possible replacement vehicles and strips all the bedsheets to wash them in bleach. It's not that we're not speaking since our conversation last night—we are. But we're doing a fairly sophisticated dance of avoiding a particular room if the other one is in it.

I can't even think of Leo's mouth without my cheeks burning. What I'm really doing in my room and have been doing since I got home last night—or early this morning— is reliving the kiss over and over in my mind from my perspective and from his. From my viewpoint, this is how it went down: it was the best five seconds of my life. Seriously. Every time I think of how gentle he was, how his breath burned like peppermint Altoids, how his tongue— soft and firm at the same time—darted out and touched my own, my knees get weak and I have to sit down and teach my lungs how to breathe, teach my heart how to beat, teach my eyes how to blink.

These feelings are going to be the end of me. Getting involved with Leo or any boy at Ant will end in social destruction for me. Saturday night made that very clear. Unless I'm willing to dig myself a bedroom behind the leafless bushes at 151 Hemlock Crescent, the only way I can survive this school is by keeping relationships at a cool distance.

Trouble is, that's now become impossible.

"He kissed you?" Mandy squeals into the phone Sunday afternoon.

"Pretty much."

"This is the guy from the changing room? The crazy chick's boyfriend?"

"Ex," I say. "I've wondered, about a thousand times, what it meant to him. Does he kiss just any old girl like that or does he actually like me?" I've also wondered whether it's really over with Leo and Carling or if he was just using me to get back at her somehow. More important, does he feel faint when he thinks of being with me . . . if he thinks of it at all?

"He might come to school wondering the same thing about you."

"You think guys are that insecure?"

"My brother sure spends a lot of time fussing with his hair when he likes a girl."

"But what if Leo went to see Carling last night? She was planning to have sex with him. That's got to be a big draw for any guy, whether he wants to stay with a girl or not."

"You'll know when you see him again," Mandy says.

"Tomorrow at school. Like it or not, the expression on his face will tell you what you need to know."

"Right. You're right. He'll either turn the other way as if it didn't happen or he'll smile."

"And then the real trouble starts. He learns who you are."

I can't think that far ahead, so I change the subject. "Any word from Eddie?"

"Just that his wretch of a fiancée is going to make her bridesmaids wear burnt orange. Can you picture it?"

"I can smell the rotten pumpkins."

"I miss him so much, Sara. I don't know if I'll ever get over him."

"You will. And I'm going to help you. Starting with our movie next Saturday. *When Harry Met Sally* is on. Nine o'clock. And I've decided we should both have the same snacks. Black licorice, sour cream and onion chips, and Diet Coke."

"I can't be alone that night. If you forget to call, you know I'll drive out to our hotel and spy on them. And then I'll see that the room is dark and I'll know they're doing it. . . ." She starts choking back sobs.

"Don't think that way for a second. I'll keep you busy the whole night."

"No cancelling to study this time, promise?"

"Cross my heart."

It's the first week of November, so Monday morning is Grub Day. Standing in front of my locker in my Docs and jeans, I fumble with my combination. There's a lot of murmuring going on in the hallways, a lot of shocked faces.

217

Like a fast-spreading brush fire, a hot piece of gossip is burning across the student body. I lean closer to the two girls whispering a few lockers down and can just make out what they're saying.

"I heard she jumped on the 1 tracks," says the one with super-short bangs as she stuffs a violin case into her locker. "And then he dumped her."

Her friend says, "I heard he refused to save her because she made out with an interior designer at the warehouse party."

"Whatever happened, one thing's definite. Leo dumped her good. I saw her begging him to take her back this morning, on the second-floor landing. You know, on *the* sofa."

"So Leo, he said no when Carling begged?"

"His exact words were, 'This time, Carling, you don't get what you want. You get what you need.'"

They walk away.

I want to believe it. I need to believe it. But do I dare?

I tug my locker door open, drop my backpack inside, and try to compose myself. I'll be sitting behind Carling in about three minutes and I need to drum up some genuine sympathy. A pair of narrow shoes appears beneath my locker door. I peer around it to find Isabella leaning against the wall, her mouth all knotted to one side.

"Hey," I say, hoping my thoughts aren't visible.

"Have a good rest of the weekend?"

"Sure."

"Get enough sleep?"

What is she up to? "I did. And you?"

She ignores me. "Did you hear about Carling and Leo? He actually dumped her."

I duck my head inside my locker and allow myself a smile. So it's true. So many emotions are swirling through my head, I've become top-heavy and can no longer stand up straight. Concern and embarrassment about Carling's begging. Pride for Leo, for refusing to take her crap anymore. Newfound respect for the universe for giving Carling Burnack a consequence for all the havoc she wreaked on Saturday night. And, yes, a bit of sorrow for the pain she must be going through right now. But, sweeping away all of these feelings, mostly I feel pure joy because Leo Reiser is officially single.

"Yeah," I say. "Pretty shocking."

"Did you get in trouble for getting home so late?"

"I was quiet."

"Cool." She hugs her books to her abdomen and blinks. As usual, her nails are filed into paper-thin ovals. On her index finger is a flat gold ring with the initials *IEL*. I wonder what the *E* stands for. Encyclopedia of Horrors? She says, "I've been thinking about where you live...."

No. Don't think about where I live. I forbid you to think about where I live. "Why?"

"It's just kind of weird. I never saw a FOR SALE sign in front of that house. Or anybody moving in or out."

My heart starts to thump in all the wrong places. My throat. My upper arms. My stomach. What were the odds anybody had ever noticed that street? Why couldn't I have picked the next cul-de-sac over? Or the one after that? I try to shrug but my shoulders don't move. "What can I say? We're speedy movers."

219

"Really." She narrows her eyes and watches me.

"Really."

"What makes it even weirder is my old housekeeper rents out the basement. Has lived there for years. She's still in touch with my mother. You'd think she'd have mentioned something as big as moving, wouldn't you?"

For a moment I consider saying we have a housekeeper tenant in the basement, but quickly realize it won't work. "I wouldn't know."

"I'll have to mention it to my mother." Isabella shifts her books to her right arm. "Something about you smells funny, London."

I slam my locker and walk away as if my life isn't crumbling into too many dusty pieces to count. "Then keep your nose out of my business, Latini."

chapter 25
not my father

Nest-maintenance workers are among the first to emerge from the nest each morning, often cleaning away dirt that may have plugged up the entrance overnight.

Grub Day is less spectacular this month. As if, this deep into first term, everyone is too exhausted to care. Mr. Curtis's class is peppered less with equestrian wear and stripper attire and more with sweatshirts and yoga pants.

Yes. *Those* yoga pants. I count three girls wearing them, including Sloane. It's churning my stomach.

Sitting behind Carling in math class that morning feels like a lie. Smiling at her, telling her everything's going to be okay with Leo, pretending I haven't been praying this would happen since Saturday night. All lies.

"I can't *believe* him," says Carling. Her eyes are puffy from crying. "He didn't even give me a reason."

"Guys are such jerks," whispers Isabella, rubbing her friend's shoulder.

Willa walks into the room and bends down to wrap her arms around Carling's neck and kiss the top of her head. "Stay strong, sweetie."

Once Willa's gone, Carling's eyes fill with tears again.

She turns to me. "You saw Leo Saturday night. Did he meet someone? Did you see him with some skank?"

"No," I say. "He definitely wasn't with a skank."

This seems to calm her.

Mr. Curtis stands up, grinning devilishly, and sets his hands on his hips. "This is about the time of year my students begin to despise me. So don't feel sorry about your malevolent fantasies about my driving my Acura into a deep-bottomed loch or my succumbing to some antibiotic-resistant skin infection. You won't be the first to feel this way about me, and God willing, you won't be the last."

All movement, all whispering has stopped as we wait to hear the bad news.

"Your midterm will be two weeks from today. It will count for thirty percent of your final grade and there will be no make-ups for those of you who need a few more days to plan a bad case of mononucleosis. Nothing short of my seeing your name on a tombstone will get you out of taking this one." He walks over to the window and forces it up a few inches. "My rules for this test will be strict. You will walk in on test day to find your exam booklets already on the desks, along with two sharpened pencils. No backpacks or purses will be permitted anywhere near your sweaty corpses—you'll drop them at the back of the class and search the desks for a test with your name on it. In other words, I'll decide who sits beside whom. Got it?" He looks straight at me.

Does he know?

I slump down in my seat to think. I'm just as guilty as Carling, aren't I? It's one thing if someone copies your answers without your knowledge. It's another thing entirely to enable it. My mouth goes dry as I recall the way I slid my quiz to the edge of my desk to allow Carling a better view. Mr. Curtis wouldn't see things my way. He would argue that I did actually have a choice.

This is all too much. The hiding, the guilt, the cheating, the lies. The roomful of yoga pants. I can't take it.

I've gotten myself into a dark and dirty corner that has no easy way out. If I confess about the test, I'll destroy things for Carling. If I come clean about my dad, he'll hear about my deception. And no matter how he reacts on the outside, it will kill him a little on the inside.

Dampness creeps along my back like Rascal's guilty fevers and I realize there is one thing I can do, today, that will hurt only me.

Standing up, I say, "Mr. Curtis? I think I have a fever."

I run up the stairs of my building two at a time. The thought of having a closet that doesn't reek of brand-new Lycra has given me energy. I don't know why I didn't recognize it before, but just knowing they were in there has been like a stone in my shoe. Not anymore. I'm going to return them to the school. Confess. Just march into the office and tell Mrs. Pelletier about my poorly thought-out plan. Let her punish me any way she wants. I slow down on Noah's landing because there's an official-looking paper tacked to his door. As I move closer, I stop.

It's an eviction notice. He has thirty days to vacate.

Dad's never really had a friend before. Not as long as I can remember. But in all their hours spent under the hoods of the VW and the Bentley, Noah seems to have worked his way into Dad's life. They swap car magazines and tools. Dad even invited Noah over one afternoon to watch tapes of some Japanese Grand Prix. It was cute, seeing the two of them groaning through the wipeouts and analyzing the pit crew. They were like excited little boys.

I don't want Dad to lose that. I don't want Noah to lose that.

They're not so different from each other. One might reek of weed and unwashed dreads and the other might smell of Mr. Clean, but they're both alone in their adult worlds and they've found a way to bond. My mother would never have approved of Noah—there's not a hairnet in the world big enough to allow a guy like him in the back of a restaurant—but she didn't always know what was good for Charlie. And in the end, she didn't care.

Behind me, I hear footsteps and turn to see Noah climbing up the stairs with a small bag of groceries. He glances at the door and shakes his head, chuckling angrily. "You know how long I waited to get into this building? Two years. You don't find rent like this so easy."

"Can you fight it?"

"With what?" He holds up his bag. "This has to feed me for a week."

"Forget that. You'll eat with us."

"I can't sponge off your dad."

"What happened?"

He swings his dreads over one shoulder and unlocks the door. "Brice Burnack's career happened. Or didn't happen. That's what I get for working without pay."

I follow him inside and watch as he sets the bag on the kitchen counter and unloads a few cans of soup and beans. A carton of milk. His place is so empty it's as if no

224

one lives here. "I don't get it. If things were this bad, why didn't you quit? Go work for someone more reliable?"

"I could've. But I worry about Carling. She may be prickly, but she's had a tough home life. Who's to say either of us, in her shoes, would react any differently?"

"Still. You could have kept in touch with her. It doesn't make sense to let things get so bad you lose your apartment."

He stops unpacking, both hands resting inside the bag. Staring at me, he thinks about it for a moment. "I guess I'm just a sucker for a family. Anyway, what are you doing, roaming free on a school day?"

"I'm headed straight back. I just needed something from my room."

"It couldn't have waited until tomorrow?"

"No. It couldn't."

He sighs. "Run up and get it. I'll drive you back to school."

Forty-five minutes later, I step into the office and place a paper sack on the counter. I'm numb, shaking. But how I feel doesn't matter. All I can think about right now is my confession. Whatever comes next can wait. One step at a time.

The office is unusually empty. Eventually an older teacher rushes out of an office with an armful of files. He looks up at me, shocked. As if I were a cheetah standing here instead of a student.

My stomach flips and I tighten my fingers around the folded bag. "Is Mrs. Pelletier around? I need to speak with her for a moment."

The phone rings and he holds one finger in the air as he answers it. "Yes, it's true. It's the third-floor science lab. Room three twenty-nine. We don't know. He hasn't said much at all. Just mutters things we can't understand and keeps right on scrubbing the sink as if he's lost his mind. It's been nearly an hour."

Dad.

I grab the paper bag and run.

I can't see past the swarm of kids at the doorway of the science lab. They're all jostling and shoving to get a better look. Somehow when they're in uniform, a crowd of Ants seems smaller, more compact. In their Grub Day clothes, with everyone wearing every color of the rainbow, they seem ten thousand strong. A wall I can't penetrate no matter which opening I try to break through.

"What the hell?" says one kid.

"He's been at it for almost an hour," says another.

"This guy's whacked."

"The office called nine-one-one."

Trying to attract as little attention as possible, I burrow through the bodies but don't seem to get any closer to the door. At one point Carling calls out to me, something about my fever, but I ignore her, busy as I am looking for gaps in the crowd. I lift myself up on my tiptoes and peer between Griff and some older girls, but my view is still blocked by heads. This is no good. I need to get in there.

The principal, Mr. Oosterhouse, arrives and starts herding students away from the door. "That's enough, people. Off to your next class. This is none of your concern." He pushes his way through the kids and finally I'm able to make my move. I duck down and follow in his wake, not stopping until I'm standing in the doorway.

There he is at one of the sinks in the long counter, rag in hand. Red-faced and sweating, Charlie is scrubbing and scrubbing at the center sink. He has a wild look about him, with hair standing on end and eyes glazed, not really focused properly. I've seen this look before. In a rain-soaked garden in front of a little red bungalow in Lundon, Massachusetts.

This cannot be happening. Not here. Not now. It was hours before Dad allowed himself to be coaxed out of the rain, out of the sloppy black grave and into the house. And even then, he didn't stop because he felt he was done. I cannot produce the real reason Dad stopped. I cannot produce my mother.

Just before we came to Ant, the sweater lost my mother's smell. Something about being packed in a carton and shipped out of Lundon—where the sweater must have spent most of its life—stripped it of its scent. The cardboard greedily absorbed my mother's essence, taking her from me for a second time.

It was the last week of school when I saw the cartons. Three days before prom. What should have been the sweetest afternoon in my life. Almost eighty degrees, sunny, and the trees had that urgent, early summer, acid-green tinge that begs you to look at them in wonder every time you step out the door. This freshness is fleeting—you know that from the year before—it lasts only until the heat of July makes their color deep and lazy.

I'd raced home after the last bell had rung and dumped

my backpack in the dining room, praying my mother would be home early enough to practice curling my hair into prom-worthy ringlets. Turned out she'd been home already but had left again. I should have guessed from the cardboard boxes and suitcase outside her bedroom door that she was leaving for good. Instead—maybe because of the silky breezes outside, or the happy prospect of a long summer of suntanning with Mandy—I stupidly entertained the idea that my parents were surprising me with an unannounced vacation. I looked at Mom's yellow plaid tote bag and green sweater placed neatly atop the big suitcase and hoped I wouldn't have to share the overnight bag with my dad because the zipper could never be trusted.

Days later I would remember other details, like all her perfume bottles and lotions were missing from her bathroom. Her antique alarm clock was gone. If I'd thought to open her closet door, I would have seen nothing but wire hangers on her side, huddled together at one end of the rod, trying to appear, to my father's jeans and shirts and bathrobe, as if nothing out of the ordinary was happening, as if they hadn't been left behind at all but were simply waiting for fresh laundry to arrive.

But, drunk with anticipation of Friday night, I turned on the shower. Dropped my shorts and T-shirt to the bathroom floor, stepped into the scalding-hot water. It wasn't until I'd lathered, rinsed, repeated, that I realized something was missing from the front hall. Without stopping to reach for a towel or to turn off the steaming water, I bolted out of the shower and slipped and skidded my way to the front of the house. I stood there dripping water onto the floor, staring at a square of red paisley wallpaper that glowed brighter than the rest of the faded old wall, thinking it should be the other way around. It was the patch where our mother-daughter photo used to be that should be faded away, if only to show a little respect for the girl who'd refused to accept what the late nights, the broken promises, the affair with her teacher really meant.

Her mother was leaving home.

A group of teachers huddle behind my father in the science lab, unsure what to do. Mr. Oosterhouse approaches, lays a hand on Charlie's shoulder, but Charlie is too obsessed to feel it. It's as if no one is around and all that stands between life as we know it and deadly microbes taking over the earth is this stainless-steel sink and Charlie's overworked arm.

I want to lay my hand on Dad's shoulder. I want to run across the room and hold him. Tell him everything's going to be okay now. That I'm starting to like it here and won't study so hard anymore. Tell him I'll stay home every night to play Scrabble with him if only he'll go back to normal. Tell him I love him even if my mother doesn't.

"You've done a great job, Charlie," Mr. Oosterhouse says. "We couldn't ask for a more pristine sink. Now what say we pack up and move on to another classroom?" He leans over and picks up Dad's bucket. "I'll give you a hand."

"No," says Dad, still erasing something that isn't there. In this light, I can see the sharp creases in his clothes from where he's been ironing his uniform. Some of the seams in his jacket, his trousers, are frayed white from repeated heat and stress. I look around. No one else is as unwrinkled as my dad. "No," he repeats. "There's a small mark."

Mr. Oosterhouse moves closer. "It's an old sink. One that has endured many science experiments gone wrong. There are many stains that will never come out."

That's not it! I want to shout. He's not scrubbing to rid the sink of stains. He's got it in his head that this spot is wicked with danger. It doesn't matter that his opponent doesn't exist, it just matters that he feels he won. That's the enigma of OCD.

At the doorway, more teachers have gathered and are herding the students down the hall. I slip past them into the laboratory. Once inside, I hear Mr. Oosterhouse whisper to a small redheaded teacher to call 911. He says Dad needs medical care. The teacher nods and shoots out of the room, slamming the door shut, her sturdy pumps making threatening *rat-a-tat-tat* machine-gun sounds as she retreats to the relative normalcy of the hallway.

The thought of paramedics racing in here and shooting Dad up with tranquilizers like some gorilla that's escaped from the zoo, only to strap him to a stretcher and whisk him off for observation at Massachusetts General, is more than I can take.

Mr. Oosterhouse, the only person besides Mrs. Pelletier who knows I exist, looks at me. "Are you his daughter?"

"I'm Sara."

The kids are gone, along with many of the teachers. I pluck the bottle of bleach solution, Charlie's liquid solace, his pacifier, from the cleaning bucket and push past Mr. Oosterhouse.

Knowing full well it's like giving the alcoholic a beer, I hand the bleach to my father. "Try this."

His wild eyes focus on me but he says nothing. Just removes the cap, douses his cloth in fluid, and wipes the sink with it. He stands back and watches the sink go from shiny and silver with wetness back to mottled and dusty-looking silver. The sound of the microbes screaming, dying, is nearly audible, and right away I see his jaw slacken and relax. It's the sanitary equivalent of having dug the perfect hole.

The paramedics' walkie-talkies buzz and hum in the hallway like a swarm of killer bees. Mr. Oosterhouse heads to the door to wave them in. As Dad bends over to pack up his things, I check the area for students, then, assured we have a split second to ourselves, I say, "Are you all right?"

He nods.

I want to kiss his bearded cheek more than anything. Smother it with kisses like Mom did to bring him out of the rain. But all I say is, "I'll see you at home, Dad. Okay?"

"Don't worry, Sara. I'm fine."

Paramedics rush in as I slip out. Dad's calm now. They won't have reason to do anything but ask a few questions and recommend he make an appointment with his dead doctor.

My heart races when I see Leo waiting in the hall. I'd forgotten all about him. It's just like Mandy said, right away I have my answer. His eyes soften when he sees me and a sweet smile spreads across his face. And, I don't know if it's my imagination or just the excitement, but it looks like he might be blushing. He stares at me and mouths the word *Hey.*

I whisper, "Hey."

I clutch the paper bag behind my back. There's no returning the yoga pants now. Not with the current state of my dad's mental health. His daughter confessing to theft, getting suspended, maybe even expelled, could make him really lose it. All I can do now is lie low. And pray.

Behind Leo are Griff and Willa. Griff asks, "How did you get a backstage pass, London?"

"I just slipped inside to help."

"But why?" asks Willa.

"Yeah," says Griff, pulling up his drooping pants. "Is Crazy Charlie your father or something?"

I shoot him a look meant to shut him up. To show him he's the one who's crazy.

This isn't like last time, when Dad's OCD plowed my social life deep into the flower bed on Norma Jean Drive, not to be unearthed and dewormed for a full two years. At least I still had a real family. I still had a real friend. Mandy was willing to stick by me even if it meant eating lunch every day with the kids who made shadow puppets against the radiators.

But nothing is real anymore. My mother is gone. My dad moved me far, far away from my rock, Mandy. And the friends I've replaced her with are cheap imitations. There's not a single, solitary student at Ant who would stand by me if Charlie's OCD showered me in muddy droplets right now. I would be completely alone.

"Well," giggles Willa. "Is he your dad or what?"

I thought they'd keep Charlie longer. The paramedics. I thought they'd look into his eyes and listen to his pulse and slide a stethoscope under his crisply ironed shirt to hear his heartbeat. I thought they'd ask him to breathe in and breathe out. Make him answer endless questions about his medical past. I thought Dad would say something about vintage ambulances being superior to modern ones and ask them if they've ever considered retrofitting an old vehicle with modern-day lifesaving equipment.

If I thought for one second Dad would be finished with them, walking out of the science lab, and passing behind me—fake friends or no friends—I wouldn't have said it.

"No." I shake my head as if Griff is the one who has lost his mind. "Charlie is *not* my father."

My eyes meet Dad's the moment the words have tumbled off the tip of my forked tongue. His face crumples like he's been shot.

chapter 26
the tiniest key

A necrophoric substance is the scent emitted by a dead ant, signaling to the others that the corpse is ready for removal.

When too many things spin out beyond your reach, the human body takes notice. Only, instead of pumping evenly timed doses of soothing serotonin, warmed up like a baby's bottle, through your veins to modulate your mood and leave you clear-headed enough to battle your way out of your problems, your body declares mutiny by hammering on your nerves and making your breath reedy and shallow. This has the cumulative effect of leaving you with a sick stomach, tingling fingertips, and a perpetual feeling of faintness.

It's a case of life imitating art. Rascal killed the old pawnbroker to make the world a better place. But her innocent, underappreciated cleaning-lady sister walked in and he offed her in the process. What I've done is no different. I thought I was killing off the OCD. Saving myself from a lonely existence. Making the world—okay, *my* world—a better place. But I axed my father's soul in the process.

I don't know how to make it up to him. How do you bring someone you've murdered back to life? Once you've stepped on an ant, just because you could, there's no going back. You've done what you've done and you simply have to live with it. No amount of apologizing will erase it.

I've told Charlie I'm sorry. I've told him I love him. I know it sounded tinny and false when I said I was proud of him, but I am. He's handling our broken situation as best he can. He's doing the best he knows how. And in some screwed-up way, his worsening OCD is part of that. He's been trying to scrub our lives clean.

His reaction? *I love you, Sara. I understand, Sara. Now don't stay up too late, Sara.*

If he'd yelled at me, if he'd grounded me—if he'd disowned me, even—it would have been easier to take. But this. This absolute acceptance. It's making me sadder than sad.

The school handled it amazingly well. Mr. Oosterhouse met with him in private. Asked Dad about his stress levels. Suggested Dad consider a leave of absence to give himself time to unwind; after all, he's had the big move and the change in schools. The principal doesn't even know about the biggest stressor of all: Mom. Mr. Oosterhouse even went so far as to give him the card of a board-approved doctor, an actual *live* doctor, to help him.

The Antmasters, they aren't so bad. Think about it— they could have fired him after an episode like that. For all they know, he could get violent. But Charlie is Charlie. To know him is to want to protect him, and Mr. Oosterhouse wants to help.

The thing is, aside from this whoopsie, Dad's been good for the school. People always say the place has never looked so good. Mr. Oosterhouse knows it. Plus the staff has grown to like Dad. And what's not to like? He's a good man.

If he takes the leave of absence, he'll still be paid. Union rules. But while spending his days at home relax ing might be good for my father in terms of resting and coming to terms with his new life, it would probably end in another unnecessary cleaning frenzy in the apartment. So when Dad refused the paid leave, I didn't argue. He did, however, put the doctor's card in his pocket and, later, tack it to our bulletin board in the kitchen. Whether he plans to call or just took it out of politeness, I don't know.

I didn't sleep Monday night because there was a terrible storm, heavy wind that tore huge branches from trees and set off more than a few car alarms. So by the time Dad calls out that it's time to go, I'm still pulling on my uniform and I tell him to leave without me.

With cleanup crews gathering fallen tree limbs all over the city, traffic is terrible. Once the bus pulls up to my stop, an elderly couple, clearly from out of town, begin arguing with the driver because he can't change a twenty, blocking my path down to the front stairwell. There doesn't appear to be an immediate solution beyond the old man stuffing twenty dollars into the fare box, so I dig through my pockets and slide three dollars into the box for them. They seem shocked and touched that a young person mustered up a little generosity and selflessness, and the woman touches my shoulder as I pass, saying, "What a sweet girl."

If only she knew.

The twenty gives me a great idea that might just help me feel I've regained some shred of control over my life. As I shuffle toward the school, I reach into my backpack for my plane ticket, wandering closer to the street, where early-morning traffic is whizzing by. The wind hasn't fully died down from last night and if I time it well, I should get a nice tailwind in the wake of the next passing bus.

It's not long before a city bus comes roaring down Charles. I hold the ticket out toward the road and wait until it starts to kick and flap like Carling's twenty-dollar bill in the T. I open my fingers and watch the ticket dart up toward the sky, then cartwheel back to earth over the street, where it gets ripped beyond recognition under the wheels of dozens of passing cars.

I trot up the school steps toward the front doors to find Isabella leaning against the chipped railing, arms folded across her chest. She looks me up and down. "Hey, London."

"Hey."

"Are you okay? You look tired."

"I'm fine."

"I hope you don't have that flu bug. I hear it can be nasty."

"What do you want, Isabella?"

She feigns shock. "What a question. Can't a good friend be concerned for your health?"

"Not if she's you."

"See, now I'm hurt. And all I want to know is why you look so terrible."

"Long story." I turn away. "We'd better head inside."

She steps in front of me, thrusting out one bony hip. "You're full of long stories, aren't you? In fact, I'm pretty certain you've been telling us a whole pack of lies." She leans closer and lowers her tinkly voice. "Is that true, London?"

"Actually, the bell's about to ring and—" I step back and she pulls me close again.

"That bell can ring and ring and ring. But if I were you, I'd listen."

I can't breathe. I suck in air but somewhere between my lips and my windpipe, it seems to vanish.

"Your father is not a brain surgeon, is he? Not unless tying the trash bags into seven thousand knots is called surgery. Your dad is the crazy new janitor. I saw you with him in the science lab."

"Just because I helped another human being doesn't mean—"

"Does 'I'll see you at home, Dad, okay?' sound familiar to you? I'm surprised you didn't ask for an increase in your allowance."

"But how did you—?"

"I was at the restroom door across the hall. Did you know it has a perfect view into the science lab? It's like being front-row center at the Old Vic Theatre in London. But then, you wouldn't know that. You're not from London either, are you, Saint Sarah?"

It's as if I've been painted over with cement. Concrete. I can't move a single body part other than my eyelids, which are blinking with panic. Finally I dislodge my mouth, knocking flakes of dried-up concrete to the ground, and whisper, "Please don't say anything, Izz."

"Now you're asking *me* to lie?"

"No. Yes. Please."

She narrows her eyes and purses her lips. "There is one thing you can do for me that might convince me to keep quiet."

"What? I'll do anything, I swear."

"Does your dad have keys to every room in the school?"

I think back to the huge key ring he stuffed into his pocket the first day of school. "I guess."

"Take them."

"What?"

"Take the keys, break into the office, and steal a copy of the calculus test for Carling. I'm going to give it to her to save her grade."

"I can't do that."

"Yes, you can. Just wait until no one's around. Sniff around the file cabinets in the principal's office and take it. It'll be *our* little secret. Carling will think I did it for her."

So that's what this is about. Isabella likes Carling completely dependent on her. It's the only way she feels secure.

I know exactly where the tests are, and they're not in the principal's office. They're in that tall wooden filing cabinet in the storage room—the one I caught my mother's sweater on when I was raiding the Lost and Found with Mrs. Pelletier on my first day of school. The keyholes stand out in my memory. I remember they were so tiny I couldn't imagine a key small enough to fit. "I don't know. What if I get caught?"

Izz starts to walk away. "Never mind, then. I *must* go

find Carling and Sloane. And Willa and Griff. Ooh, and the lovely Leo. We all have so much to talk about."

I grab her sleeve. "No, wait!" I swallow the acid that's bubbling up into my mouth. "I'll do it."

The door closes behind her and I'm alone outside, just me and what's left of the windstorm, small bits of garbage and crushed leaves swirling around my feet.

It's Monday morning and on my bed is the smallest key from Dad's key ring. It's been nearly a week since Isabella stopped me on the steps. She's given me the evil eye ever since, but I had to wait for a safe time to go through Dad's key ring. During the week, the keys stayed hidden in the pocket of his Anton jacket, which hung in his closet at night. But on the weekend, he emptied his pockets and left the contents just lying there on the hall table for anyone to see. I went through the key ring during my two a.m. study break Saturday night. Or, rather, Sunday morning. No other key seemed old enough, tarnished enough, or small enough to fit, and I'm praying I've got the right one. All I need now is about five minutes alone in the Lost and Found.

Standing in front of my mirror, rubbing granules of sleep out of my eyes and dressed in the same underpants and neon yellow Dubble Bubble T-shirt I wore to bed, I call out to Charlie to say I can't find my English essay, to go ahead without me. He tells me to have a nice day, then the front door thumps shut.

I pull on my kneesocks, then my plaid skirt, which seems to have shrunk from Dad taking it to the dry cleaner. It's hard to suck in a really good breath when your abdomen is being crushed, and today I need the O². Which is when it hits me. The only real way to be alone in the Lost and Found closet.

Unhooking the waistband, I let my skirt drop to the ground, peel off the socks, and kick my little clump of Ant armor under the bed. Out of sight. My old jeans are hanging on the back of my chair. I pull them on, stuff bare feet into my battered red Docs, slip the key into my pocket, and head out the door.

Stomping through the foyer of the school, I'm nothing but a crumpled piece of neon flotsam being swept along in the wave of woolen vests and tartan skirts and tailored trousers streaming toward their homerooms. From every direction, kids are staring at my T-shirt and boots, nudging their friends, snickering. I couldn't stand out more if I had a strobe light strapped to my forehead.

I couldn't care less.

Just before I'm sucked down by the undertow of the navy-vested workday that exists inside these walls, I fight my way to the edge and slip through the office doors.

"Sara Black," says Mrs. Pelletier, catching my eye and crossing the room to rest her impressive bosom against the counter. A thin gold cross lies on the pillowy shelf. Leaning forward, she whispers, "How's your father?"

"He's doing better. Thanks."

"Good." She smiles and pats the back of my hand, raising an eyebrow at the sight of my outfit. "You have your schedule mixed up, my dear. Grub Day's not for another three weeks."

"I don't know what I was thinking."

She glances up at the clock. "You can't go to class that way or you'll be given a demerit point. And if you go home to change, you'll miss first period entirely."

"Actually, I was kind of hoping I could dig through the Lost and Found real quick. I have Honors Math first period with Mr. Curtis."

"Ah, Mr. Curtis." She smiles, nodding her understanding. "Say no more. Your big test is coming up."

"Exactly."

She motions for me to come around the counter and follow her in the direction of the storage closet . . . and Mr. Curtis's exam. I don't know if it's her kind eyes, the cross, or her motherly bosom, but as I follow her into the storage room, I'm suddenly exhausted. I want to drop, wrap my arms around her, and confess to the growing list of lies I've told and crimes I've committed that are now threatening to swallow me whole. She opens the doors to the cupboard and starts going through the row of ties hanging from a small rod. "Now, let's start with the tie. Maybe we can find you one that looks brand-new."

The way she's so nice to me, the way she thinks I'm a good person, it makes me sad.

I reach for a tie. "It's okay. I can dig through these and find one. I like my ties a certain way—worn out enough that they aren't stiff, but not so soft they're floppy. Pretty weird, huh?"

She turns around and sets her hands on her round hips. "Not really. I'm that picky about gloves. I can't stand when they're brand-new." Walking toward the door, she says, "Go ahead, dear. But don't take too long or you'll be late for class."

And, just like that, it's me, a few hundred cartons of message pads and copier paper, a rack of used clothing, and the old wooden filing cabinet. As quietly as I can, I pull out the tiny key and hold my breath as I try to insert it into the lock on the top drawer

It fits.

chapter 27
missing polynomials

An ant that lives in the colony of a different ant species, and is parasitically dependent on it, is considered a social parasite.

Here sits the former model student and one-time valedictorian hopeful at her desk with a stolen calculus exam stuffed up the vest of her hastily assembled uniform. As I was pulling the test out of the file, I was relieved to see two more copies because there was no way I was going to be able to photocopy this and get it back into the drawer without detection. Will anybody miss one exam out of three? I have no idea. But leaving two behind has to be a whole lot less suspicious than leaving none. My next problem is how to get the exam to Isabella without raising any questions from Sloane or Carling. I lean forward over my desk—directly behind the three of them—and whisper, "I have to pee."

Isabella snorts. "Thanks for the internal update. Just don't do it in a South American river."

I say nothing until Carling turns around, then I reach out to Isabella's chair with my foot and give it a gentle nudge. She doesn't turn right away. First she makes sure the others aren't looking, then glances in my direction. I pat my vest and nod, then put up my hand.

"Yes, Sara," says Mr. Curtis from the blackboard.

"May I go to the restroom?"

"Go ahead. But be quick, we're going to be covering polynomials in a few minutes."

Isabella raises her hand. "Can I go too? I don't want to miss a minute of the polynomial discussion."

He plants one chalky hand on his waist and tilts his head. "The perfect loophole to my one-at-a-time rule. Well timed and well executed, Miss Latini."

"Thank you," she says, unfolding herself and following me out of the class.

We lock ourselves into the handicapped stall and I pull out the exam. All the answers are right there in red ink. She starts to take it from me, but I don't release it immediately. This is it. My last crime.

"Give it," she says.

"We'll be even with this, Isabella. Do you swear?"

"Yes. Even."

"This means everything is as it was, right?"

"Right." She tugs on it, stronger than she looks, but I hold tight.

"And no one is to know where you got the test. I don't want my father implicated in any way. Not ever."

She rips it from my hand and backs away, stuffing it into her waistband and heading for the door. "Don't get tough with me, London. I'll win every time."

Knowing full well I could snap that spindly neck like a fresh carrot, I walk away.

chapter 28
someone deserves rocky road

The Texas carpenter ant invades homes at night in its constant hunt for food.

Brice Burnack's new Broadway musical opened on the weekend. Not only was the theater half-empty, but the scalpers—the ones with the uncanny, near-canine ability to sniff out a play's success—got stuck with the tickets they'd gobbled up. And it seems even the critics felt invincible enough to defy Brice's finely sharpened claws and fiery hair. While reviewers applauded the lead actors' performances, calling them "brilliant" and "hauntingly soulful," they ripped Brice's music score into finely ground tiger meal. The *New York Times* said the musical "might better have been sung by muppets." *USA Today* suggested it might be "adopted by nursery schools across the country as perfect music for pulling on rain boots."

According to Brice they were too simple-minded to see the irony in his work.

Carling hasn't been seen without a mouthful of antacids all week. Unfocused and rumored to have been caught smoking in the girls' locker room at recess, she has taken to wearing Isabella as a coat of armor. Not that Isabella minds.

There isn't the tiniest part of me that wants to be at Carling's house after school. Not a fingernail, an eyelash, or a pore. With people like these, at a time like this, anything could happen. Brice himself might open the door, Carling might jump off the roof, and Isabella might find herself permanently glued to Carling's skin. Again, not that she'd mind. But there's a certain wisdom in keeping your enemies close, and I'm afraid to let Isabella Latini out of my sight.

No sign of Brice, the throbbing tiger, when the door swings open. It's Gracie herself. From the look of things I can only assume that their housekeeper, whatever her real name was, has quit. The floor is unswept, there's a stack of unopened mail spilling off the hall table, and a basket overflowing with laundry sits at the bottom of the stairs. Gracie, her hair unstyled, dressed in sweatpants she might have slept in, tries to smile. "The girls are in the basement."

Music thumps from the rec room speakers and Carling, Isabella, and Sloane are at the bar; Isabella on a barstool in a spa-like white robe and Sloane bent over doing Izzy's toes. Carling is behind the bar—wearing my mother's sweater—stuffing things into the blender and looking happier than she has in days.

Carling grins as I enter. "London. It's Pamper Isabella Day. Grab a pumice stone and start filing the girl's bunions."

"You don't *file* bunions, you cow," says Isabella, adoring all the attention. "A bunion is a swollen bursal sac with an osseous deformity at the mesophalangeal joint."

"Stay still," says Sloane. "You're messing up your pedi."

I sit down and watch Carling pour frozen berries into the machine. "Carling, when am I going to get my sweater back?"

"You're too uptight, London. I'm not keeping it." But she makes no move to take it off.

I know why everyone is treating Isabella like the queen, but have to ask, "What's the occasion?"

"Izzers just got me into med school," Carling says with a happy squeak. "She stole Curtis's math test for me, and I decided she deserves some juice."

Isabella stares at me. "If only Carling knew what things I do for her when she's not around."

My heart thumps in my throat.

"That's the best kind of friend to have," says Carling. "One who's working for me—Round. The. Clock."

"Can you believe I did that?" Isabella looks at me. "Next I might start telling outrageous lies about myself. I might even start telling people *I'm* from London. Wouldn't that be fun?"

"A riot," I say without taking my eyes off her.

She continues. "How about you, Sloaney? If you could suddenly be from anywhere in the world, where would it be?"

Sloane sips from a small bottle of sparkling water and thinks a moment. Then says, "Italy. But only because of the accent and the hot guys."

"But some people can drop their accents just like that," says Isabella, snapping her fingers. "Like London."

"I told you, I wasn't born there," I say, wanting to slap her.

"Still," she says, "you'd think you would have picked

up the accent in all your years of going to British schools, riding in British limos, fraternizing with the Royals . . ."

"I never said I knew the Royals."

Isabella says, "Don't some of the Royals have weird obsessions? I wonder if you know anyone weird, London. Anyone with strange quirks who calls attention to himself in crazy ways? Maybe even someone who can't stop—"

"Can I see it?" I blurt out.

"What?" asks Carling, pushing the juice across the counter to Isabella.

"The stolen test. Show me, I want to know what's on it."

Carling roots through her backpack behind the bar. She starts out slowly, then starts pulling out pencil case, binder, Tums bottle in a panic. "Oh my God. It's not here!"

"What isn't?" asks Isabella.

"My little purse." Her nostrils flare and her chest starts heaving. "I must have left it on the floor by my locker. I pulled it out of my backpack because I couldn't find my lipstick. I must have forgotten to put it back!"

"So you lost your Prada bag," says Sloane, sticking her finger into Isabella's juice. "Don't be so dramatic. You can get another in, like, a couple of days. And I'll hook you up with a new fake ID."

"The test was inside my purse. If anyone finds it and opens it up . . ."

Sloane looks up. "You're dead."

Ever since I got home about an hour ago, I've been in and out of the bathroom three times, certain I'm going to throw up. We went to the school and found no sign of Carling's purse, no sign of the stolen test. And Isabella made one thing clear to me as I left: if Carling gets caught, she's turning me in.

I'm leaning against the sink when Dad pokes his head in. "You don't look so well. Are you sick?"

"No. I don't know. Probably just tired."

"Would you like a sandwich? I'm making one for myself. We have the lean turkey you always ask for, and mayonnaise."

"Please. No food."

"Why were you so late getting home?"

"I went back to school to help a friend look for her purse. But we couldn't find it. Some kid probably took it home." The image of Isabella whispering in Mr. Oosterhouse's ear while pointing at me fills the air above my head and my stomach lurches. "It was a pretty expensive bag."

"Was it brown? Canvas and leather with a logo on one side?"

I look up. "Yeah. How did you know?"

"I found a brown purse on the floor beneath a row of lockers. I didn't want to invade the owner's privacy by looking inside."

"Seriously? I'll call her and tell her we have it."

He turns away and starts padding down the hall, scratching himself. "It's not here. I left it with the principal."

chapter 29
the bottled inferno

Certain species of ants are able to survive underwater for more than two weeks in an anesthetized state whereby their oxygen consumption is drastically reduced.

While every parent is unique and will psychologically damage his kid in his own special way, most fall into three fairly recognizable categories when faced with the trauma of being called into the office because their child messed up.

First there are the Hand Wringers. They could be dressed in anything from socks with sandals to a power suit, but they have one common trait: they all bought the parenting book that said you should never say no to your toddler. Other parents read this book too, but the Hand Wringers were the idiots who fell for it. These parents are flimsy and unsure of themselves and have that scared-rabbit look in their eyes because their kids now have all the power. After being invited to the office and informed little Ocean or December told the teacher to go bite herself, the Hand Wringer will wonder where he went wrong and ultimately forgive the child for her failure.

Next are the Egalitarians. These guys don't take their teenagers' bad choices personally, they just accept the bad news and move forward. Upon hearing their high-school senior skipped thirteen out of twenty days of school to stay home and play World of Warcraft, they might be inwardly worried they've raised a resident of an alternate universe, but know that saying it out loud will result in a broken kid who will never have the self-esteem to pack up his warlord fantasies and move out of the house. Instead they keep their yaps shut, start planning to retire to a one-bedroom condo one day, and confiscate Ronan's cell phone for two weeks. Not that anybody calls.

The most volatile is the Bottled Inferno. This is the parent who, while sitting across from the principal, nods and grunts and makes all the appropriate concerned-parent sounds. What the principal can't see from behind his or her desk is that the parent is gripping the arms of his chair so hard they have fused with his flesh. Other telltale signs are nostrils tensed into flared triangles and pupils that swirl with tiny tornados. The Bottled Inferno will be fairly silent during the school meeting, but you just know he'll blow once those car doors are firmly shut.

Brice Burnack is a Bottled Inferno.

Mr. Oosterhouse's door is cracked open just enough for me to see—as I drop off Mr. Curtis's attendance sheet the next morning—the Burnack family sitting across from the big desk. I can't see all of Gracie, only her slender legs, crossed at the ankle, but I can see Carling and her dad. Carling, sitting in the big leather chair between her parents, looks about twelve years old. As if she's gone back in time. Probably wishes she could. And Brice. Brice smoldering—dark, red, and ashy—in the corner.

I shift myself closer to the door and try to hear snippets of what Mr. Oosterhouse is saying.

". . . which is why I move that we deal with this incident in the same way we've dealt with your daughter's other infractions." I peek inside to see the principal reach for a stack of papers. The phones are ringing like mad in the office behind me, so I press my ear closer to the door to hear him explain, "Here are the architect's plans for the new music wing. Very detailed, as you'll see . . ."

Brice shifts forward in his seat, looking sick.

The principal is speaking again. ". . . of course, and we would hold an elaborate naming ceremony for the new *Brice Burnack Music Wing.*"

Brice's hair practically starts sparking and smoking as he shoots a look of incandescent fury at his daughter. He drops his head into his hands and rubs his temples hard. When he looks up again, his face has lost its charred toughness. "I can't do it this time," he says eventually. "I just don't have the cash."

"Brice, don't," says Gracie. "It's nobody's business."

Someone sidles up beside me. Sloane holds up a brown envelope. "For Mrs. Pelletier. Curtis tried to stop you, but you'd already gone." She peeks inside Oosterhouse's office and whispers, "This is not going to go down well. Especially after Bricey's just had his creative genius mocked in every major publication in America. If there's one thing Mr. Burnack hates, it's public humiliation. And Carling's just given him a ton."

Suddenly the principal's door bangs shut, nearly taking off the tip of my nose. Mrs. Pelletier, her hair pulled back more severely than usual, her glasses shelved on her bosom, takes our shoulders, spins us around, and propels us toward the hallway. "That'll be enough snooping, girls. Off you go, back to class before you get yourselves into just as much trouble as your friend."

It's pathetic how, after all I've seen of Carling, after all I know, I still get a little thrill from being referred to as her friend.

At the end of math class, we find Carling waiting in the hall. She motions for us to follow her into the closest restroom, and once inside, Sloane checks that all stalls are empty before sliding both metal trash cans in front of the door. They won't exactly stop anyone from barging in, but we'll hear them coming long enough in advance to stop talking.

"We only have a few minutes," says Carling, her face gaunt and pale. "My parents are waiting for me in the car."

"What happened?" asks Isabella. "Am I dead?"

"No way," Carling says. "I went down alone."

"Seriously?" I ask, relieved beyond belief that this won't be traced back to Charlie's keys. And his daughter.

"Are we going to see a Brice Burnack plaque on a wall somewhere tomorrow morning?" asks Sloane. "Or will they wait until after the renovations to christen it?"

Carling turns on the tap and splashes cold water on her face. Her hair falls into the water and she stands up with wet strands clinging to her face like leeches. "Brice offered big bucks, believe me. But Oosterhouse is being a total moron. He said to go home for today until the school decides what to do with me."

Brice offered big bucks? Not quite what I heard.

"Hey, just as long as I'm not expelled." Carling pulls a few paper towels from the dispenser and turns around, blotting her face dry. "You should have heard Oosterhouse. He was all, 'This isn't like you, *Carling*. We'd like to think our students can ask for help, *Carling*. You might want to consider dropping down to Applied Math, *Carling*.'"

"What an arrogant ass," says Isabella.

"I'm so pissed at the guy who ratted me out. That new janitor, Crazy Charlie. He found the purse and turned it in to the office. Crap for brains. Probably looked inside, saw the test, and figured he'd take me down. Ladies, it's time for punishment."

"No," I say too loudly. Sloane and Carling look at me, surprised. Isabella just folds her arms and waits. "Why would . . . Charlie look in your purse? He probably thought he was doing you a favor by giving it to someone in charge."

"He knew it was mine. My name was inside. Besides, he's hated me for weeks. One time I grabbed the stair rail to stop myself from falling and he came up behind me and cleaned the spot I touched. Like it was contaminated. From me. I can't *stand* that prick. I swear to God, if it's the last thing we do, we're taking him down."

I'm alone in the bathroom. Carling left school with her seething parents and the other two went to class. But I haven't yet regained the ability to move my feet. As I stare at my traitorous face in the mirror, my hands start to shake. This is all my fault. Charlie meant no harm. The man would rather ingest a shovelful of dirt than hurt another person. He's no match for Carling. She's volatile, capable of anything. Especially with Brice's doubly scorned ego licking her heels.

It's going to take a distraction. If she can get focused elsewhere, my father may recede to some forgotten, cobwebby part of her demented mind. I need to give her something so ultimate, so irresistible, so hurricane-huge that she disappears into it and gets too dizzy to breathe.

There's only one thing I know that can do that to a girl. Leo Reiser's kiss. As much as it will kill me, I have to step aside. To keep my father safe from Carling's twisted mind, I have to make Leo see her as desirable again.

Pushing through the swinging door, books balanced on my hip, I walk straight into Griff and Leo, scattering all our belongings across the speckled floor. "Don't say it," I say as they squat down to scoop up the aftermath. "It's too pathetic at this point."

Leo hands me my books. "Hey, I wasn't brought up to argue with cute girls."

Griff huffs. "You weren't raised to do anything with cute girls. Me, on the other hand . . ."

"Bye, Griff," says Leo, taking his mini-friend by the shoulder and guiding him away from us and toward the flow of students. "Your work here is done." As he watches Griff feign death and stagger off, Leo twists his mouth to one side in amusement. His upper lip is smudged with the stubble of a recently shaved mustache, leaving behind a stinging red nick. It takes everything I have not to reach up and wipe away the dried blood. The thought of touching him again sends currents of static through my veins.

"I was hoping to bump into you," he says. "Not literally. I do have my rugby arm to consider."

Please ask about Carling. And I'll say she's had a rough morning. That you should call her. See her. Forgive her.

"I was wondering," he continues with a bashful look in his eyes, "if you want to go to a movie with me Sunday afternoon."

For some crazy reason, the framed photo of me and Dad that sits on my desk at home pops into my mind. It was taken at my old school. Dad was in his far less lame Finmory custodian uniform and we were arm in arm on the steps of the school. His hand was resting on my shoulder, his knuckles soft, pink, unchapped.

Say no to Leo. You started this deranged situation for your father by lying about who he was instead of encouraging kids to get to know him. It's all your doing; now undo it. Tell Leo that Carling needs him. Tell him she's hurt. That she loves him.

Against my will, my lips curl back in a smile and I hear my voice saying, "I'd love to."

chapter 30
flush

Ants emit an alarm pheromone to announce a state of emergency to other colony members.

I set my alarm for 6:45 Saturday morning, so early the streetlights are still on. It doesn't matter that I didn't get four hours' sleep. Dad is going to see a few VW buses out in Brookline today, and I'm going to shock him by coming along. Not because I'm excited about choosing yet another vehicle that makes us look as if we solve Scooby-Doo mysteries on the side. But because I can't erase from my mind the look of Dad's eyes from the other day. The ache that I thought might bring him to his knees right there on the terrazzo tile of Anton's halls. That ache is the last thing I see before falling asleep. The first thing I see when I wake.

Without bothering to wash my face—I just washed it four hours ago—I pile my tangled hair into a high ponytail, pull a pair of old sweatpants over bare legs, and head into the kitchen in the same gray turtleneck I wore to bed.

Dad, sitting at the breakfast table in his Anton High custodian jacket, looks me up and down as he stirs his coffee. "You're up early."

"That's because we have to leave soon if we're going

to get to Brookline by eight. Buses don't run too often on Saturday mornings." I pour myself a cup of coffee, black, and hoist myself up on the counter across from him, thumping my heels against the cupboard doors below.

"Sweetheart, go back to bed and catch up on your sleep. You don't have to accompany me."

"I don't have to but I *want* to. You and I don't get to spend enough time together."

"Sara, it'll be nothing but peering under hoods at carburetors and distributor wires."

"Sounds delish."

"Seriously, hon. It will be hours of car talk at three different locations. You don't have to do this for me."

I drain my coffee cup and bang it on the counter, shooting him a teasing grin. "For you? Dream on, big guy. I'm doing this for me. You never know when I might want to dazzle my friends with my knowledge of air-cooled, four-cylinder boxcar engines."

He doesn't say anything right away, but his face softens. It's the kind of face that is trying to say nothing at all on the outside while it processes something sad and significant on the inside. It's the curtain that comes down on a stage—heavy and draping, soft and velvety—that blocks the audience from seeing the actors regrouping on the other side. "Boxer engines. Not boxcar."

I hop off the counter, lean down, and kiss his cheek. "Let's go, Dad. I don't want to miss our appointment."

By the time I stand up, the curtain has lifted and the actors are back onstage. He tugs on the leg of my grubby sweatpants. "You didn't have to go to so much trouble getting dolled up."

259

"Dude, at least I'm not wearing an Anton High jacket. You look like you're the oldest guy on the school bowling team."

He smiles, flipping up his collar. "We'll do a great job of convincing them we're penniless. It's the oldest buyer's tactic in the book."

We get off the bus on a street called Dresden Road. In spite of our forty-five-minute trek, it's still so early all the streets are empty. We walk up a slight hill on a sidewalk bordered on one side by a low stone wall with grass poking out from between the rocks.

Dad stops in front of a large, pale gray clapboard house—mansion, really—that looms over us. Not only is it set up on a grassy hill, but it's three stories high, with an actual turret on the right side. Shaggy bushes line the base of the house, parting only long enough to allow a steep set of steps to lead to the covered verandah.

He squints at a scrap of paper, then back up at the number above the front door. "We're here."

A balding man named Alex, dressed in old boat shoes, khakis, and a worn denim shirt with sleeves rolled up to his elbows, leads us to a four-car garage out back and opens the door. As he and Dad examine his collection of vehicles, a smiling, drooling, wiggling golden retriever races across the lawn and drops to the ground at my feet, rolling over and begging me to scratch his belly.

"This one's my baby," says Alex, walking straight past the VW bus, which I can already tell is too new for Dad, and motioning toward a small white car shaped like a bubble.

"Porsche 356 A-Coupe. Is it a '59?"

"Fifty-eight."

Dad whistles as he bends over and inspects the chrome bumper. "Not a whisper of rust. You keep her in excellent condition."

"I don't drive this one in winter. Not with all the salt on the roads. I own a car-parts company and maintain a rather large vintage division through which we buy and sell antique cars." Alex laughs. "Though I have to admit we buy often and sell rarely. We brought this one up from Santa Barbara about ten years ago and I took her home with me."

"Can't blame you. A car this special shouldn't sit unloved in a showroom."

"I can see you and I think alike." Alex unlocks the door to the Porsche and Dad climbs inside like a kid clambering onto Santa's lap.

Alex wanders over to where I am, sitting cross-legged on the smooth cement floor petting the dog. "You like dogs?"

"Sure."

"My wife breeds goldens. We typically sell all the pups, but Boomerang here kept running away from his new owners and finding his way back here. Eventually we stopped fighting him. Gave the owners another pup and let him stay. There's just something about this place he wasn't willing to give up."

I let my eyes wander around the property—across the overgrown bushes with leaves so scarlet they almost hurt to look at, the enormous tree branches that lean over the house and wrap around the roof as if embracing a child, the basketball hoop partway down the driveway. A woman pushes open an upstairs window. Her blondish gray hair is messy but pulled back, and she's wearing a white T-shirt. She looks sort of worn and comfy, just like Alex. This is no house of trial separations and envelopes full of divorce papers. This is a real family home, like you see on made-for-TV movies. I scratch Boomerang's ear and look up at Alex. "I can see why he likes it."

Dad and Alex are already acting like old friends, laughing and smiling, bonding over mid-engine tubular chassis. At one point Alex even pats Dad on the back. They're chatting about impossible-to-find antique parts—turns out Alex has never heard of this obscure vintage-parts Web site in Austria that feeds Dad parts for less. Alex writes the URL on a pad of paper beside the phone on his beautifully organized workbench, then the conversation shifts to our VW. Alex has been looking for an old van like ours to restore because he had a VW camper bus as a surf-loving teen out in San Diego, and they might work out some sort of a swap for one of the cars. While they bond with their heads buried under the hood of an ancient-looking convertible, I watch Dad lean against a dirty bumper with no concern about the microbes that might be jumping onto his palm like hardcores diving into a mosh pit.

It isn't until this moment I realize something. Cars, especially crappy old heaps, are his panacea, like the sun is to Superman. Cleaning is his kryptonite. As much as it temporarily soothes him, it ultimately destroys him.

Deep in a discussion about engine parts, Dad asks Alex about the last time the blue convertible was in the shop and does Alex have the invoice so he can see what repairs were made. Alex isn't sure and walks over to an intercom on the wall. "Honey? Is the prince out of bed yet? Ask him to drag his weary bones off the mattress and come out to the garage." He smiles at Dad. "This one belongs to my son, actually, so he's the best one to answer your questions. As much as I'd love to tinker with his car, I'm a big believer in my children making their own mistakes. He bought the car, he makes all his own maintenance decisions, and he pays for every decision he makes. It's the only way with kids. . . ."

As Alex's voice trails off, a horrified tingle spreads from my unwashed hair, along the ribbing of the turtleneck I slept in, across the fraying, secondhand threads of my Finmory sweatpants, across the gleaming cement floor to my father's overly ironed custodian jacket. It's too big a coincidence.

As I sit frozen to the concrete, Alex asks Charlie what he does. Dad's response sounds so far away, I almost believe I've floated out of the garage and am hovering somewhere up above the weathervane on the roof. "I'm the custodian at Anton High School," Charlie says before launching into an explanation involving words like refuse, toilet tanks, and HVAC system.

"Really?" says Alex. "Maybe you know my son. . . ."

A barefooted teenage boy in rumpled black T-shirt and low-slung plaid pajama bottoms pads into the garage, yawning and rubbing sleep from his eyes. With a big stretch, he blinks and looks right at me.

I don't move. I don't breathe. I don't speak. The boy standing in front of me is Leo Reiser.

*   *   *

Sitting cross-legged on the floor, stunned and mute, was how my mother found me when she came home the day I found the boxes. She just breezed straight past the cartons and packed bags and into my room as if bursting with good news. She took one look at me in my green prom dress, trying to make sense out of this afternoon, and asked why I was home so early. I pointed out it was four thirty and that she'd promised to help me pick a hairstyle for prom. She'd lost track of time, she said. Hadn't realized it was so late. Time does that, doesn't it? Vanishes. But here's the slap—it only happens when you're happy. My mother's apparent mathematical formula? Her − (Dad + me) = Time Flying.

She squished her mouth into an appropriate family-busting frown as she sat down on the rug beside me, put her arm across my shoulder. "Darling," she said, "you know I love you."

It always starts that way, doesn't it? Six words like this, seeping from down-turned lips. As soon as they hit the air, they rush around and get busy ending your world.

"But your father and I . . . you *know* it's been wrong for a long time. You *know* how he thinks. He's stagnant. I just want so much more out of life. Like I want for you. I'm at the point where staying is suffocating." She stopped and gathered my hair off my face.

I knew the answer, but it was my turn to speak. "You're leaving."

"Yes, sweetheart. But I'm not leaving you. Never leaving you."

"But I live in this house. So you sort of are."

"Don't look at it that way, Sara. You're a big girl now. You can hop on a plane and come see me—"

"A plane? How far are you *not* going? And is Mr. Nathan not going with you?"

She was quiet for a moment. "You know?"

I nodded.

She pulled me to my feet. "Come into my room and talk to me while I change. I think you'll understand what I'm about to tell you."

"Sure," I said, following her across the hall. "I don't want you to be late."

Love brings out the stupid in people. It traps fluid in the inner ear and blots out sound. My mother actually smiled at me as if she appreciated my concern for her timing. The sarcasm in my voice didn't even register.

I folded my arms across my chest, leaned against the wall connecting my parents' room to their bathroom, and watched as she tugged off her T-shirt and slipped into a pink silky sleeveless blouse. Her arms were tanned, muscular. As she kicked off her jeans and stepped into a skirt, I looked away, angered by her matching pink silky underwear. I'd never seen this bra or these panties in the laundry before.

"When I met Michael, it was as if I had a chance at life again, you know? You'll understand this when you're older, I promise. My God, you're going into eleventh grade. You're almost an adult yourself."

Keeping my eyes focused on the bathroom, I tried to blot out her words by staring at a little pile of gold by the sink. The bracelet Dad and I gave her for her birthday two years ago, her gold Wal-Mart watch from her sister. And something else. I leaned to the right and picked up a plain gold ring. It was too shiny, not a scratch or a mark on it. I turned it over in my hands and noticed something was inscribed on the inside. Holding it closer, I read the words *Mon amour.*

"Do you understand, sweetheart?" Mom asked.

She was at the doorway and I nodded, hiding the ring behind my back.

Taking my shoulders, she looked into my eyes. "Are you sure, Sara? I want us to be really open with this. And I want you to learn from my mistakes. I've given almost a quarter of my life to a man I never should have married. When I met Michael, I felt I had a chance again. Like I'd found my reason for living."

Her reason for living. Her freaking reason for living. Because she hadn't found one yet. She didn't have one living across the hall from her bedroom. Tears pierced my eyes like burning needles and I stepped back. "Could you excuse me, Mom? I need to pee."

Closing the door behind me, I dropped the ring into the toilet bowl and flushed.

The ring wasn't the only thing that vanished that day. Nor was my mother.

By the time the balloon-covered gymnasium doors opened for prom that night, every student at Finmory High knew that Tina Black had stolen the beloved Mrs. Nathan's husband. For me, it was the end of life as I knew it. The only student willing to look in my direction was Mandy.

chapter 31
flash futures

The procedure of colony members isolating unacceptable virgin queen army ants is called "sealing off."

Dad walks into our apartment first. I push past him and head straight for my room, throwing myself on my bed. How unbelievably, utterly, completely humiliating! Leo had looked from me to Charlie to me again. Then looked at his dad like he needed convincing that he wasn't still asleep. And next thing I knew, Dad was shaking Leo's hand, so pleased to meet an Ant student. So certain his daughter hadn't been erasing his very existence.

Leo looked at me, surprised, disappointed, maybe even disgusted.

But here's the thing. He wasn't disgusted that he had nearly gotten involved with the custodian's daughter. I could see it on his face. He was disgusted by what I'd done—to him, to the kids at school, and most of all to my father. Charlie asked him all sorts of intelligent questions about the Aston, and Leo gave my father the respect he deserves. It was then that I realized the truth. I'd made a terrible mistake in not trusting my father to rise above his job. An irreparable mistake. An unforgivable mistake.

I am a monster.

Charlie didn't know what was really going on in that garage. He actually put his hand on my shoulder as we left and headed for the bus stop, as if I was worthy of his trust.

Rolling over on my bed, I notice the red light on my cell phone is flashing so brightly it could be a warning for low-flying planes. I don't have to listen to the message to know who it's from. What it says. What it means. But I do.

Leo's voice. He doesn't sound happy. "Hey, Sara. Leo here. That was kind of bizarre this morning, waking up and finding you in my garage." He laughs, then pauses to take a sip of something. "Anyway, sorry but I have to bail on you. I'm not feeling so good. My mom is going to haul me in to the doctor or something. See you later."

I snap the phone shut, turn it off, and hurl it into a drawer. Of course Leo Reiser, future CEO of Reiser Industries, is suddenly feeling lousy. He almost got himself involved with me.

chapter 32
surrounded by ants

A fungivore is a being that feeds on fungi.

I don't come out of my room the rest of the day Saturday. Dad thinks I have a headache and offers—about twelve times—to bring me Tylenol. He has no idea what just happened, and I have no plans to tell him. Not ever. It would hurt him too much.

When he goes to bed early, I drag myself out of my room and into the living room, where I turn on the TV, desperate to give my misery a break by focusing on anything but Leo and the fact that my entire social life will have dissolved by Monday morning—though by now he's probably told Griff what I did. And Griff has probably spilled it to anyone who can stand him long enough to listen.

The credits to a movie roll up the screen, and as I watch the names of the actors pass by—*Billy Crystal, Meg Ryan, Carrie Fisher*—I realize with horror what I've done. I've left Mandy alone on her birthday night, the night she was supposed to have been spending with Eddie before he dumped her.

I race to the phone and dial Mandy's number.

Her mother answers, her voice taut. "Hello?"

"May I please speak to Mandy? It's Sara."

"It's awfully late, Sara. Eleven o'clock."

"Sorry. I just need Mandy for a second."

"She went out about half an hour ago. To get a coffee, she said. But I don't know why she'd need a coff—"

There is no time for the usual polite "thank you" and "good-bye" and "I hope to see you soon." This is an emergency. I hang up the phone and dial Mandy's cell. She didn't go for coffee. She went to her asshole ex-boyfriend's hotel room to see if he's there with his new girl. Mandy picks up on the second ring but says nothing. I can hear her sobbing in the background.

"Mandy, are you at the hotel?"

"Screw you, Sara."

"Don't do this to yourself! Following them around is only going to torture you. Please tell me you'll go home and—"

"Didn't you hear me? I said *screw you*."

"I know I messed up. It's just that I had a terrible day and I . . . I just forgot."

"He's in there with her right now." Her sobs dissolve into hiccups.

"You have to get yourself home. Just put me on speaker and I'll keep talking to you until you're in your driveway."

"Leave me alone."

"But you shouldn't be driving."

"I'm in my driveway, okay? So stop trying to make like you give a crap. It's pretty clear that you don't."

"I do, I swear. You want to know what happened today?"

"No. I don't." And she hangs up.

little black lies

I try to call back, but she's turned off her phone. I send text messages explaining what happened. Then I leave a voice message, begging her to call me, forgive me. My mother was right to put an ocean between us. There's something wrong with me. I was born bad. I ooze pain and hurt wherever I go. If I could take back every single thing I've done, I would. There is officially not one single sliver of my life I haven't destroyed. Not one freaking speck.

Mandy needed me and I wasn't there. All the IMs and phone messages in the world aren't going to undo it.

Monday morning I go to school prepared for the very worst. For everyone in the building to know me for the lying, cheating wretch I am. Dad went in early to get a start on some heater that needs fixing, and in some feeble and cowardly attempt to stand by him now that it's too late, I went with him. The foyer was empty when we walked in, which diminished my move significantly, but before he headed down the first-floor hall toward the boiler room, I kissed him on the cheek.

He looked at me and smiled. "You really are the perfect daughter."

It was all I could do not to weep. But a high-school student's instinct for self-preservation runs deep. I bit hard on the inside of my cheek, then said, "I don't deserve you." As I headed up to the second floor, the only sound I heard, other than my own footsteps, was my father's key ring rattling from downstairs.

The hallways are thick with students by the time I spot Carling, Sloane, and Isabella. I wade upstream in a river

271

of kids flowing in my direction. It takes twice the effort to fight the rapids, strength I just don't have today, but I drum it up to protect my father from whatever Carling might have schemed up over the weekend.

As soon as Carling sees me fighting the human flotsam, she squeals and pulls me into a huddle with the other girls, walking us toward the girls' bathroom. "London. Operation Takedown is about to launch a few days early."

I'm pretty sure I know what she's talking about, but have to ask, "What's that?"

"To take down Crazy Charlie. Our worst-case-scenario Izzy came up with the perfect plan that will ensure that his reputation is forever trashed. In fact, that's what we'll call our strategy, Forever Trashed." Aggression oozes from her body, making her seem a caricature of herself. Her square jaw line looks mannish and sharp, almost as if her jawbones have been replaced by a steel box. Muscles bulge in her neck, and her long, wild hair seems to be hissing like a nest of writhing cobras. Flanked by her brainy, kneesock-sporting thugs, with hordes of students filing around her, Carling looks ready for a fight.

"Listen up," she says. "Izzy's going to tell him there's a leaky toilet in the girls' room. Tell him the place could be crawling in germs and we need a custodian. So in comes Charlie, all bug-eyed with determination and his bucketful of bleach. Sloane is going to make sure the restroom is empty. With one exception."

"Which is?" I ask.

She pushes a gold spiral out of her eyes and grins, pressing against the doorway. "Me. I'll be waiting for him with my shirt ripped open. Charlie walks in, I count to five, then scream, 'He touched me!' Let him face a fraction of what I faced all weekend with Brice. See how he likes it.'"

In my most manic dreams, I didn't imagine her going this far. Even if Charlie had turned her in on purpose, which he didn't, it's beyond extreme. So much so it makes no sense. Noah was right. Carling Burnack is capable of anything. "It won't work," I say. "Charlie will call for the female custodian, what's her name? Jeanine?"

Sloane says, "No. That's why we're doing it now. Jeanine's not in. I heard it in the office. It's today or never."

"Then never." I hear my voice get shrieky and bounce off the cement walls. "You can't do this. It will ruin his career."

"Career?" Carling snorts. "He's a freaking Molly!"

"You'll destroy him. Think about what you're doing, Carling!"

Her eyebrows cap her turquoise eyes, which are suddenly shining with tears. The hallways have almost emptied out now, but she lowers her voice to a deep, husky whisper. "You think Charlie didn't destroy me? Huh? You think for one minute waiting to be expelled has been fun?"

"That's nothing," I snap. "And you won't get expelled. Maybe you'll get your cell phone taken away, boo freaking hoo! You can't turn around and wipe out a man's life. Charlie could end up in jail. You can't do it!"

"Why not?" Carling demanded. "Give me one good reason."

I stare at the way her lips break into a wicked smile, stretching her nostrils so wide I can practically see into her brain. I look away, if only because it makes me feel intrusive and criminal.

When I was about eleven, I used to sit folded up, with my knees tucked under my chin, in the backseat—more like a shelf—of Dad's dented orange Karmann Ghia and stare at myself in the rearview mirror. I used to isolate my features, contort my body so I could view my forehead separate from my eyes, my eyes disconnected from my nose, all the way down to my chin. It was shocking how beautiful my features were when viewed on their own. A smooth rounded forehead blended into center-parted blonde hair. A straight nose that could grace the "after" photos in any plastic surgeon's office. Heavily lashed green eyes. A small, determined chin. But when I caught sight of my face as a whole again, my perfection vanished. I was plain again. Mousy, washed out, homely.

Carling, I'm noticing for the first time, is the opposite. When offered as a faceful, her features are breathtakingly gorgeous. But if you mentally detach one feature from the rest, its glory is gone.

Her parts, like mine, are full of lies.

My throat grows thick and I choke on tightness before I speak. "You can't do it because he's my father, Carling."

Wild strands of uncontrolled hair blow and dance in front of her eyes, feeble against the air vent above her, and she does nothing to push them away. "What the hell are you talking about?"

"Charlie Black is my father."

"I should have told you, Car," says Isabella. "I figured it out a few days ago."

"Damn straight you should have told me." Carling turns back to me. "You lying little bitch. So that's how you got into Ant? Because Daddy is the janitor boy?"

"No. I took the test."

She laughs a bit hysterically. "Whatever. And all this time you've been lying to us?"

"Yes. So there you go. Now you know me for real. You should have stayed away from the start. I'm a thief and a liar."

"This is so pathetic I can't even speak. Why would you do this?"

"How else was I going to fit in? I'm from Lundon, Massachusetts. That's Lundon with a *U*. I'm the daughter of a janitor and a cook. Some fancy genetics, huh? The result of a teenage pregnancy and a marriage that never should have happened. I've never been out of this state in my entire life, and I live in an apartment above a hardware store. There you go. Those are my illustrious, so-not-Ant-worthy genes. Don't even ask why I did it, I'm pretty sure you can apply the Genius Theory to my situation and figure it out for yourself."

Carling's head shakes from side to side in a movement that is almost imperceptible. "You little bitch." Without taking her eyes off me, she says to Isabella, "Go get the Man of the Morning, Izz. I've got a lesson to teach him. And his two-faced daughter." With the hall completely empty behind her, Carling Burnack rips open her blouse and disappears into the bathroom while her friend races toward the stairwell.

It isn't easy to find Charlie. Takes a full twenty minutes. He is down in the pool area tinkering with the heater. It doesn't matter which one of us, me or Isabella, reaches Charlie first. Charlie Black, Custodian Extraordinaire,

Mopped Crusader, hears there's a terrible mess in the girls' bathroom and no amount of begging, crying, or warning on my part is going to stop him. He marches toward the restroom door as if he were heading into war, dragging his mop and bucket behind him.

"I swear to God, Dad," I say, tugging on his arm.

"They're setting you up!"

"It's a good thing you're here, Charlie," Isabella says from his other side. "Jeanine isn't in today."

"Dad!"

As if I don't exist, he turns to Isabella. "When did you say it happened?"

"Just a few minutes ago. And you better hurry. There are Niners on this floor and you know how clumsy they can be. They're like toddlers. And you know what they say about their immune systems—weak."

He walks faster.

"Dad, no! Carling's mad about her purse. There was a stolen exam in it—she's trying to frame you."

He marches on. It's like the flower-bed incident or the science-lab sink. No amount of reasoning can get through to him. The OCD acts like a filter, screening out whatever gets in the way of its twisted, imagined purpose.

A weird feeling rushes me hard, like a bucket of warm water dumped from the ceiling that has soaked me to my bones. At first it slows me down—it's not easy to chase someone with an imaginary bucket on your head—but then I see what's happening. What has needed to happen all this time. I don't quite know what to call it, but it feels an awful lot like I've aged.

I reach out to grab Charlie by the sleeve and force

him to stop, but I trip and my cell phone goes skittering across the floor. "You're not listening to me. I need you to listen."

"After I deal with the mess, Sara. We'll talk. I promise."

"No. We talk now." He looks down the hall and I step in front of him. "Dad. We talk now. You're disappearing, do you hear me? Mom's gone and that sucks. But it doesn't mean you can vanish inside the OCD like this! It's taking you away from me. You listen to it, you listen to its every command and all it does is pull you away from the one person who loves you more than anything. Me." He looks again toward the escalator. "Dad! Do you even hear me?"

"Yes. I do."

"You don't. You're still listening to it. Please believe me when I say this is a setup. You cannot go into that bathroom."

The mention of the bathroom is too much. He kisses my head and walks away from me, promising we'll talk in a few minutes.

I've never felt more useless.

Back on the second floor, the door to the girls' room pulsates, throbs with Carling's presence. Inside, she's burning with rage, her fingers holding her torn blouse shut, ready to point at Charlie as soon as he enters.

Sloane and Isabella crowd him from behind as he approaches the door, blocking me from entering with him. I call out to him one more time but it's too late. In one motion, he disappears, the door swinging closed behind him with a soft thud. Not two seconds pass, then, with Charlie caught in her trap, Carling puts her plan into action.

She screams.

chapter 33
skinned

Chitin is the strong, protective substance that makes up the ant's exoskeleton.

Carling took Charlie down, all right. When her screams didn't stop, teachers, students, even a few parents who happened to be on the second floor rushed to see what had happened. There, through the open door to the girls' bathroom, was Carling—her back against the far wall, ripped shirt gathered in her fists, wailing and keening like a wounded tiger cub. Charlie appeared so shocked, so vulnerable, so naked, he might as well have been skinned, standing before the crowd as Carling pointed at him and cried, "Look what he did to me," over and over.

Students and teachers stared at Charlie, their faces curled up in horror and disgust. Ms. Solange shouted for someone to go down to the office, tell them to call the police. Seeing my father held by two teachers, dazed and confused, was too much for me. I tried to make them listen to me, to tell them this was a lie, but couldn't make my voice be heard above the commotion. When I saw actual fear in my father's eyes, I started to feel like my skin was on inside out. Otherworldly and faint. I leaned over onto my knees and tried not to throw up on the floor.

When I stood up again, Dad's eyes met mine. He shook his head, so sad, impossibly sad, and I said, "I'm sorry."

They whisked him away.

Minutes later, Dad was in the office surrounded by cops, office staff, the principal. Mrs. Pelletier took over crowd control, trying to keep students out in the foyer, but it was like trying to stop water from pouring through a leaky bucket. Next to impossible. I told everyone what happened—that Carling had set him up—but by this time word had spread about the lies I'd told, about who I was, who I was not. My credibility was gone.

Now I stand in the office oblivious to the commotion, feeling as if I'm trapped in a nightmare. All I know is, without my lies none of it would have happened.

Poppy wanders in and stops beside me, leaning over the counter and smacking her gum as if bored. "You're some kind of new kid, aren't you?"

I don't answer.

"If you'd just gotten caught up with me, instead of that bitch Carling, life for you would have been totally different. I gave you my number the first day. If you'd called me at the start, you wouldn't have had to lie and shit."

Shrugging, I mumble, "If I hadn't done a lot of things, life would have been different. I effed up my existence way before Ant. Just ask my mother."

"Where's your mother?"

"Does it matter?"

"Guess not."

Through Mr. Oosterhouse's window, I can see a police officer moving closer to my father with a pair of handcuffs in his fist. In the same chair she sat in the day Brice admitted he was broke sits Carling, still weeping, pointing. Lying.

Poppy blows an enormous bubble, reaches for an office pencil, and pops it, pulling the shredded gum back into her mouth with her tongue. "He's a pretty cool guy, your dad."

"Yeah. He is."

"One time after school my bike lock was jammed. He stayed late to fix it. Could have just snipped it off with the school's lock cutters, but he didn't want me to have to spend the money to buy a new one." She looks at me. "He's just a guy who really cares."

I nod sadly.

"So don't go thinking I'm doing this for you."

"Doing what?"

She shoots me a look that says *Watch me,* and steps behind the counter to tap Mrs. Pelletier on the shoulder. When the vice principal looks her way, Poppy says, "This is one big waste of taxpayers' money. It didn't happen." One by one, people stop talking. Heads turn to face Poppy. "Charlie didn't touch Carling." She holds up her camera and smacks her gum. "I have the whole scam on film."

I could kiss her.

When Mrs. Pelletier and the camera disappear into the principal's office and Poppy follows, I stop her. Thank her. I dig inside my backpack and pull out a paper bag. Inside it are the yoga pants. "Take these," I say. "Someone decent should have them."

I hand it to her and she looks inside, crumples the bag shut, and hands it back to me. "I'm not like you, Sara. I don't need to profit from my choices."

280

chapter 34
plain old high school

The booty cache is where army ants temporarily store their prey after a raid.

By lunchtime, everyone knows the truth. That Charlie did nothing but enter the girls' room and ask about the mess. That Carling had planned to take him down because of the stolen math test. That Poppy's camera finally proved to be something more than an annoyance.

The funny thing is, it was Sloane's laziness that saved Charlie. Her sleepy manner meant she checked most of the stalls in the girls' room, but never bothered to look into the last stall on the left. She bumped it open, Poppy said, but never poked her head in to see someone squatting on the toilet seat. Poppy had been in the end stall filming the graffiti on the walls to make a short video about adolescent poetry when Carling came in with her blouse ripped open and ready. "I figured the bitch was up to something," Poppy explained to the police when they came out of the principal's office. "Why not get it on film?"

It's a full hour before the office is cleared out, the police gone. Dad and I are told we can collect ourselves in the principal's office, which looks nothing like you'd expect from a man who heads up one of the most elite high schools in the country, with its painted cinderblock walls, buzzing overhead lights, and sick plants on the window-sill. I would have expected a roaring fireplace maybe. A wet bar and a leather chair that smells of stale cigar smoke. As it is, the only thing worthy of such a room it the brass banker's lamp on Mr. Oosterhouse's desk—but it looks embarrassed by its humble surroundings. This office could be in any other school, even Finmory.

Mr. Oosterhouse is still with the police, so Dad and I are alone for the first time since the incident. Neither of us speaks.

Outside the window, fat snowflakes drift down from the darkened sky. As I nudge Charlie to look outside, I notice a crowd gathering at the window of the outer office as well. People are smiling and pointing. It's the first snowfall of the year.

I finished *Crime and Punishment* last night. There's a moment at the end, after he's confessed, where Rascal looks around at the other convicts in prison. He's kind of astonished by how much these guys appreciate life, even while locked up. How much they appreciate simple things—trees, sunlight, babbling streams. For a moment he thinks he's different. That he's oblivious to whatever life there is around him. But a few pages later he sits on a river-bank, on a log, looking out at the sunshine and listening to a song coming from a gypsy camp. It is here that he finally appreciates life. Sadness, too, because he must wait seven more years to live free again and finally be with his girl.

People aren't as different as you'd think. Anyone, whether from Lundon or Boston, would find this office depressing. Anyone, with the exception of the most determined snow haters, would get a little thrill from the beauty of these snowflakes. If I hadn't lied, I would still be looking at these snowflakes, wishing I could taste them. Would it have really been so bad to have tasted them as the janitor's daughter?

Just like Rascal's prisonmates, the Carlingettes would have sneered at me anyway. They sneer at everyone! My lies never bought me Carling's respect. My brains did. The *janitor's daughter's* brains.

Wait. Did I just disprove the Genius Theory?

The office is silent but for the stuttering *tick-tock* of an ailing clock on the desk.

"Dad?" I scoot my chair closer until our knees touch. "About what happened. No, not about what happened. About what I did . . ."

Placing his hand behind my neck, he pulls me forward and lays his cheek against the top of my head. "I know you're sorry."

"You don't know *how* sorry, Dad. I'd come up with a list of reasons why I lied, but there won't be one single reason that will even come close to explaining it away or making it better. Plus, I stole your keys and snuck into the office. . . ."

"You were absolutely right."

"To lie and steal? You might change your mind when you hear what I took."

"What you said back in the hallway this morning. About me. You warned me about that girl and I didn't hear you. All this time you've been telling me something and I've chosen to block it out. I'm sorry for that."

I stare at his hands; only one bandage remains on his knuckles. For the first time I notice he's taken off his wedding ring. There's no white strip of skin where it once was, always was. Which means I've been too busy counting his bleeding knuckles to notice my father has taken at least one big step toward moving on already. I reach forward and wrap my arms around his neck. "I wish it would just vanish—the OCD."

He kisses my head and releases me. "It doesn't work like that, Sarie-bear. I wish it did. But I think it's time your old man gets himself some help."

The principal glides into the room and hands me my cell phone. "I'm told this is yours, Sara. It was found on the floor. Looks like it's taken quite a beating."

I try to turn it on but it's dead. "Thanks."

He drops into his chair, leans forward onto his desk, and smiles at us. "I am truly sorry for all of this. Charlie, you've been here a relatively short time, but the staff has come to care about you. I hope you'll accept the school's apologies for what happened."

Charlie shakes his head. "Not necessary."

"I hope it hasn't turned you off our school?"

"No, no," says Dad. "Anton's a fine place. A bit toilsome when it comes to homework, but a fine school."

"Good. Nasty business, all this. All over a stolen exam. We come down hard on cheating in this school. With all the pressure, it can be tempting for students to look for the easy way. But it's bad for our reputation and with all the fuss that's gone on today, you can be sure we'll be conducting an in-depth investigation with regard to the theft."

I squeeze the arms of my chair and try not to faint. I'm going to need my strength.

The principal reaches for a sheet of paper and slides it across the desk to my father. "I'd been planning to speak with you for a few days now, but thought, with what's happened, I'd better catch you before you go home because I'm hoping you'll consider what I have in mind. This facility has never looked better since you've come aboard. You're exactly the sort of dedicated professional we've been looking for, right down to your pressed uniform."

Dad glances at me and winks.

"There was a certain incident a little while back, but if you're willing to guarantee you will seek help through a school board–approved doctor, we have an offer for you. What I'm hoping you'll consider is a promotion to head up our custodial staff." The principal taps the edge of the paper. "It will mean more money and a definite step up." He wiggles the paper on the desk.

Dad studies it for a moment, then pushes it away and shakes his head. "Sorry. It's a kind offer, a good offer, but I can't accept."

No. He can't keep avoiding promotion. He can't keep clinging to failure. "Dad, don't keep doing this! You just said you were going to listen. You were going to change."

He pushes my hair off my shoulder. "I was planning to tell you this tonight, sweetheart. But I guess now's as good a time as any. I've been speaking with Alex Reiser, the man selling the cars over in Brookline. Leo's father."

I look at him, stunned. And terrified. "About what?"

"I asked him for a job. In Reiser's vintage-cars division. He said he's willing to give me a chance. It's a division he's never really staffed properly and I convinced him we

285

might be able to make it profitable. If he ever agrees to sell any of the cars, that is."

"Seriously? You'd be working in an office?"

"More of a garage slash showroom. But you, of all people, will understand there's not much, other than looking at my daughter's face, that makes me happier than being under the hood of an antique car."

I'm still too stunned by the morning to smile, but I'm happy for him. "Wow. I can't believe it."

The principal clears his throat. "Well, I can't exactly compete with Reiser Industries. I don't suppose you'll miss the cleaning."

Dad laughs. "My daughter always says it's the dirtiest thing I could do. I finally agree with her."

"We certainly won't be happy to lose you, Charlie." Mr. Oosterhouse frowns, then turns to me. "Sara, I do hope you'll consider staying on with us. From what I hear, you're a solid student. Your teachers are all quite happy with you."

"I haven't signed anything yet," Dad says to me. "Not until you give your approval. Because if I take the job, it'll mean leaving Anton High. Moving to New York, starting over yet again. What do you think, Sara? Maybe try to get into another one of these schools for geniuses in New York?"

Mr. Oosterhouse interrupts. "I'm not sure they'll take a new junior, even if she could pass the entrance tests. Not without a parent on staff." He shoots me a smile. "But if you'd like, we can make a few phone calls and find out. You're a good student and we'll help any way we can."

It's time to end the charade. I can't stand one more person thinking I'm a decent human being. "I'm not sure you'll feel that way when you hear what I've done."

Dad and Mr. Oosterhouse wait for me to continue.

"Carling had the test because I stole it."

"You?" The principal is shocked. "But your grades are the highest in your class."

"I didn't take it for me."

He looks away, blinking fast. "I don't know what to say. It's the last thing I expected."

"If anyone gets expelled, it should be me." I set the yoga pants on his desk. "And while I'm at it, it's not something I set out to do, but I stole these from the Store."

It's as if I've grown warts, fangs, and two extra heads. His expression is one of horror mixed with sorrow. "I'm afraid stealing the exam means an automatic expulsion. Now, it does appear you're leaving anyway, but an infraction of this magnitude will mean the better high schools in New York will be out of the question. Your record will reflect your . . . misdeeds."

"You mean, I can't go to *any* high school?"

"Only the designated public high school for your neighborhood. A regular school for regular kids."

"This record, will it follow me to college?"

"I'm not going to lie, Sara. Even with your grades, it is likely you'll get passed over by more than a few colleges."

But not *all* colleges. Surely he doesn't mean *all* colleges.

It's as if he reads my mind. His face softens. "Don't worry. There are plenty of good schools out there. You'll find your place in the world."

My place in the world. I'm not sure that will ever exist.

chapter 35
a thump in the thorax

Appeasement substance is a chemical emitted by a social parasite in order to reduce aggression.

As we were leaving the office, I started to explain to Dad. How, while it might be difficult to believe, the yoga pants, the test, it was all connected. True to his word, he listened. And when I finished, he said I'd suffered enough. That we were not going to refer to my crimes again. Life at Ant was a thing of the past.

Dad offered me a ride home in the green VW Beetle he bought from Alex Reiser, but I told him I had to clean out my locker and would meet him at home. In truth, there's nothing much in my locker I really care about, but I wasn't ready to sit in a car that Leo may have driven around in. Not just yet.

Leo hasn't been at school. He'll come back to hear I was expelled. Nice. I'll never see him again. Not that it matters. I lied to him as much as anyone else, and that's pretty much unforgivable.

More than a few kids refuse to speak to me on the way to my locker. Griff turns away when I say hello. As if he's never met me, never come on to me. The itchy, rashy Benadryl girls trot by in a fit of accusatory sniffs and

288

wheezes. A few guys from math class toss me a grenade: "Way to fit in, *Saint* Sarah." Needless to say, no one calls me London.

All of this is fine; I can't say I don't deserve it. Most people are accepting of Charlie and that's all that matters at this point. But for my choices, it could have been this way from the start.

Poppy, however . . . Poppy's final reaction hurt. I passed her on the escalator up to the third floor and smiled. I don't know what I was thinking. It's not as if, now that I'm the rejected one, I have the gall to try to befriend her after avoiding her all this time. It was more a smile to say *thank you*. A smile to say *I'm sorry*. But she looked at me and winced, as if the thought of communicating with me offended her to the core.

I'd have loved one last peppermint.

Carling is nowhere to be seen. I overheard in the halls that she's being questioned at the police station. But I'm not too worried about that girl. She always seems to find her way.

chapter 36
powder on the floor

*A symphile is a lone ant or insect that is accepted by the colony of a
different species.*

The best part about living above a hardware store?
Moving out. When you run out of packing tape to seal
up your cartons, there's plenty more three flights down.
And, lucky for us, Heritage Hardware has a great selection
of cleaning products, so Dad can be certain he's leaving
the floor beneath the stove so spotless the next family can
climb underneath and eat their dinner right off the yellow
linoleum. Should they desire to do so. And should they be
extremely flexible and tiny and not own any dishes.

It's wrong that Charlie needs to scrub this place silly
before we leave next week. But I'm biting my tongue. What
is it they say? You have to pick your battles. Besides, I'm so
proud of his new career move and his willingness to find a
doctor I figure I can look the other way on the unnecessary
scrubbing. I will say this. Whoever moves into this place
won't have to clean for a year.

I've never been to New York. Neither has Dad. He
went on the Internet and found us a new apartment close
to his work. We saw pictures. It's even smaller than this
place, if that's possible, but it's the entire top floor of an

old brownstone, and there's a patio on the rooftop we're allowed to use. And my room? Nothing like my lopsided lair. Nothing like Rascal's coffin-shaped garret. My new room has one tangerine-colored wall and a huge bay window that overlooks the street. I like the sound of that. There's a flowering tree out front and I'll be able to open my window and smell the blossoms in the spring.

"I'm going to leave the linen closet for you," calls Dad from the kitchen. "You're so good at folding fitted sheets."

"Nothing more than simple household geometry. It's all in the angles," I shout from my room, where I'm packing up the contents of my desk. "And the thread count."

"That's my little van Gogh."

What? I toss a dictionary into a box full of my desk contents and head into the kitchen, where Dad is wiping down a cupboard we never even used. "Dad. You can't be serious. Van Gogh wasn't a mathematician. He was the—"

"I know." He pauses to douse his sponge with Mr. Clean, then goes back to work. "The Dutch painter who cut off his left ear. I was just messing with you."

I eye him teasingly. "Since when did you get so fancy?"

"I was in charge of cleaning the art department at Ant. A guy's bound to pick up a few things. If he's listening."

"So germs are *not* the only thing you think about when you clean. Interesting." He's staring down at the floor by my bare feet. "What?"

"Footprints."

Sure enough, I've left powdery marks on the floor. "Dad, I just showered. That's baby powder. It's not dirt."

"Still." He gets down on one knee and leans over to erase them.

Before he does, I grab his wrist. "Don't do it."

He looks up at me, blinking. He tries to pull his wrist away but I squeeze tighter. We stay that way for a minute, staring into each other's eyes. I can see how hard this is for him. He needs to wipe up the slhupou of my toes, my heels. It's too much for him. Just as I release his wrist, there's a knock at the door. I kiss Charlie on the cheek and stand, knowing what will happen the moment I leave the room. The floor will be polished. And polished. And polished.

I open the door to find Carling Burnack herself standing in the hall. She looks terrible: her hair's unwashed, the circles under her eyes seem like smears of mud. It's a good thing Charlie's busy. He'd be liable to take a mop to Carling's face. Keys jangle in one hand as she crosses her arms. "Is it true?"

"How did you know where I live?"

"Don't screw around with me. I know."

"Know what?"

"What everyone's talking about. That you're seeing Leo. Griff told me you guys went out last weekend. Is it true?"

"Why would Griff . . . ?"

She steps into the doorway and hisses, "I called Leo myself, you know. I told him everything. So if you think you have a chance with him now, you're out of your mind. He'd never get mixed up with someone like you." She steps closer but I block her from entering.

"Because I'm a janitor's daughter?"

"Because you're a liar, a thief, and, yes, a total fraud. So tell me, are you seeing Leo?"

"No."

"Swear you never will. You owe me that much."

"I don't owe you anything, Carling. Especially not that."

Then I, little Sara Black from Lundon, Massachusetts, do something I never would have imagined. I thump the door closed in Carling Burnock's face. For the first time, I don't give her what she wants. Though in a way I guess I do. If making me sad was her intention, she scored big-time.

It isn't until the sound of her footsteps stomping down the wooden steps has gone silent that I realize I'll never see my mother's green sweater again.

Charlie is no longer in the kitchen, but the sponge is lying on the counter. Before I turn back to my packing, I stop and stare at the floor, a proud smile crinkling one cheek. The floor is still covered in my powdery footprints. Which means one thing. Big Charlie resisted wiping them away.

chapter 37
boxful of junk

The Texas shed-builder ant chews up vegetation, spits it out, and uses it to form canopies over aphids, which they care for because of their honeydew secretions.

The driver hangs out the window as he backs the flatbed truck—beeping like a terrible alarm clock when morning has come too early—down our alley. Beneath his elbow are the words ATLANTIC TOWING. When the truck jerks to a stop, the beeping is replaced by an angry hiss and the bed of the truck rises on an angle at the front, which lowers the back like a ramp right under the hood of the black sedan.

The Bentley is being repossessed.

Noah and I stand shivering in T-shirts and jeans and watch as the driver climbs out, his breath forming cartoon cloud puffs, and sets about attaching chains and gizmos that will pull the car up onto the truck.

"Will you miss it?" I ask him.

He takes a drag from a joint so skinny it looks like a twist tie and speaks while holding his breath. "A little. What I'll miss even more, believe it or not, are the Burnacks. And the paychecks. However rare they were." He laughs a little and holds up his joint. "A guy's got to get his greens."

I snort. "There's some twisted logic."

"Yeah, well. Not all of us have your smarts."

"Will you keep in touch with her?"

"Carling? Hell. I've been around since she was a kid. If she calls, I'll pick up the phone."

We fall silent while the Bentley is pulled, creaking and groaning, up and onto the truck. The gleaming car could not look more out of place, squatting on the back of the rusted tow truck with a look of disdain on her front grille.

The cement steps beneath our feet rumble as the tow truck revs its engine and begins to creep forward. I hear a cough above our heads and see Dad poking his head through his bedroom window three stories up. He salutes the departure of the Bentley with a slow whistle. "There goes one beautiful vehicle," he says, watching it glide past the Dumpsters and disappear down the lane. "You're going to miss poking around that engine, Noah. So am I."

"Can't argue with that."

"What about you?" Dad asks him. "Where will you end up?"

I can't tell if Noah frowns or smiles; maybe it's a bit of both. "As long as I'm behind a wheel or under a hood, one place is as good as the next." Which makes me sad for him. A hunk of metal, no matter how fancy, cannot provide much in the way of companionship. Noah squints up at Dad. "However hard I fall, I'm sure to land on my ass."

"Sounds painful," says Dad.

I have an idea. "Thanksgiving's coming up, Dad. Maybe Noah can come stay with us."

"Noah's always welcome." The phone rings from our apartment. Dad waves with two fingers before disappearing inside.

295

There's an open carton full of magazines, books, bundled newspapers, and cardboard at Noah's feet. He's been clearing out his apartment, preparing to move. I bend down to look through the box and pull out an old coffee-table book with a cover shot of a horse wearing a striped blanket. Ironically, the photo looks like it was taken in England. Silvery mist lying low over mossy hills. Stone stable with a thatched roof. The title is no-nonsense: *Sensible Horse Management.* "Is this yours?" I ask Noah.

He looks at the book and chuckles. "The last tenant left it. I used it to prop my bathroom window open all summer."

"Would you mind if I take it?"

"You buying a horse?"

"No." I smile. "But I might just have a window that needs opening."

Dad's looking out again, this time with a strange expression on his face. "Sara. You better get upstairs. Your mother's on the phone. She's here in Boston."

chapter 38
strawberry fields forever

After mating, the queen loses her wings and becomes an isolated being.

She has a scarf around her neck. It's light green and silky with the pattern of a garden trellis all over it. Classy looking, like something Gracie would own. It makes me feel sad for her. My mother is so dainty and elegant and pretty, she should have had such a different sort of life. Then again, maybe she's having it now.

"You'd love it there, Sara," she says as the waiter sets two Caesar salads in front of us. "Paris is so different. We live for the day. We walk to the market every day and pick up fresh food. You should see my fridge. It fits right under the counter."

"Wow. Sounds cool."

"Even what's considered beautiful is different. People don't work so hard to look plastic. People appreciate a clean face. A strong body. Simply cut clothes of good material. If you can believe it, I am actually considered a beauty among the other students in my course."

I can believe it. She looks wonderful. Her hair is loose, falling around her face. She's put on a couple of pounds, not enough that anyone but me would notice. Just enough to round out her cheeks a bit, make her look healthier.

Happier. The only makeup on her face is a swipe of red lipstick. I try to commit the shade to memory, so I can try to find something like it at the drugstore. "You really do look beautiful, Mom."

"So do you, sweetie." She takes my hand in hers. Her skin is so soft it could be liquid. "God, I've missed seeing you, holding you."

"Me too."

"Sara?"

"Yes?"

"Mike is here in Boston with me. He spent the day back in Lundon visiting with Tori. We were hoping you might come to a show with us tomorrow." She leans closer. "Do you think you might be okay with that?"

Hmm. You know what would be just as much fun? If I pick up my water glass right now, bite into it, and swallow the glass shards along with the ice cubes. "I don't know," I mumble. "I'll have to check with Dad. There's a lot of packing to do. And stuff."

"Okay. I understand." She leans back in her seat. "Has it been terrible for you? All this change? And now you're moving again. . . ."

Something tells me she doesn't want the truth. The truth of me doesn't fit in with her market-fresh food or the cut of her new clothes. I tell her what she wants to hear. She did, after all, come an awfully long way just to eat salad with me, when it sounds as if there is perfectly good lettuce closer to home. "It's been fine."

And her eyes shine with relief. "Next time you'll come to visit me, okay? When you're ready. You still have that ticket?"

"I might have lost it."

"No problem. We'll have one reissued. Hopefully your new school won't be quite so demanding. Maybe over spring break?"

"Maybe." I poke around on my plate for a smallish piece of romaine lettuce, one that will fit in my mouth without too much effort.

"Great. The weather should be better by then. Spring comes earlier there, from what I hear. I forgot, when I signed up for this Boston Culinary Arts Seminar, how cold it can be in Massachusetts. All I brought to keep me warm was a thin blazer I found in—"

"Wait. You're here for a conference?"

"Yes. And to see you, of course."

As she babbles on about lightweight clothing and the chill in the presentation rooms and the firmness of her hotel mattress, I lay down my fork. Creamy garlic with chopped anchovies is no longer a good idea. Not with the way my stomach has just turned inside out with my own stupidity. My mother didn't get on a plane so that she could come to see me. I wasn't the plan. I was convenient.

She notices I've gotten quiet and stops. "Honey, are you okay?"

"I don't know. It's a lot of garlic." It's a good excuse. I could complain a bit more, then tell her I should probably go home and lie down. She'd put me in a cab and I could go home to my father. Help him with the last of the packing. We have to get up early tomorrow to load up the trailer. It would be nice to be rested.

"Here." She pulls a white roll from the linen-covered bread basket, butters it lightly. Holds it out for me. "Just nibble on this. And if your stomach calms down, we'll order you something else, okay? I hear the minestrone soup is excellent."

As I stare at the roll, I realize it's all she has to give. She doesn't have all of herself to offer me, not like Dad does. She has what she has, so what's the use in expecting more? More won't happen. I can either accept it now or I can torture myself forever. It could be worse. A bread basket between us is still better than the gutter of a tenth-grade science textbook.

As I reach for the roll, I know I might not miss that green sweater at all. "Okay. Minestrone sounds good."

My purse starts blasting "Strawberry Fields Forever" when Mom's in the restroom. My phone's still dead, so Charlie gave me his in case I wanted to be picked up early. I debate not answering. The display number isn't home, so it's not Dad. And no one else would be calling me on his number. But the ringtone is insanely loud and I can't find the mute button.

"Hello?"

I hear crunching. "Dude. Did you find it in a Dumpster?"

"Mandy?"

"There was a dried-out noodle between two pages. Spaghettini, I think. In some kind of funky hardened pink sauce."

"But the book's cool. It had all these 'Be Your Own Barn Dominatrix' instructions inside." All around me conversations grow quiet and heads turn in my direction. "I thought it would be perfect for you."

"I'm kidding," Mandy says. "It's a great book. Thanks."

"No problem. And I almost did find it in a Dumpster."
I'm talking so loud the waiter shushes me. But I don't
shush myself one bit.

"Sweet."

"I'm the sorriest person alive. You realize that, don't
you?"

"Sorry apologetic or sorry pathetic?"

"Pick either one and we'll go with it."

"Can I pick both? Because, you know, there was that
noodle."

I grin. Mandy's back in my life. Sarcastic, funny, pink-
streaked Mandy. I can handle almost anything—even
Michael Nathan—with Mandy on my side. "Yeah. There
was that noodle."

chapter 39
halfway

The virgin queen is unmated and, as such, is the potential creator of a brand-new colony.

The next morning, the weather complicates our move. Icy rain buckets down on us as we load up the trailer. Dad didn't like the way we were tracking muck up into the clean apartment, so we came up with a tag-team system. Dad treks up the stairs, then back down again with his arms full of cartons and small appliances. I wait in the lobby, at the door—which I've propped open with a telephone book—for the next load before stepping out into the rain and racing to the trailer with it. It's so cold outside I can see my breath, although, from beneath the dripping hood of my yellow windbreaker, it's pretty hard to see anything at all.

As I carry a particularly towering stack of boxes through the storm, a small *S*-marked box, the box I filled with my precious things—my jewelry box, the I ♥ NY mug from when Mom once went to a concert there, the clock radio with broken alarm, and matches—threatens to slip off the top of the pile. I step forward, wet hands reaching upward, and just as I save the falling carton, my right boot floods with icy water.

"Ugh!" My waterlogged boot now weighs about fifty

pounds. I spin around to show Dad, but he's already gone upstairs. I haul myself into the U-Haul and pull off my rubber boot, standing on the metal floor in my sopping wet sock, before turning the boot upside down and dumping out enough water to fill a fish tank. Rain is hammering down on the metal roof, but I hear the sound of footsteps running along the sidewalk, then someone swings around and jumps up into the trailer. All I can see is a jacket and wet jeans. I pull back my hood to see none other than Leo staring back at me.

He reaches up to wipe water from his grinning face. "Finally!"

I'm too stunned to speak right away. Still holding my boot, I manage to whisper, "Hey."

"You're a tough one to get hold of. I've been calling you for days." Small clouds puff from his mouth as he speaks. I want to inhale them.

"My phone's broken."

"I finally get my voice back and find out you're moving to New York."

"You were that sick?"

He points at my boot. "Shouldn't you put that back on?"

"Yeah." I don't move.

He steps closer. His denim jacket is soaked right through. "I wouldn't have cancelled our plans for anything that didn't require serious meds. You believed me, right?"

I pause too long.

"Please don't say you thought I ditched you because of what happened in the garage?" he says, groaning. "I *knew* it."

"Well . . ."

303

"Sara, we both admitted to a few white lies."

"Yeah, but mine were more black."

"Will it make you feel better to hear mine?"

"You totally don't have to . . ."

"You know those scars on my chest?"

"Yes."

"It was unbelievably stupid. It was a hot summer day. I found a bottle of my mom's nail polish and bet my neighbor I could make it explode."

"Nail polish is so flammable. It can totally explode."

"Yeah, so I learned. This kid, Oliver, he was two years younger than me. We'd been in his pool earlier and were both in our bathing suits. I should have known better than to involve anyone else, but I found a sunny spot on the driveway and pulled out a magnifying glass. Anyway, it took a long time, but eventually the bottle exploded."

I cringe in horror. "You got burned?"

"What happened to me was nothing. Oliver lost sight in one eye. It's the biggest regret of my life. *So* stupid."

"God."

"Yeah. He jokes about it now, but only because he's a good guy."

Instinctively, my hand goes up to his chest and rests on his wet jacket for just a moment, as if my touch might penetrate through the fabric, might smooth away the scars.

"Will you ever hang out with me again?"

I look around at the stacks of boxes. "I'm moving."

"I know. I live with the president, remember? You better tell Charlie my dad is one tough boss. After graduation this June, he's sending me to work in the Manhattan office."

"You'll be living in New York?"

"If you can call sleeping on an air mattress at my brother's apartment living, then, yeah," he says with a grunt. "So? What do you say?"

The rain slows down and the hammering on the roof grows softer. Outside, a tiny sliver of blue sky peers through the clouds. Water dribbles down his face, drips from his chin. I want to wipe it away but I don't. Instead, I squint in the brightening light, halfway between my old life and my new, and smile. "I'd love to hang out with you again."